PRAISE FO

(AS

"A great debut novel th[illegible]at I love in my romance novels ~ sweet, angsty, sassy, and a hot ass rocker! I can't wait to see what Bishop brings us next."

-Erin Noelle, USA Today Bestselling Author

"Finding Flynn was a sweet, slightly sexy, romantic read. I loved the pacing of Ashtyn and Flynn's relationship--it was perfectly appropriate for their ages. The rest of the band members are great characters too--Jax, Hudson, and Jude are like brothers to Flynn; they're his chosen family. Add in the craziness of Chloe, Ashtyn's best friend, and it's an instant party."

-Give Me Books Book Blog

"Alexandria Bishop delivers a wonderfully dramatic and angsty young adult romance that will have you wondering where you can find your own Flynn. A wonderful debut novel for this beautiful author."

-Meghan Quinn, Author of the Bourbon Series

"Alexandria's debut novel was hard to put down once I started reading! I love the angst along with the fun the characters, Ashytn and Flynn experience together."

-Anne Carol, Author of the Faithfully Yours Series

“Finding Flynn is a sexy, sizzling read full of tantalizing moments, laughs, and heartache.”

-YA Book Madness Blog

“This is an endearing book with a super-sexy, bad boy rocker as the hero.”

-BFF Book Blog

“Flynn and Ashtyn are young and adorable lovers. They are the summer relationship that every girl wants and dreams of.”

-Mira Day, Author of Playing House

Falling FOR Hudson

XOXO

Also By
Alexandria Bishop

Ashland Series
Finding Flynn
Falling for Hudson
Freeing Jude
Fighting for Jax

Dating Trilogy
Dating in the Dark
Sinking in the Shadows
Loving in the Light

ALEXANDRIA BISHOP

This book is a work of fiction. Names, characters, businesses, places, events, and incidents are either the products of the author's imagination or used in a fictitious manner. Any resemblance to actual persons, living or dead, or actual events is purely coincidental.

ISBN-13: 978-1724348289
ISBN-10: 1724348280

Cover Design by Mischievous Designs

Edited & Proofread by Indie Solutions
Formatted by AB Formatting

Third Edition:
10 9 8 7 6 5 4

To anyone that has lost someone,
I hope that you've been able
to heal or are healing.

"The course of true love never did run smooth."
-William Shakespeare
A Midsummer Night's Dream

PROLOGUE

Chloe

Ashtyn, my best friend, is a wreck. She's been crying all of her makeup off and reapplying it I don't know how many times. I get it. She's upset. Her boyfriend, Flynn, is moving to the opposite end of the state with his band Marlowe; her feelings are valid. But not once has she asked me how all of this makes me feel. I'm losing someone too. She hasn't been paying attention and is lost in her own problems. Her mom dragged her to Ashland, Oregon, away from our home in Santa Barbara, California. Ashtyn's parents are getting a divorce, but her mom, Audrey, forgot to mention that little detail when she brought her up here.

My parents decided to go on a cruise, leaving me with two options: spend my summer vacation in Kansas with my grandmother, or run away to Oregon and join Ashtyn.

Since I got here, I've been spending the majority of my time here visiting with Jax, the guitar player for Marlowe, while Ashtyn's been off with Flynn. One night in particular pops into my mind.

Jax, his brother Hudson, and myself are sprawled across their couches and are having a movie marathon. Hudson is the drummer for Marlowe, and he left shortly after Jax turned Point Break on. As he left the room, he was mumbling something about Jax being a narrator. I didn't get what he was talking about until the movie started and he started saying all of the lines with the characters. It was cute at first but got kind of annoying pretty quickly. After he repeated some line about cum, I'd had enough.

I slowly work my way down to his end of the couch, but he's too engrossed in the movie to realize what's going on. I curl myself into his body, blocking his view from the TV, but he doesn't seem to mind. "Lets go up to your room."

With a shrug of his shoulders, he turns off the TV and leads the way upstairs. As we pass Hudson's room, I can hear loud, angry music blaring through his bedroom door. I wonder if he's upset about something? Jax opens the door to his very messy bedroom and then closes it behind me. He has a typical guy's room. Clothes, which I'm hoping are clean, are scattered on the floor. Band posters are placed in between super models in bikinis. At least his bed is made. He sits down on the edge of his bed and turns his TV on. Not happening. I straddle his lap and go in for the kill. My lips graze his once, twice, three times before I give in and kiss him.

"Chloe." He groans as he fists his hands in my hair. I

tease him with my tongue and he greedily opens his mouth to me. My body is on fire with each tangle of our tongues, and I push him back onto the bed without breaking contact.

"Chloe, stop. I don't think we should do this."

Rolling off of him, I release a frustrated sigh. "I don't get it. Why not?"

"Because I respect you too much for what this is."

"And what is this?" I sigh in frustration and motion my hand between the two of us.

"I don't know what you want from me, but I know what it can't be. I can't be in a relationship after how things went down between Erin and me. And I' m not willing to have a one-night stand with you. Chloe, you deserve better than that. You deserve better than me."

I'm pretty sure that was the night I started falling for him. It's not going to help anything to bring it up now, so I take a couple swigs of tequila and set the bottle on her dresser before heading into the bathroom.

I instill an overly bright and cheery tone to my voice. "We should get going soon. Tonight's supposed to be fun and not about goodbye. We'll do that tomorrow. So cheer up, buttercup."

The guys recently signed a record deal with Oliver Morris. Apparently he used to work for Flynn's dad, Carl Wilson, who is the owner of Lost Souls Records and also Audrey's employer. Oliver lives in Portland, which is nearly five hours away, so the guys are all moving up there tomorrow so they can get started on creating an album.

She rolls her eyes at me. "I know that, Chlo. But I'm allowed to feel sad. I'm in love with him and he's leaving me. I can't imagine not being able to see him whenever I want."

Continuing to stick with my fake happiness, I say, "Don't worry, Ashtyn, the school year will fly by. Besides, it's not like they're going off to war, just the other end of the state."

"What about all the slutty ho bags out there? I told you how the starfuckers acted when I first got here. He can have his pick of girls out there. He'll get tired of a cold bed and find someone else to keep him warm."

"How could you think that?"

She shrugs her shoulders.

"He would never cheat on you. That boy is madly in love with you. You're it for him. It's written all over his face whenever you're around."

Her face lights up with nothing but happiness. "You really think so?"

"Really, Ashtyn? I know so. No more crying. Let's go to that party and have the time of our lives. That gorgeous boyfriend of yours is waiting."

"Hey, you watch yourself there." She smiles and goes back to finishing her makeup.

"You know I don't want Flynn. But I can appreciate a gorgeous man when he's standing right in front of me."

As if on cue, Flynn shows up and Ashtyn agrees to ride with him to the party on his motorcycle. I guess I'm getting her Jeep all to myself tonight. As they're heading out, I take a couple more gulps from my tequila bottle and then stash it back in my duffle bag. I'm a little lighter and warmer now. Hopefully this will be nothing but a fun night.

They're still kissing and being cutesy when I get out to

the driveway, so I take off first. I plug my phone in and blast "Closer to the Edge" by 30 Seconds to Mars. Oh man, Jared Leto is so hot. The things I would do with that man if I had him alone for a night. I reach over to turn the volume up and swerve a little on the road.

Oops.

I guess I took a few swigs too many. I finally get there and park the Jeep. Rather than wait for Ashtyn, I go off in search of my favorite Hartley brother. It doesn't take me long to find Jax hanging out near the dock. Bumping my shoulder against his, I pull his attention away from wherever his head was at. He's all smiles when his eyes land on mine. He pulls me into a tight embrace and I relax into his arms. He smells faintly of campfire and cologne. "Chloe, you're here."

I giggle and beam up at him. "Of course I'm here. Where else would I be?"

He shrugs and steps back, breaking our embrace. "I'm so stoked we're leaving tomorrow. Only focusing on the band is going to be epic."

My happiness falters, but I quickly shake that away. I can't fault him for his happiness. "Well we need to do a celebratory drink, then."

"Hell yeah we do. What's your poison for the evening?"

I open my mouth to answer him before I'm rudely interrupted.

"Jax. There you are. We've all been waiting." A harem of skanks comes strolling up and breaks us out of our little bubble. The lead skank holds up a bottle of peach schnapps.

"We're doing body shots, remember?" She smiles at Jax before turning daggers on me.

I give her a smile as sickeningly sweet as the liqueur in her hand and tuck myself underneath Jax's arm. He automatically wraps him arm around my shoulders and kisses me on my temple. I melt a little right there, and the bitches scowl and continue with their daggers. "I'll be over in a minute." Her entire face lights and she opens her mouth to say something but must think better of it. She makes a point to smile extra widely in my direction before turning to walk away. "Oh, and Brooke?"

"Yes, Jax?" she says in a sultry voice that makes me want to gag.

"Grab something a little stronger. I don't do the sweet stuff."

Her smile falters and I turn my face into his chest to hide my laughter. Jax leans down and kisses me again. "You're okay with me heading over, right? Hudson's around here somewhere. And we can take that shot later."

I force my pain to the back of my mind and give him one of my megawatt smiles. "Of course. This is your night. Have fun, but don't forget to come find me later. You've been fighting me on it all summer, but I will be in your bed tonight."

His face breaks out in a half-cringe, half-smile. I can tell he's internally fighting between what he wants—what we both want—and what he feels is right. "I leave tomorrow, Chlo."

"More reason to finally give in to what we've both been feeling. No more talking about this. Go do your shots with the skanks, but you will be mine later." To really put my point forward, I pull his face down to mine and slam my lips onto his. He stiffens slightly, but I knead my fingers on the back of his neck underneath his hairline and dart my tongue out along his bottom lip. He groans and pulls my body to his own while bringing his hands to my ass. All too soon I break the kiss before we end up having sex right here in front of everyone.

He presses his forehead to my own. "Whatever you say, babe." And then he walks away like nothing even happened.

Making my way to the patio, I spot my good old buddy José Cuervo. I grab the bottle of tequila and head back toward the grass. I'm chugging the bottle when Hudson comes by and snatches it out of my hands. "What the fuck, Hudson?"

I reach for the bottle again, but he holds it back from me. "If you continue hitting the bottle that hard, you'll end up sick or passing out in less than an hour. Why don't you take it easy?"

He looks legitimately concerned, but I don't care right now. I reach for the bottle again, and this time he relents. "Why do you even care?"

Grabbing my hand, he leads me over to the fire pit and we take a seat. "I care, Chloe. I can tell you're hurting and I'm sorry."

I look over at him and his whole face is full of remorse. "What do you have to be sorry for?"

He grabs the bottle from me and takes a generous chug himself before placing it on the ground in front of us. I pick it back up and cradle the bottle like it's my baby. I know

I've reached the point of word vomit, but I'm drunk and I don't care. "Why are you even over here, Hudson? I'm sure Jax isn't going to sleep with all of those girls, at least not tonight. Why don't you go find your hookup for the night? I guarantee you, Jax is already living up to the rock star persona. Just gearing up for skankri-la."

"You don't get it, do you?"

I know I'm drunk, but I have no idea what he's talking about. I get it one hundred percent. Jax is an asshole and I fell for him. I'm the idiot, just like all the groupies surrounding him. I thought I could tame the untamable.

What a fucking joke.

I'm not drunk enough to spew all of those thoughts, so I ask him the only thing I can think of. "Don't get what? What is there to get?"

He looks over at me and opens his mouth but immediately slams it shut. What is going on here? His focus moves away from me and out onto the lake. He lets out a sigh and stands up.

"Never mind. It doesn't matter—"

I nod my head and ignore whatever else he says. It isn't important anyway. I continue nursing the bottle until I hear a shrieking laugh coming from the other side of the yard. From over here, it looks like he's just moving down the whore line doing body shots. The shrieker gets a little bold and slams her lips to Jax's. And he is all for it. She wraps her legs around his body, pulling him flush against her. She's dry humping him and he isn't doing a thing to stop it. They're practically having sex right here in front of everyone. It makes me sick.

Why am I still here? Why am I watching this shit? Fuck

it.

I don't notice Ashtyn approaching, and she breaks my concentration when she asks, "Hey, Chlo, what's going on? Why are you sitting over here?"

Looking around myself, I realize Hudson must have left. I guess he got bored with me ignoring him and only paying attention to his brother. One more thing that I can add to the list of stuff Jax is fucking up tonight. Why did I have to fall for him? Stupid fucking heart.

She looks down at the bottle in my arms and I twirl it around. "Hey, Ash. I was hanging out with Hudson, but he got bored with me, so he left. Everyone's leaving me these days. So I'm hanging out with my buddy José tonight. He always likes spending time with me."

She reaches for the bottle and I don't even fight her when she takes it. I need to leave this place anyway. Wasn't I already leaving? "Why are you upset, Chloe? What's going on?"

Throwing my arms out, I stumble out of the chair. My breathing is a little erratic and I just need to go. Fuck! "I can't do this anymore. I really like Jax. I thought something could actually happen between us. Something real."

"Every time I've asked you, you've told me you're just hanging out." Is she that oblivious? I mean, yeah, she's been focusing on Flynn a lot lately, but she's always been able to see through my lies in the past. "Yeah, well, I lied. He's over there livin' it up with all the 'see you next Tuesdays.' I've never been the girl to care, but somehow my stupid heart got involved. I need to leave."

She grabs my arm. "Chloe, you can't leave like this."

I stumble away, cursing under my breath. "Just watch me."

"The plan was to stay the night. If you had told me you wanted to leave, I wouldn't have started drinking tonight. I'm sorry you have feelings for Jax, but you're right, I don't see him settling down anytime soon. Sorry."

Way to stab me in the heart right now. If she's trying to get me to stay, she's fucking failing big time. I'm so over this right now. "I need to get out of here. I need to get away from Jax. I don't feel like sitting here watching him pick his whore for the evening. He's ripping my heart out of my chest. I feel like I'm suffocating, and I need to be as far away from him as possible."

"Chloe, calm down for a minute. Let's talk about this. You never told me you felt that way about Jax. You always acted like you were having fun."

"I don't want to talk this to death right now, Ash. I need to get out of here."

I take off and don't look back. I drove here, so I still have the keys to her Jeep. I hop inside, and luckily, no one blocked me in. I'm starting up the car when Ashtyn flings open the door and gets in the passenger seat. After she shuts the door, I don't even wait before peeling out of there.

"Chloe, pull over. We can figure everything out. We've both been drinking and your emotions are going a little haywire right now. It sucks Jax is an ass, but you knew that already. He's the epitome of a player."

"Yeah, and I was another one of the stupid girls thinking they could tame him. I hope someone rips his heart out and stomps the shit out of it someday."

My phone starts ringing and I'm looking all over for it. I don't remember taking it into the party with me, but I can hear it close.

Where the fuck is it?

I look over at Ashtyn and notice that she's typing something on her phone. That's when I spot mine still plugged in. I pick my phone up to answer it when Ashtyn says, "Hey, right now isn't the best time to be on the phone—"

I don't let her finish before I answer my phone. Even in my inebriated state, it crosses my mind that it's a strange time for my grandma to be calling. "What's going on? Isn't it like three a.m. over there?"

Her voice comes over the line after a pause that makes my heart sink. "I know it's late, honey, but I have some bad news."

My heart stops sinking because it hits the pit of my stomach.

"Chloe, are you still there?"

I nod at the phone, but I know she can't hear me. I can't get the words out of my mouth. In my gut I know something isn't right, but I don't know how to respond to her right now.

"I'm sorry for telling you this way, but there was an accident, Chloe. Your parents didn't make it—"

I don't even hear anything else that she tells me. All of the air leaves my body. My face gets wetter and wetter, but I don't actually feel as if I'm in my body anymore. I feel as if I'm traveling higher and higher, away from my body.

I feel like I'm watching it all in slow motion as the Jeep swerves on the road and slams into a tree. My body flies forward and slams into the steering wheel before falling back into my seat. I spot Flynn and Hudson charging toward us. Oddly, it occurs to me that must have been the text Ashtyn sent.

There's gut-wrenching screaming coming from somewhere, and I look over and notice Ashtyn crumpled at an awkward angle. It's only then that I realize the screaming is coming from me and I can't stop. I'm vaguely aware of someone trying to get my attention and pulling me out of the car. It's almost as if I'm two separate people right now: the one coherent about her surroundings, and the other who can't quite connect and is a full-blown mess.

My arm suddenly burns with a sharp pain, and my disconnect starts coming back together. Rather than stick around and watch everything unfold, I start to close my eyes, and I see Hudson's broken face before I shut them and allow the darkness to pull me under.

CHAPTER ONE

Chloe

One Month Later

Drinking all night long always sounds like a good idea at the time. Not so much when you wake up to the bright and fucking shiny sun to remind you of the mistakes from the night before. For example, my clumpy mascara and my black eyeliner are caked and crusty, making it difficult to open my eyes, my mouth tastes like I drank a gallon of vomit rather than expelled it, and there's an unknown piece of man meat currently trapping my body.

I hope this isn't going to be a coyote ugly moment.

Carefully, but not so gracefully, I attempt to wiggle free. Said man meat lets out a muffled groan and continues to spoon me even tighter. The muscular arm holding me down is hopefully a good sign of an attractive guy wrapped around me. Letting out an exasperated sigh, I turn slightly to see what kind of a situation I need to work myself out of. I hold my breath in anticipation until I see Hudson's floppy mess of sandy blond hair.

He looks kind of cute while he's sleeping. So innocent and not a care in the world. His entire face breaks out into a giant grin; he must be having quite the dream. If I hadn't seen his face, the very obvious thing poking me in my butt would have let me know. And with that, I don't even care about waking him up; I jump up and out of bed.

Grumbling, he looks over at the clock and back at me. "Chloe, it's five in the morning. Why the hell are you up?"

Getting my wits about me, I'm suddenly a little dizzy and sit back down on the edge of the bed. "If you must know, Little Hudson decided to make his presence quite known this morning, and right into my ass crack. I don't know about you, but that's an exit only zone."

He lets out a small chuckle. "I'm going to pretend you didn't just call my dick Little Hudson. And I had no intentions of sticking it anywhere, because I was in a deep sleep. Now, please, can we sleep for a little bit longer before we absolutely have to get up for school?"

Shit. I forgot about school. First day of senior year.

It's funny how you can have an idea in your mind for your entire life what this day would look like. Brand new wardrobe, a great tan from being beachside all summer long, and your parents to wish you luck on your first day. Of course all that went to shit the moment my parents died.

Not much matters anymore. This is just another day, in another year of my miserable life. Or at least it is now. If there were any liquor around, I'd drink to that. Instead I'll just comply with Hudson's wishes and climb back into bed. He pulls me toward him and wraps his muscular arms back around my body.

I sigh into his chest. "You know, one of these days, you're going to have to stop taking care of me. You'll start giving the ladies the wrong idea."

"No way. And give up on sharing my bed with a hot babe every night?"

I roll my eyes. "C'mon, Hudson, I know you'd rather be getting laid than snuggling with a drunken mess. I'm not your responsibility. You can stop taking care of me."

Leaning toward me, he kisses my forehead and gazes into my eyes. "Nobody is forcing me to do anything. I'm here because I want to be and I don't give a shit what anybody else thinks about it. Now close your eyes and go back to sleep. We have to be up in an hour anyway."

I have no intentions of going to sleep, but I don't tell him that. As his breathing evens out, I contemplate how I even got here. I went from a near perfect life to a fucked up one. Life can be real hilarious sometimes; I just wonder what I did that made it want to play this game with me.

It's mocking me and saying, *Hey, Chloe, nobody gets perfection. Everyone needs a little drama and suffering in his or her life.*

You know what, though? Joke's on you, life. At this

point I don't even give a shit anymore. I'm going through the motions, but honestly, nothing even matters anymore. How's that for a little cynical life contemplation on my first day of my last year of high school?

Happy fucking senior year, Chloe.

I don't know when it started, but I notice tears are dripping down my face. Hudson must not have been asleep like I thought he was. He pulls me in tighter, and I let everything loose. My entire body wracks with the sobs I'd been holding back, and I don't understand how there are any left in me.

All I've done is cry.

Every day since the day they died. So far, Hudson is the only person I've let see me cry. Not even Ashtyn knows what I'm going through. She's my best friend, cradle to the grave and all of that nonsense. I'm sure she has an idea, but she hasn't heard it from me. She also hasn't seen me either. I went straight from the hospital to Hudson's house. Her dad and sister came up from Santa Barbara after the accident, and they're staying for good. No more divorce, just one big happy family, and I can't bear to be around that right now.

I know Hudson's been updating Ashtyn, but he doesn't want me to know, so I haven't said anything. If they want to keep it a secret from me, then so be it. I don't care either way.

Snuggling into his chest, I hold on to him for dear life and hope he never lets me go. He's been my comfort through the storm that is my life. I shouldn't lean on him, but I'm so damn selfish right now. I'm falling apart and hanging by a thread. Hudson is the only one keeping me going day in and day out.

One of these days, I'll need to acknowledge my disastrous life. Today will not be that day. Today I will take one step at a time and just try to get through it without breaking down. Maybe tomorrow or the next day, but not today. Definitely not today.

An hour later, as if on cue, the alarm on Hudson's phone goes off. It's blaring some song that I don't recognize. Grumbling, he rolls over and shuts off the alarm before returning and snuggling back into me. I shouldn't be enjoying the feel of his strong muscular arms around my body, but it's hard not to. I feel safe and protected with him, and he's about the only person who makes me feel that way lately. "How can you have your alarm set to music? I think that would annoy the shit out of me."

"Well, if it annoyed you, wouldn't that help you wake up?"

I contemplate that for a minute before answering. "Nope, I'd just shut the song off and roll back over and go back to sleep."

"You don't know how an alarm works, do you?"

I just giggle. I've never liked getting up early. I would always hit the snooze button over and over. Eventually, Mom would have to drag me out of bed. It never took much effort on her part, because she'd bring with her a skinny vanilla latte from Starbucks. I push that thought to the back of my mind. I don't want to bring that pain and emotion up right now. Instead, I change the subject. "So, what was that song that was playing? I mean, yeah, it was kind of loud and annoying, but I kind of liked the sound of it."

He rolls over and looks at his phone. "I don't have a song set for my ringtone. It just plays a random song from my music selection. It looks like this morning we heard 'Right Where We Belong' by Boymeetsworld."

"I've never heard of them before." I think about that for a minute because I never seem to know any of the music that Ashtyn or the guys listen to. "Should I have? Are they connected to that old nineties TV show or something?"

He chuckles. "No, pretty girl, there's no reason for you to have heard of these guys. They're an unsigned band. And they don't have anything to do with the show, either."

"Then how do you know who they are?"

"I saw them at Warped Tour in Portland last year. They're pretty good. I have a feeling they'll be signed soon though."

"Well, aren't you just an expert on unknown bands."

"Something like that."

I turn over so we're facing each other and just get lost in his ocean-blue eyes. Some days I wish I had talked to Hudson first instead of Jax. Maybe things would be different right now. Maybe they wouldn't be. I don't know. I reach my hand up and run my fingers through his soft hair. He has a little bed head, but it looks so adorable on him. It's just long enough to have something to grab on to. I tug it slightly and he lets out a little groan before rolling onto his back. "Why do we have to go to school again? We could just lay in bed all day and never get up."

I laugh softly. Hudson is not the type to just ditch

school, especially on the first day. He hasn't said anything to me, but I know he's excited for today. I get the feeling Hudson's pretty popular. Then again, he and Jax did go to school together for a couple years, and I can pretty much guarantee Jax was the king of that school. It would have been interesting to know him back then. Back before that bitch broke his heart. I'm curious to know what she's like. Apparently her older brother owns the record label they signed with, so I'm sure I'll meet her at some point. That will be quite the conversation.

I flop myself onto his chest so we're face to face again. Little Hudson isn't currently present, or else this would make for an even more awkward situation. I look up at Hudson and he's beaming down at me. "You know, I would be perfectly fine with skipping the day." I ground myself down into him a little. "I could think of something a lot more fun we could do today. Hell, I would be fine with skipping the year. You were supposed to finish this year online anyway. Why don't we just do that?"

After the accident, Flynn threw a huge fit, or so I hear. He told Oliver, the owner of the label that signed their band, that there was no way he would move and leave Ashtyn behind. So Ashtyn got her way and Flynn isn't leaving, Hudson gets to finish his senior year with his friends, and I'm not really sure where that leaves me. If this were before, I would be ecstatic, but I just can't find the desire to feel much of anything these days.

He shakes his head slightly and presses his lips together in a slight grimace, almost as if he's in pain. He looks around the room before finally falling back onto me.

"I don't think that would be good for you. We need to get out of this room and have some human interaction. I know I haven't talked about it, but I'm looking forward to this year, and I want to graduate with my friends."

He's been coddling me so much lately he couldn't even tell me he was excited for his senior year. Sure, I'm not, but that doesn't mean he can't be. I'm fucking miserable and making life for everyone around me just as depressing. I should just go to Kansas and be miserable with my grandma. At least that way Hudson wouldn't have to take care of me, and he could find himself a girlfriend and be happy.

I'm not even going to think about why that thought knots up my stomach.

Turning to look up at him, I say, "You should enjoy your senior year. I don't know why I'm even here anymore. I'm not even talking to Ashtyn, and her parents are supposed to be my guardians. I should just go to Kansas and get out of everyone's hair."

He places his finger on my lip and says, "Don't even talk like that. You aren't in anyone's hair. If you left, then I wouldn't enjoy my senior year. So stop acting this way. I want you here, Chloe. I don't want you to be anywhere else but here in my arms. I'm content with never letting you go."

His ears turn pink with his admission, and I wish things were easier. I contemplate leaning up and pressing my lips to his. I could easily lift my hand and run it through his hair and down his face. We could both give into the tension radiating off of our bodies and let go. Biting my lower lip, I look up into his eyes and I'm blasted with the desire shooting from them. As if on cue, Little Hudson comes to attention and breaks me out of the daze I was in. "Do you want to take a shower first or should I?" The third option is hanging out there, left unsaid.

Clearing his throat, he closes his eyes as if in pain. "I'll jump in the shower real quick. Let you relax a little bit longer or whatever. I can just get out of your hair so you can take as long as you need to get ready."

He jumps up and rushes into his en suite bathroom and shuts the door. I roll over and throw myself back onto the pillows. My whole body smells like Hudson, and I don't want to get in the shower and wash him off me. I'd rather walk around with him wrapped around me for the day. It will be like I'm not going at this alone. Ugh, that makes me sound like a crazy person. I guess at this point I'm pretty fucking crazy. I should just go with it.

I should shower. Maybe I can catch him by surprise and jump in with him? A way to distract me from the horrible day we're embarking on. Plus, a little morning sex never hurt anybody. I don't even have the chance to contemplate further. He whips the door open and comes walking out. If his hair weren't wet, I would assume he didn't even shower while he was in there. I can't help myself as I sit up and trail his body from head to toe. His tight t-shirt is clinging to his body and leaving little to the imagination. Beating the shit out of drums builds up some great upper body muscles.

"Hey, I'm done. I'm going to get some coffee. Just meet me downstairs in the kitchen whenever you're ready." He leaves the room before I have the chance to respond. I'm left blinking and feeling like the clock skipped ahead without me noticing. I swing my legs over the edge of the bed and grudgingly tromp to the shower. The sooner this day starts, the sooner it can end. Fortunately, I'm done with the community service that I had to do after the accident. Hudson's dad worked out a deal for me since I got the phone call while I was driving, but the fact that I had been drinking underage did not go unnoticed. His dad is a miracle worker. Besides the community service, I got off with a warning, but if I get any tickets or accidents in the next year, my license is gone. Since I don't have a car of my own, that shouldn't be a problem.

CHAPTER TWO

Hudson

After the morning we had, I figure the best way to get through the day is a monstrous pot of coffee. I leave Chloe in my room to shower and get ready. Of course that was after taking the shortest and coldest shower of my life. The idea was to shock my body out of its stupor, and tame Little Hudson, as Chloe called my dick. I could deal with the only thing standing between Chloe and me being Jax. But her parents dying, I can't cross that bridge. She needs a friend, not some horny guy wanting to get in her pants. But I'm not just a horny guy, and it's so much more than that.

When Ashtyn brought her best friend from out of town to our house that first night, I was a goner. Of course she set her sights on Jax from the beginning, but she didn't spend every minute with him.

"What are you doing down here all by yourself?"

I jump half a foot in the air and fall off my stool. "Holy shit." Turning around, I see Chloe standing by the door with her hand over her mouth, trying to hold in a laugh.

"I'm...sorry...I didn't mean to scare you," she spits out in between giggles.

I puff out my chest all macho-like. "You didn't scare me."

She nods her head in agreement, but her eyes tell me otherwise. "So, what are you doing down here?"

I rub the back of my neck as I stand up and motion her over to me. "Come here. I'll show you." She tilts her head to the side but walks over anyway. Sitting her down on my stool, I pick up the drumsticks and place them in her hands. "I like to come down here and play random beats. It's fun to not focus on making anything. That's usually when I come up with my best stuff."

Her gaze trails up and down the sticks in her hands. With a shrug of her shoulders, she starts beating the shit out of the drums. She has no idea what she's doing, but judging by the laughs leaving her mouth, she's having the time of her life. After about thirty seconds, she drops the sticks and leans herself back into my chest. "How can you do that for so long? My arms are burning."

"Lots and lots of practice. That and I don't aimlessly hit the drums like a crazy person."

She spins around on the stool. "You did not just call me crazy." I open my mouth, and my words get caught in my throat. My heart starts racing and she starts grinning like crazy. "I'm kidding. I was beating the shit out of your drums." She brings her hands up to my face and lets out a small gasp at the contact. Biting her bottom lip, she pulls my face down to hers and I lay my forehead against her own.

"You're Jax's girl."

She leans back, and her ocean-blue eyes are burning with desire. "I'm nobody's anything." Instead of leaning back in for that almost-kiss, she gets up and leaves me frustrated, confused, and alone.

Down in the kitchen, I find Jax, luckily alone. He never cared about flaunting his latest conquests around, but since Chloe has been staying here, I haven't seen a single one. I'm extremely grateful, and I wonder if he even knows he's doing it. "Hey man, what are you doing up so early?"

Looking up from his overflowing bowl of Cap'n Crunch, he says, "Chloe isn't exactly a quiet crier. But I'm used to it at this point. I don't have anywhere to be, so I can just sleep all day."

"Sorry about that. I think it's just hitting her a little harder today. Stuff like your first day of senior year is important to girls like Chloe. It's the first major life moment that her parents are missing."

"I get it, dude. I haven't said anything because she's going through shit right now. I'm not a major asshole, or at least I try not to always be."

Oddly enough, I think that's the first normal conversation we've had in a long time. The Hartley brothers don't have heart-to-hearts, as funny as that sounds. Honestly, if it weren't for the band, I don't think we'd be as close as we are. That's about all we have in common. The silence drags on, and although it isn't uncomfortable for me, Jax can never have it be silent for too long. He always has to fill the silence in some way.

One night when I was watching TV, Jax came in, and just like any older brother he took the remote and changed the channel. I thought about arguing, but I was too exhausted and went with it. Five minutes after he found something, I could hear mumbling. I looked over and his mouth was moving. "What the fuck are you doing?"

"I don't know what you're talking about, dude. I'm not doing anything. What are you doing?"

"Yes you are. Wait…are you saying all of the lines?"

"No. Why would I do that? That's weird."

After another five minutes, he started up again. He was oblivious to the fact he was doing it, or he couldn't hold out any longer. Either way, it was some pretty funny shit.

"Do you think the Flash can turn his dick into a human vibrator during sex?"

And there it is. What the fuck? I stare at him incredulously. "Where do you come up with this shit?"

He holds up his juice glass, and I notice it's adorned with the members of the Justice League. "C'mon, just think about it."

I shake my head. "I don't know. I guess that makes sense."

"Dude, that would be awesome."

I can't believe we're even having this conversation right now. "Just don't tell the ladies your theory."

"Why not?"

"Because then they'd be disappointed in your lack of vibrating abilities."

"Trust me, brother, no chick has ever left my bed disappointed."

"Dude, I don't want to know how any girl feels leaving your bed. That's between you and whoever your latest hookup is." He opens his mouth to say something, but Chloe walks in the room and he shuts it right back up. I don't know what was going on between Chloe and Jax over the summer, but it stopped after that night. The two of them don't even talk to each other anymore. Or more like Jax doesn't talk to Chloe. I think he feels responsible for the accident, but I've told him time and again it wasn't his fault.

On the nights she doesn't drink herself into a drunken stupor, Chloe tosses and turns in her sleep. I'm there every time just to hold her and soothe her into a less restless sleep. I don't know what I would do if I knew it was going on but couldn't be there to help her through it. I wish she would talk to somebody about it rather than hold it in and try to numb the pain with alcohol.

She goes to grab a mug for coffee but hesitates and puts it back in the cupboard. I've never seen her drink coffee before, at least not from here. I like to drink it strong and black. Chloe is more of a frou-frou coffee drinker. Lots of extra sugary shit. I don't know how she drinks it. "Do you think we can stop and get coffee on our way in?"

"Sure thing. There's a Starbucks on the way." Even if it were out of my way, I'd say yes to get a hint of a smile on her face. I can't stand the thought of her being so unhappy, and I've been doing everything in my power to try to make her happy. If that includes some girly coffee drink, then I will deliver.

"Okay, I guess I'm ready, then. Oh shit! Do I need anything?"

"Nope, it's all been taken care of."

She looks over at me and asks, "What do you mean? What's been taken care of?"

Sighing, I look over at Jax, who is extremely focused on his half-empty bowl of cereal, before looking back up at her. "Ashtyn's mom enrolled you both in school. Ashtyn is bringing you a backpack with everything that you need in it."

I half expect her to start yelling. For her to be furious that we were all going behind her back. For her to show any kind of emotion. Unfortunately, I don't get the reaction I want. Instead, I get absolutely nothing. "Whatever. I guess we should go, then."

And that's that.

The new Chloe. So numb to everything. I mostly watched the old Chloe from afar, but the two of them are like night and day. She used to be so lively and happy. Truly happy. Not a care in the world. I toss her my keys. "Why don't you meet me in my car. I'll be out in a minute."

She doesn't even reach to catch them. They fall to the floor and she reaches down to grab them. Other than that, she again has no reaction. She just turns around and heads outside. "What am I going to do, Jax?"

He opens his mouth to speak but then shuts it immediately and shrugs his shoulders. I turn to walk away because I don't know what I'm going to do either. She's not dealing with anything, and I'm pretty sure I'm hurting her more than helping her. I just don't know what I should be doing. Turning my attention back to the coffee pot, I finally fill my travel mug with the only thing that will help me get through this day.

The steam wafts up to my nose, and I savor the smell of the rich nectar I'm holding in my hands. We went on a family trip to Sydney over the summer, and I always love picking up good coffee wherever we go. There were some pretty epic coffee shops there and some of my favorite coffee so far. And Chloe wants Starbucks instead? That girl does not know what she's missing. Then again, if she wanted some of that weasel-shit coffee, I would gladly go and find it for her. Even if the thought of that makes me want to gag. Anything to make her day a little brighter.

If Jax could hear my thoughts, he would be all over me about how whipped I am. It's true but fucking sucks at the same time. One of these days I will get back the girl I fell in love with. The girl who brightened my day every time she smiled. Hell, her smile was more like the sun, perfect and blinding. I'd give anything to get my daily fix of Chloe's smile. Anything.

CHAPTER THREE

Chloe

Why did I think school here would be any different from back home? Sure the people are different, but then again they're not. Maybe different faces but not different people. It's like you could pluck someone out of any high school and plop him or her in another and everything would still be the same. There are still cliques and plenty of bitches to go around. I almost had a cat fight on the first day of school. Apparently the queen bee around here is some chick named Brooke Mitchell. Honestly, the funny thing is, I was her back at my old school in Santa Barbara. I would have done the same thing too. Some new girl who is potentially prettier than me—major red flag and definite threat. Our little showdown was pretty laughable though. And made me realize how dumb the stupid drama is.

I'm putting some of the shit that Ashtyn's mom got me away in my locker when the click-clacking of heels stops right behind me. The cheap heels start tapping and someone pokes me on the shoulder. I'd rather not talk to anybody, so I pretend like I don't notice and continue organizing what little I have in my locker. It doesn't take long before I hear a whiny voice say, "Excuse me, you're being rude."

My arm freezes in midair as I start putting a notebook away. Dropping it in place, I clench and unclench my fist, tempted to turn around and bitch slap this chick in the face. I'm in no mood for any high school bullshit. Forcing a sweet smile on my face, I turn around. "Oh, I'm sorry. Did you need something? I didn't hear you behind me. New school and all. I was so focused on getting my locker all situated."

She sneers, marring her otherwise pretty features. "I'm watching you. I'm the queen of this school, and you better not have any ideas about dethroning me. You're nobody. You got that."

I cover my mouth with my hand, mostly to hide the fact that I stuck my tongue out behind it. "Wait, I know you. Body shots girl, right?"

Holding her head high, she turns to her posse and back to me. "I have no idea what you're talking about."

"Sure you do. We met this summer at Hudson's house. You let Jax do body shots off of you." I lean in close and whisper in her ear, "I'm sure you thought you'd be his hookup for the night. Too bad he dropped you and came running for me when I needed him."

I lean back with my smile still plastered on my face as she scowls at me. She does this weird thing where she points her fingers to her eyes and back to me. Then she and her posse walk away. She's walking a half-step ahead like a true queen would. Wow, girls are bitches. What's the point of all that bullshit?

I continue organizing my locker, when a half sheet of paper flutters out of my binder to the floor in front of me. I reach down and pick it up, realizing it's my schedule. I glanced at it this morning, but I didn't really pay attention to any of the classes that Audrey, Ashtyn's mom, registered me for. It doesn't take long before my eyes zero in on my first class of the day: theater. My heart rate picks up and my hand holding the schedule starts to shake. I can feel the tears start to build. I slam my locker shut and run in the direction of the bathrooms to let myself break down in private.

I'm standing here at my locker, thinking about the first day of school. The first week has flown by, but I still can't get what happened out of my head. After my breakdown I convinced myself dropping the class would be the best idea, but then the bell rang and I didn't want to be late. We're already a week in, and for some reason I just can't drop the class. I'm lost in my thoughts when Hudson comes up and taps me on my shoulder. Shaking out of my daze, I look up at him and ask, "Hey, what's up?"

With his brow furrowed, he asks, "Where were you? You seemed like you were somewhere else just now."

I wave him off. I'd rather he didn't know about my huge breakdown earlier this week. "Oh, it's not a big deal."

"C'mon, Chloe, just tell me. If it wasn't a big deal, you would tell me. So what's going on?"

I sigh dramatically. "If you must know, I was thinking about something that happened."

"What happened?"

"Seriously, Hudson, it's no big deal. Some girls here were marking their territory." If anything, I'd rather he think I'm upset over Brooke and her bitches than really know what's going on with me.

"What are you talking about?"

I guess he needs me to spell it out for him. Guys can be so dense sometimes. "The body shots girl from your party this summer. She put me in my place and said I wouldn't be 'dethroning' her. Her words, not mine."

He nods his head and rubs the back of his neck. "Got it. You were introduced to Brooke and her posse."

I lie like I don't know who she is. "We didn't exchange names, if that's what you're asking. Like I said, no big deal. I don't feel threatened by her or anything."

"Are you sure?"

I nod my head and go back to opening my locker, what I was doing prior to getting lost in my head. I seem to be doing a lot of that lately, which is not always a good thing. I'm putting all of my stuff away when Hudson clears his throat behind me. I finish what I'm doing, slam my locker shut, and turn my attention back to him. "Are you going home with Ashtyn today, or are you still avoiding her?"

I roll my eyes. He's asked me the same question every single day since I left the hospital. Or something along those lines. I'm not specifically avoiding Ashtyn, I'm avoiding her entire family. She's my best friend, my sister, and it kills me to even look at her. Her family is like my second family, and the fact that my parents are gone becomes very relevant when they're around. It's not their fault they're back together and happy while I don't have a family. I don't feel like shitting on their happiness with my fucked up sadness. Is it wrong to put that on Hudson?

Absolutely.

Doesn't change the fact that I'm sad and he's here. He truly wants to take care of me, and I like how that makes me feel. Hudson makes me feel loved, and I could use a little extra love right now. I'm selfish and greedy, but I'm not going to stop relying on him anytime soon. That is until he kicks me to the curb because he's sick of my moody bullshit and wants a real girlfriend. Until that day comes, he's stuck with me.

"Is that your way of asking me if I'm going home with you?"

Rubbing his neck again, he asks, "Why are you avoiding her? She's your best friend."

"I'm not avoiding her. And I don't feel like going into all of my drama right here in the hallway. I don't know these people, and I don't want them to know more about me. Other than the shit they're most likely already assuming and making up. I'm sure I can thank

Brooke in part for whatever rumors are already floating around."

"Okay, so you're coming home with me? And I haven't heard anything, so I'm sure people aren't talking about you."

"Yes, I'm going home with you. It shouldn't even be a question at this point."

Hudson leads the way to the parking lot where his black Range Rover is. We start pulling out of the school when I see Ashtyn and Abbie getting into her crimson Jeep. I don't know why it slipped my mind that Abbie was in high school this year, but it did. It's actually nice to see them together. They've never had a super close relationship, and maybe I've been to blame for that. I always considered Abbie a tag along, and Ashtyn left her out because she annoyed me when we were younger. I was such a bitch. Since I'm out of the way, it looks like they've gotten the chance to get closer. Or at least they're getting the chance.

I turn my head as we drive by. In my mind, if I don't look at them, then they can't see me. Obviously Ashtyn knows what Hudson drives, so it's kind of pointless. Oh well. Nobody said it had to make sense. I don't feel much like talking, and a broody song comes on, so I turn it up a little. I have no idea who these guys are, but I'm feeling it right now. My curiosity gets the better of me and I turn it down slightly to find out who it is. "I'm liking this song. Who are these guys?"

Incredulously, Hudson looks at me. "Seriously? You're a fan of this song? Isn't it a little harder than what you're used to?"

"You know what, I take offense to that. Sure, I'm a lover of T. Swift, but that doesn't mean I can't appreciate some broody rock music. Who are these guys? The dude's voice is super sexy."

"Ahh, it all comes out now. You don't like the song—you have the hots for the guy." He chuckles. "This particular song is 'Goodbye Agony' by Black Veil Brides. Not sure about the sexy part, but I agree it's a good song."

Ending the conversation, I turn the song back up and close my eyes. If I just focus on the words he's singing, then I don't have to focus on anything else. Especially all of the shit going on in my head right now. And I was right, this dude has a sexy voice. I wonder what he looks like. I'll have to remember to Google these guys later.

As I'm focusing on the music, the typically long drive flies by. We're pulling into Hudson's driveway and I notice the emptiness of the house. Except for the one cruise my parents went on without me, we always traveled together. I can't imagine growing up with your parents always gone. Hudson and Jax act like they don't mind, but it would bug me. Their parents are always gallivanting around on one weekend trip or another. Makes me wonder why they even had kids in the first place.

Turning the SUV off, Hudson turns to me. "Home sweet home. Any plans for the weekend?"

I look over at him, and I'm hit with an urge to kiss him senseless. I pull my bottom lip in between my teeth and focus on his lips. They're so plump and look incredibly kissable. I wonder what it would be like to just nibble on his bottom lip rather than my own. I could easily reach across the center console and pull him to me. My breathing quickens along with the rapidness of my heart rate. I want more of it because it's the first thing I've felt besides pain in months. He must realize my thought process or feel the sudden thickness of tension in the car because he turns away and lets out a cough. "Right. So we should get inside and…uh…yeah, let's get inside."

He's out of the car faster than I can respond, so fast he didn't even take his keys. I reach over and pull them out of the ignition before following his retreat. Ugh, maybe I just need to get laid. I haven't had sex since I left Santa Barbara this summer, and I think it's finally catching up with me. Why else would I be throwing myself at Hudson so much? I'm in no place to be getting involved with anybody. At least not seriously, and Hudson is the kind of guy to be very serious about relationships.

Inside, I hear the very familiar sound of his drums beating. Their studio or practice room is supposed to be super soundproof, but I can still hear whenever he plays the drums. Maybe it's not my hearing so much as I can feel the vibrations of it. He seems to be hitting them pretty hard today.

I've been living here for over a month, but it still doesn't feel like home. Home is back in Santa Barbara. There's nothing back there for me, but it's familiar. It's where I'm from, where I spent my entire life. I know Ashtyn's mom took care of all of the arrangements for my parents, but I never allowed myself to be a part of it. I was still in the hospital when it all happened. I only know this because Ashtyn visited me every day until I left. I only talked to her one time, just to let her know that nothing ever happened between Jax and me, but that was it. I had no desire to talk to anyone while I was in the hospital.

At one point they had a shrink visiting me, but I never said anything to her either. If I were staying with Ashtyn right now, I'd be having daily or at least weekly visits with that same chick. There was no way I was going to let that happen. That's why I'm here with Hudson. Nobody is forcing me to do anything. I can do whatever I want and I don't have to worry about anyone. Maybe not talking was my way of healing? I'm not sure, but I can tell you I still don't feel like I've been healed. How do you even know? Do you just wake up one day and say to yourself, I'm better. I've done my healing and everything is better now? I'm not sure.

I start climbing the stairs when I see Jax at the top of them. "Where's Hudson?"

I turn my body and nod toward the basement. "He's downstairs, hitting away at his drums."

Shaking his head, he asks, "Are you going to check on him? Or should I?"

I honestly don't even know what happened. One minute we were in the car and the next he fled. Did I do something wrong and I don't even know it? "I'm heading upstairs. If you want to go check on him, that's on you. I'll be in the shower."

Jax nods his head and starts heading down the stairs as I'm heading up. I make it to the top before he says, "You know he has feelings for you. If you don't feel the same, you should say something now. I don't want to see my brother get hurt."

Why does this have to fall on my shoulders? I never said anything to Hudson to make him think I was interested in anything more than friendship. Maybe I'm being selfish for leaning on him, but he's the only one who seems to make me feel better lately. I can feel tears start to build up. I take a deep breath and swallow them back down. Calming myself down, I turn around and say, "No, he doesn't. Besides, I'm in no place to have any kind of relationship right now. Your brother knows that. If he doesn't, then that's his fault, not mine."

"Either you're dumb or in denial, but it's still true." He looks at me for a second longer before turning around and walking away. I don't know why it's my responsibility to make sure Hudson doesn't get attached to me. He knows what I'm going through, and he shouldn't expect anything from me. I go into his room and toss my backpack on his bed. I feel like washing the shit of the day off me, so I head into his bathroom with my cell phone in hand.

Hudson doesn't have any good soap, but I fill up the bathtub anyway and pour in some of his body wash. Being surrounded by the smell of Hudson will either calm me down or turn me on. I'm not sure which is better, but either one has to be better than the way I currently feel. A nice hot bath to soak in sounds like heaven right about now. I plug my phone into the sound dock and switch on "Fighter" by Christina Aguilera. Slipping into the steaming hot bath, I clear my mind of any of the stressors of the day and focus on the anthem flowing from Christina's voice. I hope someday I'll be stronger than I am now. I can't currently see that in my future though.

I know I told Hudson what Brooke and company said didn't bother me, but it still kind of does. The last thing I need right now is the bitch crew starting problems with me. I have enough problems of my own without having issues at school. Hopefully they'll quickly learn I'm not a threat and just back off. I guess only time will tell on that front. I sink lower into the bathtub and wonder how far I can sink under.

Is it possible to push myself under the water and just not come up? I could just slowly sink under right now and let the water take over my body. I'm sure if I held myself under long enough, I would naturally just come up. I'm not a suicidal person; at least I didn't used to be. Maybe life for everyone around me would be so much better if I just weren't here anymore. I push my butt forward a bit and slowly start slipping my body underneath when the door flies open. Hudson comes walking in covered with a new sheen of sweat. He obviously worked out everything he was feeling on those drums of his.

"Oh shit, I'm sorry, Chloe. I didn't know you were in here." He brings his hand up to cover his eyes and his cheeks turn bright red.

I giggle, slightly hysterically, because I'm completely covered. For one thing, I filled the bathtub with stifling hot water and Hudson's body wash. For another, I was slowly slipping under and contemplating drowning myself. There's nothing of my body to see here. Before I have the chance to say anything, he turns around and walks back out. Well, so much for that. I guess I'll just have to try to kill myself another day. I lean forward and pull the drain stopper on the tub and watch as the water goes down. Getting up, I wrap a towel around myself and look in the mirror.

"What are you doing with your life, Chloe Weston?" Fuck if I know. Sighing more loudly than necessary, I turn around and head off to get changed and find Hudson. I don't know why, but I feel a strong need to apologize. Maybe I'll try to figure that out later, but not right now.

CHAPTER FOUR

Hudson

Someday I'll get used to the fact that Chloe shares my room and bathroom with me. I can't believe I walked in on her. I can't get the picture of her naked, soaking in my bathtub, out of my head. Little Hudson, as Chloe referred to my dick, starts coming to attention. Right about now I'd be taking a cold shower, but Chloe is currently soaking that smoking body of hers in my tub. Shit, I need to get a hold of myself.

I don't even think, I just go. Walking out the back door, I slip off my shoes, socks, and t-shirt. I contemplate leaving my pants on, but I add them to the trail of clothes behind me as I run full speed over the dock and jump into the freezing cold lake. It's a shock to my body, but I force it to stay under. My previous problem shrivels up from the cold, but I continue holding myself under. I slowly sink and plant myself on the bottom. I open my eyes and look around the murky water that prevents me from seeing much further than a couple of feet in front of me. My lungs are screaming and my brain sets into panic mode.

I shove my feet down and quickly swim to the surface, breaking free with a giant inhale of air. My breathing is ragged as I turn around to swim back toward the dock when I notice Chloe sitting on the end. Her feet are dangling in the water, and if I thought she looked gorgeous soaking in that tub, that's nothing compared to right now. Her hair is hanging down her back, the ends still dripping. Her white t-shirt clings to her body in all the places she didn't dry off.

I'm still in the freezing cold water, but I can feel stirrings below the waist. I am so screwed. I continue swimming toward the dock, but at a much slower pace than before. Forcing my brain to think of anything other than the gorgeous girl in front of me is a lot harder than I thought. My train of thought sucks. I try thinking about football, watching some games with the guys on Sunday. Jax isn't a huge fan, but he loves looking at the cheerleaders in their tight uniforms. I bet Chloe would rock a cheerleading uniform. Especially the ones the professionals wear. Shit.

I think we have some popsicles in the freezer. Maybe I should go eat one of those. It might cool my temp down even more. I wonder what Chloe looks like while eating a popsicle? I bet it's sexy as hell. I can just imagine her mouth going down the popsicle and bringing the whole thing in her mouth. The things she could—

Yep. Fucking screwed.

"I saw you jump in, so I brought a towel down for you."

I close my eyes and pretend to wipe water out of them. "Thanks. You didn't have to do that."

"The water is freezing and it's not exactly a hot summer day. What were you thinking?"

Before I even think about lying, the truth comes out. "I needed to cool off. I figured a quick swim in the freezing cold lake would do the trick."

"Cool off from what?"

"I was a little too worked up."

I glance up at her and see her mouth has formed into an O. I guess she gets it now. I pull myself onto the dock and attempt to not get Chloe wet with the gross lake water while I reach for the towel. As I pat myself down, I look over at her and have to do a double-take. Her eyes are fixated on my body, and they're blazing with desire. What the fuck do I do now? I know what my brain is telling me, but it's not connecting with what my body wants right now. What I want right now. I turn away from her and clear my throat a couple times before I speak up.

"Thanks for the towel. I…uh…I think I'm going to go take a shower now. Rinse some of this shit off of me."

I turn back around as she's shaking her head. She looks up at me with a fake smile plastered on her face. "Oh yeah, that's a good idea. Just let me know if you need anything else."

I don't even have to say anything else before her face turns beet red. I can think of plenty of reasons why I would need her in the shower with me, all of them one hundred percent selfish and too fast for her. It's not that I think she's a virgin or anything like that. I just don't think she's emotionally ready to get involved in a relationship. Because when we finally do something about this attraction we have, and we will be doing something about it, I won't be letting her go. At least not easily. She'll have to fight me for that.

One time with Chloe would not be enough for me. Hell, I don't think a thousand times would be enough. That's a need that I don't think could ever be quenched, but I'm sure we'll have more than enough fun trying. Before I change my mind and do something stupid, I start walking away. When I get up to the patio, I find all of my clothes folded in a neat little pile on the table. Turning around, I see Chloe is still looking out with her feet dangling in the water.

After my incredibly unsatisfying shower, I make my way downstairs, where I find everyone waiting for me. Funny thing is we're usually waiting around for Flynn. I guess since he lives closer he doesn't have a reason to be late. Plus my impromptu swim in the lake and my crappy shower took me a little longer.

Always the one to be incredibly serious, Flynn says, "You'd think that since you live here, you could be on time."

I start to open my mouth when Jax horns in. "Oh, he took a little dip in the lake." Turning toward me, he waggles his eyebrows and asks, "Did you need to cool off a bit?"

I know he's just kidding, but he doesn't know how close to home he hit. I turn my back from them and go sit at my drum set. "Are we ready to practice now?"

"Seriously, dude? What happened?"

I don't want to get into this shit right now, but knowing Jax, he won't leave me alone until he gets an answer from me. "If you must know, Jax, I walked in on her when she was in the bathtub. I obviously couldn't take a cold shower with her right there, so I dove into the lake. It didn't help though."

I expect him to start giving me shit or laugh in my face, but I'm surprised when he doesn't do either. He just shakes his head and says, "When are you going to stop torturing yourself? I realize she's a little emotional right now. So either suck it up and go for it or let her go. We all know Ashtyn would gladly step up and take her back. She is her best friend and all."

I bow my head and incessantly rub the back of my neck. Looking back up at the guys, I see nothing but pity in all of their eyes. When did I become the one they pitied? They've all had their share of shit, and I've always been on the sidelines, the cool and collected one who helped everyone pick up their own pieces.

"You don't get it, Jax." I turn my attention toward Flynn. "If this were Ashtyn, would you pawn her off onto Chloe? Or would you be by her side doing anything you could, knowing how much it was killing you inside that you couldn't have every part of her?"

He doesn't even hesitate before answering. "No question. I didn't leave her hospital bed, did I? But I lo—oh shit."

Jax looks confused and asks, "Oh shit what?"

"Yeah, oh shit what?" I ask.

"You're in love with her." Jude pipes up from over in the corner where he's been fiddling with his bass.

Shaking my head, I sit down on my stool. "I don't even know what love is. How can I feel something and not know what it is?"

Jax lifts his hands in the air and takes a step back when I look at his face. Flynn shrugs his shoulders, but Jude puts his bass down and takes a step toward me. "Let me ask you something. Is she the first thing you think of in the morning? The last thought that runs through your mind before you go to sleep at night? Would you do anything for her even if it meant being apart? Knowing it's the best thing for her no matter how much it kills you? If you can answer yes to all of those questions, then you are without a doubt in love with her."

"Fuck…I'm in love with her."

The grimace that flashes across Jax's face goes unnoticed by everyone except me. Shaking it off, I shift my gaze across the room and lock it with Jude's, who has moved back to his original spot. There's an eerie quiet to the room now, and I need to hit some shit. Preferably my drums so I don't break anything. I can't handle all of the pity heavily weighing on my shoulders. I'm choking, and the only way I can breathe is to let it all out. Let out the frustration of the situation I'm in. Let out the intense love I feel for this very broken girl. Just let it all out. "Can we just play now?"

Everyone nods their heads and we play. Typically, during practice, we attempt to write new stuff while perfecting some of our better songs. It won't be long before we get in the studio and record our first EP. Oliver wanted us to come up with at least fifteen kickass songs, that way he could hear them all and we would choose the best ones. The songs that would make it a cohesive album.

Today that's not even close to what's happening. With the tension in the room, we play a lot of cover songs. These guys truly are my brothers. They know what I need and just let me waste this practice. Technically we aren't wasting it, we just aren't playing our own shit. Flynn starts us off with "Pain" by Three Days Grace, and it's so fucking ironic. I lose myself in the song and just go with it. Our hour-long session goes through a variety of songs harder than what we play. Some Papa Roach, Avenged Sevenfold, and we end the night on a few of The Sinners' songs.

By the end of practice, I'm a little less frustrated and a lot more relaxed. Just being in a room with these guys and doing our thing always does that to me. We can get lost to the world while we're playing. My parents keep pushing me to go to college next year, but I know I wouldn't want to be doing anything else. This is where we're all meant to be. This is our future.

I'm drenched in sweat and need another shower, but I don't care. We have quite literally put our blood, sweat, and tears into this band. The fact that it's paying off is a bonus. If I never earned money from making music, I would still want to play. It isn't about the money. It's about the high that I get while playing. The adrenaline that flows through my body. There's nothing better than that. Well, maybe sex with Chloe, but I haven't had the pleasure of experiencing that yet, so I'll have to come back to it. Right now, the best feeling in the world is when I'm playing the drums.

All the guys look back at me as we finish our final song and I just nod. If I needed it, they would have stayed here all night to play. Luckily for them, I don't need to stay up all night. "Thanks, you guys. I needed that."

Being serious for too long always makes Jax uncomfortable, so he says, "If we would have played our own stuff, you would have sounded like shit. You just needed to pound on some shit. Although you'd feel better if you were pounding in Chloe."

I chuckle. He may not be eloquent with words, but he's still my brother. He gets it, most of the time. As everyone files out of the room, I stay sitting. I'm feeling good right now and I don't want that to go away. As soon as I go upstairs and see her face, that longing will return. I'd rather stay here for a little bit longer. Soak in the feeling I get while in this room.

CHAPTER FIVE

Chloe

I don't know what it is, but I always seem to find myself sitting out on this dock when I'm alone. Ever since school started, the guys are getting into more of a routine with practice, and I find myself without company most nights. I think I'm just naturally drawn to the water. Back home, if I was upset about something, I would always be down at the beach. I don't have an ocean nearby now, so I settle for the lake.

Hudson is the kind of guy I could truly see myself falling in love with. He has all of the best parts of Jax without the manwhoring side as well. But Hudson is way too good for me. Jax is the kind of guy I will end up with. Not that I'm complaining. I'd gladly choose a Hartley boy to be mine.

Of course his ears must be burning because Jax chooses that minute to come strolling out. He plops himself on the deck next to me, but I don't even have to look up to know it's him. My body hums whenever a Hartley boy is around, and I have a feeling Hudson won't be coming back out here. "That was a quick practice today."

He chuckles. "Yeah, well, if you'd give it up already maybe Hudson wouldn't be so sexually frustrated." I whip my head around. There's no way he just said those words to me. He winks at me. Fucking winks. "You know I'm just fucking with you. Well, mostly."

"If your brother wants me so bad, maybe he should do something about it."

"Damn right he should."

I turn my attention back out to the lake. The breeze is dancing over the water, putting a slight chill in the air. I should head back inside, but it's peaceful. Pulling my legs out of the water, I hug them to my chest and relish in the silence. Jax and I haven't had a conversation since before the accident. Sure, we've said hi and bye in passing, but that's nothing compared to the long conversations we used to have. As much as I'd like to bask in the sounds of nature, I need to clear things up with him. "I don't blame you for the accident. You know that, right?"

Shaking his head, he leans down and lays it in his hands. "I don't know what to think, Chloe."

I lift his head up and force his eyes on mine. "I was drunk and irrational that night, Jax. I wasn't thinking straight and my emotions weren't even close to being in check."

He raises one eyebrow as he asks, "Why did you get so pissed and leave? That's what I don't understand."

"It sounds ridiculous to say now, but I was mad at you."

Waving his arm in a circle, he says, "Okay, want to clarify a little further?"

I don't want to clarify that further. I don't want to tell him that I had feelings for him. That I still have feelings for him. How messed up is that? I share Hudson's bed with him every night, but part of me wishes it were Jax. I know I can't have them both. I know that. Doesn't stop me from thinking about it, from wondering what it would be like to have Jax want me just as much as Hudson does. "I like you, Jax. Or I liked you. I don't know much of what I'm feeling these days."

"We're friends, Chloe. I would hope you like me."

"Not like that, Jax. I may have…started falling for you."

His eyes bug out of his head. "What are you talking about?"

I let out a small chuckle and shake my head. "See it from my perspective. I'm a pretty girl."

He lifts his hand and his eyes go wide. "That's a little vain, don't you think?"

I can see why he'd think that, but that's not how I meant it at all. I sound like a stupid bitch, but I need to complete my thought so he knows where I'm coming from. "I'm not being vain, just honest. I know I'm pretty and I've never had issues finding a guy who thought so as well. But that's the thing. Any guy I've ever gotten to know just wanted me for sex. But not you."

"So you figured since I didn't want to sleep with you, that meant you loved me or could love me? I'm not following. That doesn't make any sense."

"Something like that, but not totally. You wanted to talk to me. You wanted to spend time with me for me and you didn't want anything out of me. Just my company, nothing more. I loved spending time with you and I looked forward to it. Especially when Ashtyn was going through all of her Flynn drama. One minute they're all over each other, the next she hates him, and then they're all over each other again. I didn't want anything to do with all of that."

He's rubbing his chin excessively and says, "Okay, so we spent some…um…time together. Did…uh…I lead you on? Make you think that I wanted something more?"

I've gone about this whole conversation the wrong way. I'm trying to take any blame or fault off of Jax, yet he still feels he is to blame. "No, you never did that. It was just how I felt. We were friends, and after developing a friendship I started having other feelings. The night of the party I was crushed. I was confused about what I was feeling for you, yet you were surrounded by a harem of skanks."

He turns away laughing and playfully knocks his knee against mine. "Give me a little more credit than that."

I press my lips together in a tight line. He can't actually be serious. "Jax, they were trashy. Even you can admit that."

He opens his mouth and then shuts it as another whip of the wind rips over the lake. My body spazzes out in an uncontrollable shiver, and Jax gets up and walks away.

What the fuck?

I watch his disappearing form as he wanders over to the fire pit. I don't move, completely transfixed on what he's doing. It isn't until I see the fire pit lit up that my brain connects with what he's doing. Quickly I get up and venture over in his direction. I don't realize how cold I am until my body starts tingling with the touch of the heat against my skin. Slowly I start thawing out and let the warmth envelop me. "Thank you."

He waves his hand and asks, "What were we talking about?"

"The starfuckers, the night of the party."

He does a double-take and rolls over laughing. "The what?"

"The starfuckers. You know, like groupies. I like the way that sounds better. It just rolls off your tongue."

Now he's rolling with laughter. I'll have to thank Ashtyn for that one later. Late night browsing of UrbanDictionary.com is always a fun time. "Well, either way, I didn't do anything with any of them."

"Please. Before I left, you were doing a line of body shots."

The tips of his ears turn red and he looks a little sheepish. "That may be true, but I wouldn't have taken it any further than that. I was having fun, sure, but I didn't sleep with any of them."

I hate to state the obvious but…yeah. "First off, you were all over Brooke. And yeah you didn't, because of the accident."

Adamantly shaking his head, he sputters out,

"That…that wasn't the only reason. Sure, I like to flirt. It's fun, but contrary to what everyone seems to think, I don't sleep with any girl that's willing. I'm broken, but I'm not that broken."

Sadly nodding, I say, "I think that's why I was originally drawn to you."

His eyes widen. "Because I'm broken?"

How I wish he weren't broken. Underneath all of the shit and the armor he's built around himself is an amazing guy. Unfortunately, Jax is pretty screwed up and only shows the asshole side of himself to most people these days. I know I was one of the lucky ones who have gotten the chance to see the real him. Before that bitch broke him, I know everyone got to see the real Jax. All he's doing is protecting his heart these days, and he refuses to get close to anyone. I hope someday a girl will come along and break down that tough exterior. I'd love to see the day the real Jax comes out to stay. "Yeah. I don't know, it sounds crazy, but I thought I could be the one to heal you. Help you realize that not all girls are selfish bitches like Erin was."

He cringes at the mention of her but recovers quickly. "I don't think anyone can heal me. I'm pretty sure I'm stuck like this."

"You're only that way if you want to stay that way. Part of me still hopes you'll let me be the one to heal you."

"You should be with Hudson. He's the better one between the two of us, and he can take care of you better than I ever could."

Dropping my head in my hands, I blow out a frustrated breath. "You know it doesn't work that way. Just because you tell me to be with Hudson doesn't mean I can just drop the feelings I have for you. It's a fucked up situation and I know that. I care for both of you, just in different ways."

"I don't know what you want from me."

"If I knew what I wanted, I'd let you know. I don't even know what the fuck I'm doing anymore, Jax." I don't know anything anymore. My heart is racing like it's going to rip right through my chest. Having no heart would be preferable to the pain mine is currently causing me. My entire body shudders as the first sob rips itself from my body.

Why did she have to leave me?

Each tear that rips down my face is like a shock to my body. One right after the other and it's never-ending. I'm suddenly aware of my body being jostled around as Jax pulls me down onto his lap. I curl into him and hold on like he's my lifeline. My hands fist his t-shirt as I sob into the crook of his neck. He pulls me more tightly to him as he rubs his hand up and down my back. Through my sobs I can barely hear his whispers. "I'd switch places with you in a heartbeat. You don't deserve this and I wish I could heal you. I love you."

I lean back and his eyes are wide. "What did you just say?"

"I…I don't know. Fuck. I was just talking and then—"

"And then you said you loved me."

Clearing his throat, he lifts me back up into the chair and moves away from me. The tension is rolling off his body as he paces in front of the fire pit. "It wasn't that big of a deal. I don't even know what I'm saying. Let's just forget it."

Pushing up from the chair, I move over to him and grab his arms. He shrugs out of my grasp but doesn't move to continue pacing. "It's a fucking big deal, Jax. What do you mean you love me? Not even ten minutes ago you were telling me I should be with Hudson."

He rips his fingers through his hair like he's going to pull every last piece out. His shoulders are hunched over with tension and growls before replying. "You should be with Hudson. He's the one who's good for you. I could never be good enough for you."

Nodding my head, I take a step back. "Because you still love Erin."

He looks up and sighs. "Because I still love Erin."

"Then why'd you say it?"

Dropping his head, he refuses to look at me when he whispers, "Because I love you too."

All of the air whooshes from my body and my stomach knots itself a million times over. Reaching behind me, I find the chair and plop myself back down. What the fuck just happened? And what am I going to do about it?

CHAPTER SIX

Hudson

It's weird to think just a few short months ago, we didn't even know much about Jude's home life. I feel stupid thinking back now, but it never came up. We hung out, we practiced, and we went our separate ways. To know that I was sleeping in a warm bed and Jude was sleeping in his car makes me feel like complete shit. He never said anything, but I should have known something was going on. Fortunately, Flynn helped him out as soon as he found out.

Now, today, everything is going to change for him. For the better. When Dad found out about what was going on, he started getting everything going to get Jude emancipated. There was no way any of us would let Jude's mom near the band. No way in hell. After months of the court dates being pushed around, today Jude is finally going to get what he needs. We're all on edge, waiting. Jax has been pacing and Jude is sitting in the corner not saying much. Not that that's any different from normal, but the stress level is off the charts today. I get up and walk over to him and take a seat.

"How are you doing, man?"

He sighs and leans his head back against the wall behind him. "As good as can be expected, I guess. Abbie's pissed at me. I get why she wanted to be here for me, why all the girls did, but I don't want them anywhere near this. I didn't even want you guys with me."

"Yeah, well, there was no way we'd leave you to deal with this on your own."

"That's why I didn't argue about it."

We go silent after that, and shortly after, the courtroom is opened up. I know the girls are pissed, and like Jude said, he didn't want any of us here today. We weren't going to leave him alone. We're family and we're all in this together. Even though it's not why we're here, what happens today affects the band greatly. It could be the difference between starting now or putting our dreams on hold for a couple of years until Jude turns eighteen. None of us want that, especially not Jude.

We've been sitting in this courtroom for hours as the judge handles one case after another. There have been a few divorces. One in particular was kind of ridiculous. The man was a plastic surgeon, and from what I could tell the wife didn't do much. They were dividing up homes, vehicles, his practice locations, and even a plane. My parents are well off, but that was just over the top. After a few custody cases and an adoption case, it's finally our turn. Or Jude's turn.

The judge calls the next case. Dad and Jude shuffle up toward the front of the room, and that's when we finally get a look at her. Jude's mom looks like the kind of woman who used to be pretty before life and drugs beat her down. Her golden hair is extremely stringy, her clothing is saggy on her frail body, and there's a horribly covered up bruise on her cheek. There's no way the judge could look at her and not award Jude his emancipation. After getting his opening spiel out there, Jude's mom raises her hand like she's in a classroom. "Judge Wilmoth."

"Yes, Mrs. Winters?"

She stands up and pushes her lackluster chest out as far as she can. Where does this woman think she is? "I'd like to request this be a closed courtroom. This is a family matter, and I don't feel like it's appropriate for my son's friends to be present."

Jude goes to stand up, but the judge puts his hand out. Plus, Dad reaches his arm up and tugs Jude back down to his seat.

Clearing his throat, the judge says, "If one of the parties is uncomfortable with the court being open to the public, then we close the room. Everyone else present and not applicable to the case, please leave."

I glance over at Jax and Flynn. We're all struggling with this and don't want to leave Jude behind. Luckily he has Dad by his side. After a little grumbling, we all three get up and shuffle out of the room. A bailiff follows us, and as soon as we exit the room, the door closes behind us. So much for being here for support. Ready for an even longer afternoon, we park ourselves in some chairs near the window and wait. After a couple of hours of alternating between staring off into space and fiddling with our phones, Jax finally breaks the silence between us.

"So, do you think we'll be here all day? Or—"

Jax doesn't even get to finish his thought before we hear a commotion coming from inside the courtroom. "Jude, baby! Don't let them take me away. I'm your mother. Please!"

We all look at each other and get up and move toward the courtroom. As we're getting closer, Jude comes strolling out with Dad. We're all standing around in complete shock, unsure how to handle this. Jax is the first one to speak up though. "What the fuck is going on?"

Jude just shrugs and nonchalantly says, "She's an idiot. She was leaning far over, trying to flash her cleavage to the judge, when a baggie of meth fell out of her bra. Fucking idiot forgot it was even in there. They had to verify what was in the bag before anything could happen, so we've mostly been waiting around for confirmation."

The three of us glance between ourselves. Man, Jude comes from a pretty fucked up family. That shit is intense. Who even does that? It should be obvious what happened next, but I'd rather he give us all the details instead of us assuming. So I ask, "Okay, and then what happened?"

He runs his hand over his face and through his hair, tugging on the ends. His jaw is clenched as he tightens and releases his hands into fists at his side. "Basically what you just saw. Any argument she had went out the door. They're whisking her off to jail and I was granted my emancipation. She should never have shown up. She could be sitting at home smoking her precious drugs instead of going through withdrawals sitting in a cell."

It's not the time or place, but we can't hold back our hollers, which rewards us with the stink eye from people around us. Always being the smart one in the group, Flynn states, "Yeah, so let's get out of here before they decide to arrest us for disturbing the peace." That gets some more hoots and hollers out of us, but we quickly make our way out of the courthouse. We all agree to meet back at our house to have a mini celebration. Flynn and Jude head off to pick up Ashtyn and Abbie while Jax, Dad, and I head home. It's been a good day.

We're all pretty quiet on the drive home. Flynn has constantly been telling us that "Weightless" by All Time Low is our mantra. We all have given him shit for it at one time or another, but he's right. Everything has been falling into place, and it's happening more quickly every day. I have absolutely no reason to doubt him anymore. When we pull into our driveway, I start to get out of the car, but Dad stops us. "I'm going to head into the office and get some extra work done. I'm glad I was able to help out your friend today. You guys have fun. You have a reason to celebrate today."

Mom's out of town at some spa retreat or shopping trip. Whatever it is she does in her free time. Jax nods his head, gets out of the car, and heads toward the house. I'm compelled to talk to Dad further. "Why is Mom always gone? Or for that matter, why are the both of you always gone?" He becomes the picture of a broken man as he leans his head down against the steering wheel. I turn in the passenger seat and face him head on. "Do you want to talk about this right now, Hudson?"

With a question like that, right now is the best time to have this conversation. Something is up and I'm determined to find out what. "Yeah, I do. What's going on, Dad?"

"I had an affair."

My head whips back like he slapped me. "What the hell? What are you talking about?"

Raising his head, he turns his sad eyes to mine before choosing to look out the window instead. "Earlier in the summer…it's so fucking cliché and I never meant for you or your brother to find out. I had an affair with my secretary. Business was slow and I was so stressed out that we might lose the house. So one night it happened, but as soon as it was done I felt even worse than before. I immediately came home and told your mom what had happened."

"No offense, Dad, but why the hell didn't Mom leave you?"

"I begged her to stay. I got down on my knees and I begged. I love your Mom and I love you and your brother. I screwed up and didn't think. Anyway, we've been in counseling ever since. One of your mom's friends from college has her own practice in Seattle, and she lets us see her on the weekends. I'm paying an astronomical amount, but it's helping."

"So that's every weekend? That doesn't explain where Mom always disappears off to."

"I guess we screwed up with this whole situation. Your mom has been staying up in Seattle while we work through our issues."

My hand involuntarily clenches and unclenches. My body is buzzing with adrenaline and I'm so tempted to hit Dad. I've never wanted to hit him before. "What the fuck, Dad? You didn't think it was necessary to tell us that Mom isn't even living here?"

"Honestly, we didn't think you'd notice. You have all of the band stuff going on. It's not like it's going to be forever. Just until we can fix our issues."

"I get that. But you still should have told us."

"Yeah, we should have. I'm sorry about that. Please don't tell your brother though. I'd rather it come from me and your mom."

I hang my head. Why did I have to even ask? I could have just left it alone, and now I'm keeping something from Jax. I can't lie to him forever. "Just as long as you promise that you'll actually tell him."

"I will. I promise."

He takes off after that and I head into the house. What the fuck just happened? What's even worse is what I find once I enter the house. Both Chloe and Jax are sitting in the living room, a little too close for comfort for me. They seem to be deep in conversation about something but stop when I come in. "Hey! Jax just told me the good news." My face must show confusion because she continues. "That the judge awarded Jude his emancipation."

With the conversation that just happened, I forgot about going to the courthouse and Jude's emancipation. I shove the conversation I had with Dad to the back of my mind and plaster a smile on my face. "Yeah, isn't it great? Did Jax tell you Flynn, Jude, Ashtyn, and Abbie are coming over?"

Her smile falters, but she quickly puts it back up. "Yeah, this calls for a celebration." She brings her hand up and it appears the celebration has already started. There's a half-empty bottle of rum sitting on the coffee table. It's going to be one of those nights. Just what I want.

Fuck it.

I grab the bottle off the table and chug directly from it. If we're celebrating tonight, then I'm joining in the celebration. Screw being responsible for once. Chloe cheers, and with each additional chug I forget about the conversation I had with Dad. Tonight is all about Jude and celebration. "Hey, let's take this celebration downstairs. What better way to celebrate tonight than drinking and playing some kickass music."

Jax raises an eyebrow. "Sounds good, bro. What's going on with you?"

I shake off his inquisition. "What? I can't be happy for Jude? I can let loose every once in a while."

"If that's all it is, then let's go. I'll shoot a quick text to the guys and let them know where to find us."

I don't wait for either Jax or Chloe to follow me. I start heading out and turn around. "This bottle's going to be empty soon. Make sure to bring some extras down with you." I don't wait for a response, and I continue on my path downstairs. I'm feeling better and better. My body feels lighter and it's tingling all over. Reaching for my drumsticks, I get the adrenaline coursing through my body that only they can bring me. Sitting down, I start just whacking the shit out of them and slowly get a good beat going.

The energy around me feels amazing, and I close my eyes and feel the music flowing out of me. I'm not even paying attention to what I'm playing; I'm just going with it. I always second-guess myself and try to perfect my beats, but right now I don't care about any of that. It's like I'm a different person right now and it's exhilarating. All of the shit and stress in my life is gone, and all that's left are the drums in front of me.

Sweat is dripping down my body and my arms are screaming at me, but I don't stop. I can't stop. The beat vibrates up my arm and my heartbeat matches itself to every hit to the drum. My breathing becomes labored, but I push myself through it. It's like I'm running a marathon and I can't stop until I reach the finish line. The burn coursing through my body only propels me to continue.

Don't stop.

Don't stop.

Don't stop.

With one final hit to the drum, my stick shatters in my hand and goes flying. At some point you have to stop and can't keep going on. My arms continue shaking as if they're still moving, and my heart is pounding so hard. I take a deep breath and then another. Opening my eyes, I see that everyone has arrived. They all have varying expressions of the same face—eyes wide, mouths hanging open, standing there staring at me head-on. Taking my shirt off, I wipe away the sweat on my face and neck. "Well, don't just stand there. Let's do this." I get up to grab a new set of sticks and take a chug from one of the many bottles they brought down here. Situating myself back down at my drum set, I continue beating away everything I don't want to think about right now.

Slowly, everyone starts picking up their instruments, and we start an epic jam session. Ashtyn and Abbie sit on a sofa against the far wall, and Chloe is sitting across the room from them on the floor. She's nursing a new bottle of rum and ignoring them. Rather than think about that drama, I close my eyes and let myself feel the music again. This is Jude's night. No drama tonight of any kind.

CHAPTER SEVEN

Chloe

October used to always be my favorite month. School is in full swing with homecoming and Halloween just around the corner. But this year it's just another month. Even if I had a date to homecoming, I wouldn't go. The only thing I feel like dressing up as this year for Halloween is myself when I was happier and had parents.

So there's that.

Or maybe I should dress up. Be somebody else for a day. Somebody happier and more carefree. Someone who doesn't care and doesn't have any drama in her life. Particularly drama from crazy bitches. I shook off that first interaction with Brooke, but of course she couldn't leave it at that. It didn't take long for me to realize that she's threatened by me not because I could "dethrone" her, but because she likes Hudson. He's oblivious and it's one hundred percent one-sided. And that has nothing to do with me.

She gives me the stink eye any chance she gets, and it's gotten to the point of being hilarious. Even if I weren't in the picture, he still wouldn't want her, but instead she's putting that rejection blame all on my shoulders. Not like it matters to me, but I'm having a whole lot of fun rubbing it in her face. For example, Hudson and I are sitting in the cafeteria right now—his doing, not mine. Being Mr. Popular, we're sitting at the "popular" table, which means Brooke and her bitches are sitting right here with us along with some jocks and theater geeks. I don't get the hierarchy here, but whatever. That's not the point.

I'm half listening to her complain about some party getting canceled for Halloween this weekend. How her life is ruined and it's so unfair because it's her senior year. Blah, blah, blah. Just a bunch of whiny bullshit. I start to get up and walk away when Hudson wraps his arm around me and tightens his hold. When I catch sight of Brooke's scowl, I squeeze myself tighter into his embrace. "I just…I don't know what we're going to do, you guys. We can't not have a Halloween party. It wouldn't be right."

I don't know what compels me to do it, but before I can catch myself, I say, "I can throw it." Everyone looks in my direction and I see a variation of mouths open and eyes wide. I guess I don't talk much around these people, or anyone at school for that matter. Her lips tighten into a flat line before a smile breaks out on her face. "Oh, thanks so much for offering, hun. We need a big party house, though, and I'm sure you can't provide that. Maybe next time." She turns her back to me like I've been dismissed.

Not so quick, little bitch.

"Actually, sweetie, I live with Hudson. I'm sure his house is more than adequate." His body stiffens when I look up at him. "You don't mind throwing a party, do you, babe?" He cocks an eyebrow, but his body relaxes into mine.

"Sure, babe. Whatever you want." I turn back to the shocked crowd and I'm met with daggers from Brooke. "Well then, it's settled. Hudson and I would be more than happy to host the party. Plus his parents won't even be there. So it's perfect." I flash a saccharine smile and go back to my lackluster salad.

I've spent most of lunch just pushing it around my plate. Who wants to eat wilted lettuce, half-frozen carrots, soggy cucumbers, and ranch that I can only assume came from a bag. My entire body shudders. Not me, that's for sure. I could seriously go for an In-N-Out Burger right about now. I start to get up, and this time Hudson releases me. Just for Brooke's benefit, I lean down and kiss Hudson on the lips and put my all into it. Running my fingers through his hair, I lose my concentration on what I was doing and put all of my focus into this kiss instead. Tingles spread throughout my body, and I gently caress Hudson's bottom lip with my tongue. I moan as he grants me access, and the clearing of somebody's throat brings me back to reality. Opening my eyes, I say, "I'm heading out to my locker. I'll see you later?"

He nods, and out of the corner of my eye, I watch as

not one but four sets of murderous eyes bore into me. Well, at least the minions are loyal. Shaking himself out of his daze, Hudson stands up. "I'll come with you." I start to wave him off but see the determination in his eyes and stop myself. He's pissed about the party, but I know if I bring it up to Jax, I can easily get him on my side. He's always up for a party. We're kindred spirits. After tossing our trash and heading out of the cafeteria, Hudson leads the way to my locker. We walk there in complete silence, which is normally fine but somehow feels awkward right now.

As I shuffle around the books and notebooks in my locker, I pretend I'm doing something. Anything to prevent the conversation that is starting to build. Is he pissed at me? With nothing else to do, I slam the locker shut and face Hudson square on. "So…what's up?"

The tension builds between us as he steps forward. With a grin plastered on his face, he clears his throat and says, "Why don't you tell me. What was that about back there?"

I'd rather not step into any kind of trap, so I simply ask, "Which part?"

"I don't know, babe?"

"Oh, that. I can't stand Brooke."

"You want to clarify that a little bit more?" he asks.

"It should be obvious. She has a thing for you." He chuckles and I continue. "No, seriously. She and her posse shoot eye bullets in my head any chance they get. She likes you and they think I'm the reason you're not together."

"That's ridiculous. I don't think of her that way, and you're not standing in the way of anything."

I laugh and reply, "You don't have to tell me that. If you wanted to be with her, you would have been way before I got here. Doesn't change how she feels."

"So, back there?" He pauses before continuing. "That was you throwing whatever this is—" he motions between us "—in her face?"

My cheeks heat up slightly and I turn my focus to my feet. "Well, when you put it like that."

With a harsh tone, Hudson says, "The next time you feel like doing mean-girl shit, don't use me to get back at anyone."

I watch as his back retreats away from me. Looks like Hudson got a little peek into the old Chloe. It felt great in the moment, but now I feel nothing but guilt. Sure, Brooke is a bitch. That doesn't mean I have to go around acting the same way she does. It also doesn't mean I should be using Hudson and throwing it in her face. He's been nothing but nice to me, and I'm pretty sure I know how he feels about me. As my thanks, I turned around and did that. The bell rings for class and I start heading in that direction, contemplating what I'm going to do to make it up to him.

On the way home from school, Hudson starts going on about canceling the party and having someone else host it. There's no way that can happen, especially because after all of my brainstorming, I came up with the perfect costume idea.

When we get home, I go off in a search of Jax, and it doesn't take me very long to find him. He's sitting, still in his superhero pajama pants, at the breakfast bar eating a bowl of cereal. His hair is disheveled, and if I had to guess, he just woke up not too long ago. Wish I could sleep in until three in the afternoon.

"Jax, please tell your brother that a Halloween party is a genius idea."

With a mouth full of cereal, he says, "Why would I do that?"

"Girls dressed in lingerie and throwing on animal ears as a costume." For emphasis, I run my hands down my body. His eyes light up and I know I've got him hook, line, and sinker.

"Dude, we have to have a Halloween party."

"We don't need to have anything," Hudson says with a scowl.

Crossing my arms over my chest, I say, "I'm pretty sure you were just outvoted. Two against one means majority rules."

With a huff, he turns and walks away. Over his shoulder, he says, "Whatever. When it comes to parties, you two always gang up on me and get what you want. Doesn't matter what I have to say anyway."

I start to go after him but think better of it. He's in a mood right now and I'd rather not deal with that. Instead, I grab a bowl and park myself next to Jax. I pour myself whatever he's eating and start chomping down. I can't remember the last time I had a bowl of cereal. After a few bites, I look over at Jax and find him staring back at me. "So, what did you do today?"

He chuckles slightly and motions down to his clothes. "What do you think?"

"Yeah. Must be nice."

"So what's the deal with the Halloween party?" he asks.

"Okay, so you know who Brooke is, right?"

He laughs. "How could I not? That chick tried to attach herself to me, but Erin stopped that shit real quick. What does she have to do with this?"

"Not to mention she was one of your body shot girls, but that's beside the point. She's after Hudson. Like hardcore after him and seems to think I'm the reason they aren't together. Anyway, she's been giving me shit about it." Jax's nostrils start flaring and I throw my hands up. "Hold up, I can take care of myself, no big deal. She was whining about her Halloween party getting canceled, so of course I couldn't let that happen. I swooped in and saved the day. While mentioning that Hudson and I would gladly host since we live together."

"Shit, you don't mess around. I would have loved to see the look on her face."

Nodding my head, I say, "Oh, you should have seen it. It was priceless. While she and her bitches were scowling and staring daggers at me, I had to plant a kiss on Hudson before walking away. And trust me, it was hot."

I look up to a scowling Jax, and I'm not sure what just happened. "What's your problem, Chloe?"

"I don't even know what you're talking about."

"Yeah, that's the problem." He gets up and storms out of the room without even cleaning up his mess first.

What the fuck just happened? Standing up, I clear up the cereal mess and contemplate my next move. Upstairs, both Hartley boys are pissed at me for some reason or another. I could go up there and try to fix whatever is going on with either one of them. Or I could go find a bottle of something and light up the fire pit. Drama or no drama? Yeah, I think I'll go with the latter.

After hunting, I find a bottle of rum. I grab a can of Coke and a glass. I'm okay with it just being a party of one this evening. Screw boys and their confusing drama. I'm just fine being by myself, and that is precisely what I'm going to do.

CHAPTER EIGHT

Hudson

I don't know how the two of them constantly talk me into this. The last thing Chloe should be doing is drinking away her problems, yet here we are at yet another party being thrown at my house. Somehow Chloe convinced both Jax and me that Halloween is reason enough for a party and we can't not have one. Although, it didn't take much convincing on Jax's part. All Chloe had to do was mention girls in lingerie and glide her hands down her damn body for him to be all for it. It was like he'd spent all day at Warped Tour without a drop of water. He was salivating at the damn mouth for her.

It doesn't help that Chloe came waltzing down the stairs in a Black Canary costume. Talk about a fucking fantasy come to life. I'm not sure who she was trying to impress with that: me or Jax. Either way we were both ready to drag her back upstairs. Good thing neither one of us made a move, because that would have been pretty awkward. Jax dressed up as The Flash, which only makes me think that after our conversation last month, he started planning his costume. I guess I should be happy Chloe didn't come dressed as Iris.

Flynn and Ashtyn showed up as Han Solo and Princess Leia, gold bikini and all. How he got her to agree to that costume, I'll never know. But they look good. I don't know how everyone found the time to get a costume. The stupid party is at my house and I didn't have enough time to find something. They all picked out stuff weeks ago. Even Jude and Abbie look awesome. I'm not sure who's doing it was, but they showed up like Link and Zelda. Their costumes are totally kickass. I just threw on some faded destroyed jeans, boots, and a flannel. My hair isn't super long, but it's shaggyish. I used Chloe's straightener and made it a little longer. Then I threw some of her gunk in my hair to make it look messy and greasy. Everyone keeps calling me Kurt Cobain, so it works.

This whole house is jam packed with people, and I can guarantee you I don't know most of the people here. But Chloe was right about one thing. All of the girls here are wearing variations of the same costume: lingerie and accessories to make their costume legit. I'm not sure how someone could fight fires in six-inch heels and garters. And wearing a plaid mini-skirt and rhinestone bra doesn't qualify you as a teacher, even if you carry a ruler around. Jax got what he wanted though. He's in Halloween-slut heaven.

I peek over at Chloe for the millionth time and watch her dance. She's just been swaying her body to the music and hasn't had a single drink yet. I'm surprised but relieved at the same time. Usually she starts out these parties already a few drinks in. Maybe tonight will be different and she'll actually go to bed sober tonight. I, on the other hand, have been chugging waters all night. I search the room for Jax and finally find him standing in the middle of his admirers and head over to him.

"Dude, I'm going to the bathroom. Can you keep an eye on Chloe while I'm gone?"

He rolls his eyes and turns his attention back to the brunette standing in front of him. She's shameless with her costume choice for the evening. She's legit dressed up like a Playboy bunny. I guess there had to be at least one in the mix. "She's fine."

I clench my hands into fists and spit out, "I don't care if she's fine. Will you keep an eye on her?"

"Yeah. Calm it down. I'll watch out for her," he says as he brings his hand up to pat me on the back.

"Thanks." I turn away and head downstairs. Outside our practice room, I grab the key out of my pocket and unlock my door. One thing we agreed on a long time ago when we started having these parties was to get deadbolts on our bedroom doors and our practice room. I would never be okay with finding some random couple hooking up in my bed, and we have way too much expensive equipment in here to let just anyone come in. Gross. Shutting and locking the door behind me, I head into the attached bathroom.

After finishing up, I sit down at my drum kit and take a deep breath. Pounding on my drums always helps cool me back down, and I'll need it after the way the night is already heading. I beat the shit out of my drums, not playing any song in particular, and I eventually stop when the sweat starts beading off of me. My breathing comes out labored, and I lick my overly dry lips with an even drier tongue. It's like using sandpaper, making my endeavor pointless. I down a water bottle from the mini fridge and clean myself up the best I can in the small bathroom before I check out the time on my phone. Shit, I've been down here for almost an hour.

When I make my way back upstairs, there's a commotion in the kitchen, and when I get in there, it doesn't take me long to figure out why. Someone has "Pour Some Sugar on Me" cranked up, and Chloe is on the island with a bottle of something or other. Fortunately she was smart enough to take off her heels. She's kind of all over the place and has reached the point of way too much for the night.

Where the fuck is Jax?

The only reason I agreed to this damn party in the first place was that if I wasn't watching her, Jax would be. I leave the room and this is what I come back to? I spot Jax over in the corner, talking with Erin. Guess that's where he went off to. I didn't tell him I invited Oliver and Erin. Since they're both in town, I felt it would be rude not to. From where I'm standing, it looks like she's decked out in a hot Black Widow costume. She's always known about Jax's love for superheroes, so I wonder if this is her way of trying to win him back? Not that it would make any sense, because she left him, not the other way around.

Much to everyone's disappointment, I pull Chloe off the counter and remove the bottle from her hands. Taking a quick look at it, I see she was working on what is now a half-empty bottle of Fireball. I just hope it wasn't full when she started. Pulling her with me, I start heading back upstairs. She wiggles and attempts to struggle from my grasp, but I'm holding on tight. "Chloe, I think it's time to head upstairs now."

"Oh, Hudson, you're no fun. Where's Jax at? I'm sure he'd like to dance with me." Somehow she's gotten another drink in her hands and takes a giant chug before turning to walk away, but I spin her back around to face me. She wobbles slightly on her feet, and I realize that wasn't the best choice on my part. When she steadies herself and turns back toward me, she's smiling and wraps her arms around my neck. I don't know the song that's playing, but Chloe doesn't seem to care. She's swaying her body and no longer has the drink in her hands. "Ecstasy" by the Late Nite Reading comes on, and I squeeze her tighter to me. We continue dancing in our slow circle when her body stiffens and she stops moving. Dropping her hands away from me and taking a step back, she asks, "Who is she?"

I don't even have to look up to know she's talking about Erin. But I do at the same time I tell her. "That's Erin." She and Jax are still deep in conversation, and I'm kind of curious what they could still be talking about. "I saw her when she came in. She's freakin' gorgeous, and Jax gravitated straight to her." I shouldn't be surprised, but it's still like a punch to the stomach that her immediate thought was to start drinking because Jax's attention is elsewhere. I thought she'd moved on from that…but I guess not.

I don't even realize what's happened until I look up and see Chloe stalking toward them. Oh no. This can't be good. There are a shit ton of people here, and she makes it to Jax and Erin before I can catch her. I'm only seconds behind her, but I clearly hear her say, "Why are you even here?" Jax's eyes go wide and Erin switches to a defensive stance with her body turned toward Chloe and her hands on her hips. "Excuse me?" she asks.

Clearing her throat, Chloe says, "I said, why are you here? Nobody wants you here, and I think you should leave." She motions toward the door and takes a step back, clearing a path for her. Somebody turns the music off and the entire room becomes dead silent as everyone is watching this interaction. The majority of them don't even know what's going on, but I'm sure they're all just hoping to see a girl fight.

Erin looks over at Jax, ignoring Chloe, and asks, "Who the heck is this girl and why is she telling me to leave? Are you going to say something to her?"

Jax opens his mouth to say something, but Chloe beats him to it. "This girl lives here. And I know exactly who you are, Erin. Don't you think you caused enough trouble when you left Jax in the first place? He doesn't want or need you anymore."

I pull Chloe back to me, and Jax finally gets the chance to speak up. "You should leave, Erin. In fact, I think everyone should leave." Louder, he says to the entire room, "I don't care where you guys go, but you can't stay here any longer. Party's over, everyone." There are a few grumbles and somebody turns on that old Semisonic song. But they all shuffle out the front door until all that's left in the living room is Chloe, Jax, myself, Ashtyn, Flynn, Jude, Abbie, Oliver, and Erin. Talk about awkward. Jude turns toward the iPhone we have plugged in and turns it off. I guess he was the funny guy who turned the song on.

Oliver takes this moment to step forward. "What's going on here?"

I've got my arm tight around Chloe's body. She's not moving, but I have a feeling she might just snap at any minute and I'd rather be proactive and hold her back. "That's what I'd like to know. The blonde came up to me and started telling me I need to leave. I don't know who she is or how any of this is her business," Erin says.

Chloe starts struggling in my arms and I start to say something, but Jax beats me to it. "Chloe lives here with Hudson and me. She's Ashtyn's best friend." He points to where Flynn is standing with his arm wrapped around her. "Yeah, well, she's acting like a bitch," Erin says back.

Oliver whistles loudly, causing everyone to turn his or her attention back to him. "Can someone please explain what the fuck is going on?"

Everyone is a little dumbfounded, so I say, "Chloe here is a little drunk."

"No, Hudson, I'm not drunk. I'm thinking very clearly. And I don't know who you are." She squeezes herself out of my grasp and turns her attention toward Oliver.

"I'm Oliver. The guy who signed all of these guys to my label. Although I'm starting to wonder if that was such a good idea."

Chloe doesn't even hesitate before replying,

"Okay…nice to meet you. This girl right here," she motions to Erin, "obliterated Jax. I wasn't there when it originally happened, but I've been witnessing the aftermath. What she did is not okay and I don't think it's helpful to anyone for her to be here right now. I don't even know why she's here."

My turn to speak up. "Because I invited her."

Chloe whips her body around and stares me down with daggers. "Why the hell would you do that?"

Clarifying, I say, "I actually invited Oliver and I said he could bring her along."

That causes Chloe to whip back around and stare her death daggers at Oliver. She is on a manhunt tonight. "Okay, why would you bring her with you?" she asks.

Shrugging his shoulders, he states, "Because she's my sister."

I look around the room for confirmation, and all of the guys are nodding their heads. Chloe throws hers back in a cruel laugh. "Well, that's just fucking hilarious. Apparently I don't even know what's going on here. I think I'll just go to bed and leave you all to this ridiculous drama."

She turns to walk away, and Jax says, "Chloe, wait. Thank you for trying to help. I know you were doing what you thought was right."

"You're welcome, Jax." She turns her attention to Erin. "I don't like to see you in pain, and every time anyone mentions her name, that's exactly what happens."

Erin cringes and Chloe turns back away, getting exactly what she wanted. She heads upstairs as we all stand around in complete silence. What a fucking night.

CHAPTER NINE

Chloe

Another month of school flies by. Not that anything exciting has happened or that I would even care if it did, but either way it's over and done with quickly. At this point, I feel like I'm just going through the motions, and it's more for everyone else than it is for me. Don't get me wrong, I don't want to be a high school dropout, but at the same time, I don't even care.

This is such a minuscule part of my life, and why does everyone care so much? In ten years, it won't matter who was the homecoming queen or the quarterback of the football team. Why does any of this matter to anyone? We sit in these classrooms day after day for years of our lives, but will anyone remember what we learned? I'm gonna go with a big fat no. It's all so pointless.

For example, I'm sitting in my theater class right now, which is one giant joke. I get it. Ashtyn's mom registered me for classes and she knows the old me. The old me would have been buzzing with energy as soon as I stepped foot in this amazing theater that's way too good to belong to a high school. The teacher drones on and on about auditions, volunteer opportunities, internships, blah, blah, blah. The acoustics make it sound like he's standing right next to me rather than one hundred feet away on the stage. Basically perfect.

A packet is passed onto my desk: "A Midsummer Night's Dream." I pick it up and run my fingers along the title and wait for the adrenaline rush and butterflies to flutter through me. My favorite Shakespeare play is within my reach. I could stand up on that stage and pretend to be Helena. Steal the show and have everyone fall in love with me. But as I look at that stage, all I feel is the darkness closing in. I feel like I'm standing in front of an audience as they judge me and not a single supporter among them. There's a hole where Mom should be, and rather than let the panic start up, I toss the script to the side.

It's one of my favorite Shakespeare plays. I always preferred the comedies to the tragedies, and when you throw in a little love, you have something there. With the proximity to the Shakespeare Festival, I get the idea that the theater program is pretty competitive here. I wish I cared enough to see how good I am.

"Mr. Hemmer, are you requiring everyone to audition for the play again this year?" I try to ignore the annoying sound coming from Brooke's mouth, but my ears perk up nonetheless.

He clears his throat and rolls his eyes. No one else is looking at him, so I'm the only one who caught it, but at least I know I'm not the only one that can't stand her. She's so fake it's disgusting. "No, Brooke, that turned out to be a disaster last time. No one will be required to audition, but everyone here will be required to help out in some way, whether that is working on the sets or any of the other backstage jobs. I do hope you all consider auditioning for a part though."

She can't even hide the ridiculous smile that is plastered all over her face. In the most saccharine voice, she says, "That's good. I'm sure there are some people in here that just aren't meant for being on stage." I turn to look at her, and she's staring straight at me. I hold her gaze and refuse to back down from her. I match my sickeningly sweet smile to hers, although mine's a little more serial killer than cheerleader. It works though. Her mouth opens in horror and she turns back around.

I toss the script to the side and go back to drowning out the noises around me. If I could get away with blasting music in my ears right now, I totally would. That's a little more than frowned upon though. Instead, I listen to the song playing inside my head. Hudson's phone every morning, without fail, gets a song stuck in my head throughout the day. The upside is I'm going outside of the box and learning new music. That's the only upside.

Today, Hudson slept through not one but two songs, so I've been going back and forth between them. Right now I've got an All Time Low song on repeat. I can relate to those "Kids in the Dark." I'm sure Ashtyn would be so proud. I keep singing the song over and over as I shuffle out of the classroom. I don't think the teacher even noticed me, or any of my teachers for that matter. But I'm perfectly okay with that.

Speaking of Ashtyn, fortunately I only have one class with her. She's still giving me my space right now. I think she gets that it hurts too much to be around her. Some of my best memories growing up were when our families were together. I should just suck it up and be her friend. I feel bad that she doesn't know anyone here, but I just can't do it right now. Part of me needs her, needs to know that everything will get better. But the other part of me, the bigger part of me, is too damn selfish to focus on our friendship. To focus on anything else other than the giant empty hole inside of me.

That particular class, English, is the one we're sitting in right now. The teacher is a bitch, and I think she gets off on seeing her students suffer. I haven't been subject to her torture, and luckily I've flown under her radar so far.

I'm about ready to turn around and punch the chick behind me in the throat. She's been nudging me on the shoulder for a good solid thirty seconds. Looking up, I see all eyes turned to me, including the teacher. Shit, what did I miss?

"Sorry, did I miss something?"

The older woman purses her lips and stares me down. This woman is such a bitch. She brings the phrase "resting bitch face" up to a whole other level. If she doesn't want to teach, then why the hell is she here?

Clearing her throat, she says, "Thank you for joining

us, Chloe. I asked what everyone thought about the poem you were supposed to read for homework last night."

"Ms. Potter, I don't think—"

Even though I've been ignoring her, Ashtyn is still coming to my rescue. I interrupt her before she even gets out what she was trying to say. I think I can answer a few questions about some damn poem.

"No. It's fine. Which poem was that again?"

She purses her old lady lips again, and I know I've pissed her off at this point. So I didn't read some stupid poem. I'm sure it will take me all of thirty seconds to read it over and answer whatever stupid questions she has about it. Then I can go on and pretend I'm invisible all over again.

"Open your book to page three hundred and forty-five. It's the Emily Dickinson poem."

I look around the room and notice everyone else has their books out and open. My face reddens slightly. Way to go, Chloe. No wonder the woman called on me. I pull my book out and open to the page she referred to. Staring right back up at me is, "Because I could not stop for Death." I've never been much of a poetry reader, or a reader in general, but I scan through it quickly.

Now I get why Ashtyn didn't want me to read it. My hands are shaking and my eyes are welling up with tears. I swallow that down and then look up at Ms. Potter. She has a blank expression on her face, and I know she's waiting for me to respond.

Taking a deep breath, I ask, "What was the question?"

She lets out a deep sigh and shakes her head. "You should pay better attention in class, Chloe. What do you think the poem means? If you can't answer that question, I can have someone else answer it. You've already wasted enough of our time as it is."

I ball my hands into fists underneath my desk. Who does this woman think she is to talk to me like that? She doesn't know anything about me or what I've been through. What gives her the right to be so damn judgmental? I don't even filter myself when I bark out my response.

"I will gladly answer your question."

I stand up so I don't have to worry about holding back.

"Plain and simple, Death is a bitch and Ms. Dickinson knew that. It doesn't matter how many plans you have in life or if you haven't done everything you wanted to do. If Death wants you, Death will have you. It fucking sucks, especially for those you leave behind. But you know what? Death doesn't even care. Death doesn't have to deal with picking up the pieces after you're gone or dealing with the wreckage that's left behind. Death just swoops in and takes you away. Death is a piece of shit."

I can feel my whole body shaking, and the tears are pouring out of me now. The entire room is closing in around me and my heart is racing. I can hear the BOOM, BOOM, BOOM in my ears. The room is eerily quiet and I don't even look at anyone else. I pick up my stuff and rush from the room.

I can hear voices calling behind me, but I just continue running. I don't know where I'm going, just that I need to get out of there. I need somewhere empty and somewhere quiet. And I know just the place. With it being a holiday weekend, the theater will be empty. I can sit in there and compose myself before I go home with Hudson in an hour.

I burst into the theater and immediately feel calmer. The smell of the fabric, the coolness of the room, it settles me. The quiet is very zen. My heart rate is slowing down and my breathing is evening out.

I toss my bag up on the stage and sit with both legs hanging over the ledge. I haven't stepped foot on it yet, and honestly I figured it would be the last place I needed. Who knew that the one thing I avoided the most would be the one thing I actually need?

Sitting in here has memories flashing back to me. I don't want to think about any of that right now, so I grab the pint of 151 I've been keeping in my bag for emergencies. This feels like an emergency moment. I open the bottle and feel the horrible burn as it goes down. I wish I had some sort of chaser with me, but I guess I'll have to settle for the rum flavor until I can no longer taste it. I haven't touched tequila since the night of the accident, and I don't plan on changing that anytime soon. The only reason I drink now is to forget.

Forget that night.

Forget my life.

Forget it all.

The quicker I can become numb, the better. That's when the happiness sets in and I can feel a little more like normal. The old me comes out a little, and I don't have to deal with anything real. Deep down I know that's not helping anything, but it hurts too much to acknowledge anything. It's hard enough to wake up in the morning sober. Maybe that makes me an alcoholic, or maybe it just makes me sad. Either way I'll just stay in denial as long as I can.

I sit there, taking sips from the bottle, and eventually my tongue and throat become so numb that I can't even taste or feel it anymore. I don't even remember why I was so upset in the first place. Oh well, no big deal. I pull out my phone and open up my music app. I turn on "Riot Girl" by Good Charlotte and put it on repeat. I'm singing along because I'm obviously a riot girl. I giggle uncontrollably but continue belting out the song anyway. It feels good to just let go and not think about anything.

CHAPTER TEN

Hudson

After waiting in my Range Rover for fifteen minutes, I hop out and slam my door out of frustration. Chloe wanted me to take her home and repeatedly told me that she wouldn't keep me waiting. Pulling out my phone, I notice a text from Ashtyn waiting for me.

Ashtyn: Hey, I just wanted to let you know that Chloe had a rough time in English today. Potter was being a raging bitch and Chloe left class super early. I'm not sure if she's with you right now but I thought you should know.

What the fuck? That woman needs to get laid or something. Maybe she doesn't know about what's going on with Chloe, but I'm fucking pissed she made her cry.

Me: Thanks for the heads up.

Ashtyn: Of course. Take care of my girl for me.

I'm tempted to text her back and correct her. Chloe is our girl. Not just hers. Fuck that, she's my girl. I don't feel like going into a whole long conversation right now about it. Finding Chloe is my number one priority right now. I call her up, and of course it goes straight to voicemail. I toss my phone on the passenger seat and let out a growl of frustration. She can't make anything easy on me.

I'm tempted to just leave, but I know that's not who I am. Of course that's something Jax would do, and he's already been lucky enough to earn her heart.

Not that he deserves it.

I don't know how I found myself in such a fucked up situation. My brother loves Erin, Chloe loves Jax, I'm in love with Chloe, and I don't know how the fuck Erin feels. If I weren't so miserable, I would laugh at the irony of it all. Here I am, a theater geek living in Ashland, Oregon, and my life is like a Shakespeare play.

Maybe we should all go hang out in the woods for a bit. We'll all come back, in love with the right person, and lose a little dysfunction in the process. After a little magic and mind control from some crazy fairies. Yeah, that's the shit that dreams are made of.

Passing by her locker, I'm very much aware of the lack of people in the hallways. It's crazy how quickly this place empties out on a holiday weekend. I love Thanksgiving just as much as anyone else, and I know Mom will be pissed if I'm not home soon. She always gets crazy over the holidays.

If you were to ask anyone about the number one important holiday in the Hartley household, everyone would say Thanksgiving. Mom goes overboard with all of the planning and cooking. It's always been her favorite holiday, and she cooks a feast to feed twenty families. It's intense but so delicious. Even with the issues going on with Mom and Dad, there's no way she would miss out on our usual family Thanksgiving.

I rub my belly at the thought.

I'm out of ideas of where to look when I hear the screeching of a dying cat. Maybe that's too harsh, but Chloe shouldn't be allowed to sing. Ironically enough, I find her sitting on the stage in the theater. Maybe we can find our way into that forest after all.

Unfortunately, my damsel is singing away, horribly off-key, while downing a pint of something. Great. She's drunk. I guess she wants to start off her holiday by getting hammered.

Fuck.

I'm a complete idiot. This is the first real holiday she's celebrating, or lack thereof, without her parents. She feels like complete shit right now, which is why she's drowning her pain yet again. Honestly, I don't blame her. Even if she had been healing through all of this, getting wasted is a little understandable.

Thanksgiving is a holiday surrounded around giving thanks. What is there to be thankful for when you just lost your parents? Not a whole lot. Especially in Chloe's case. She still hasn't noticed me, but then again, she's too focused on screeching at the top of her lungs and ruining a Good Charlotte song. Just because she's getting drunk at school, that does not make her a "Riot Girl." I'm sure I have Ashtyn to blame for Chloe knowing their music. Not that it's a bad thing, just when it's coming out of her mouth. Her singing is just awful.

For some reason, her singing aside, I can't help but love her. This beautiful broken girl. Unable to stand in the shadows any longer, I start striding down the aisle. "There you are. I've been looking all over for you, Chloe."

She jumps half a foot in the air. I can't help but laugh as her eyes go wide and focus on me. "Dammit, Hudson! You just scared the shit out of me. I think I just peed myself a little too."

"TMI, Chloe. Seriously though, let's get out of here."

With an overly dramatic sigh, she grabs her bag and starts to get up. I hear voices coming up the hallway outside and my entire body stiffens. I bring my finger up to my lips and Chloe pauses where she's at. Swiftly but quietly, I move up to Chloe and get on the stage. Her entire body is stiff as a board as I whisper in her ears, "Don't say a word. I heard some voices outside the door. We're going to head backstage and hang out in one of the dressing rooms. The last thing we need is for you to get caught drinking on school property."

She slowly nods her head as I grab her hand and pull her backstage with me. Five minutes ago she was laughing and screeching at the top of her lungs without a care in the world. I guess the thought of risking what little she has left sobered her up pretty quickly. As we step behind the curtain and continue our path to the dressing rooms, my breath leaves me as the door to the theater is opened. Chloe releases an audible gasp as muffled voices carry their way toward us.

Our palms are sweaty as I continue dragging Chloe behind me. I make my way all the way to the end of the very narrow hallway and around the corner. This dressing room is never used, so hopefully, even if someone heard us, they won't be able to find us. I quickly open the door, shoving Chloe inside before joining her and shutting the door behind us. She hasn't said a word, but I'm very aware of her quickened breathing in the darkened room.

I turn away from the door and run my hand along the wall until I find what I'm looking for. I flip a switch, and the lights on the vanity light up. Chloe's transfixed on it. Quietly, she whispers, "Won't they be able to see the light from under the door?"

I shake my head but realize she's still looking at the vanity and not at me. "Nobody comes back here anymore. All of the other dressing rooms were remodeled, but this one has been left untouched. Besides, I turned on the vanity instead of the overhead lights so it wouldn't be as bright."

At some point while I was talking, she switched her focus to me, but after nodding her head, she's looking back at that damn vanity again. Why is she so focused on it? It's old and beat to shit. Nothing special with it at all. While she's still in her trance, I pull my phone out of my pocket. It's almost four o'clock. I'm not sure how long we'll be waiting, so I grab the chair from in front of the vanity and take a seat. Chloe is still glued to her spot, off in her head somewhere.

Instinctually, I get ready to send a text to Jax, but then I notice my lack of bars on my phone. I'm in here often enough—well, I used to be—that I should know you don't get reception in here. I don't know the details exactly, but something with how they wired the building makes it impossible to use cell phones anywhere within the theater. It's fucking genius, but I could use my phone right about now.

Shaking her head, she comes out of her trance and pulls up a chair from the corner of the small room. "So, how long do you think we'll have to wait in here?"

I bring my right hand up and rub the back of my neck. Shoving my phone back into my pocket, I move my gaze over to Chloe. She has her body all huddled up in that chair while she's hugging her bag. At least she realizes the seriousness of the situation. For both of us even. Just because I wasn't drinking doesn't mean if we get caught they won't put the blame on both of us. Fucking Chloe. "I don't know, Chloe. But you should have thought about that before you decided to bring fucking liquor to school. What were you thinking?"

Her eyes start to glisten and she turns her head away from me. She takes in a few deep breaths and sniffles a couple of times before turning back to me. "I wasn't thinking, Hudson. I haven't been thinking a lot lately."

"Well, maybe you should start."

With her gaze straight ahead and fixed on my face, she replies, "Yeah, maybe I should." She sticks her tongue out and slowly drags it along her bottom lip, and her eyes intensify with heat. The temperature rises in the room as both of our breathing becomes labored and I lean my body forward. Relaxing her body, she lets go of her bag. It clatters on the floor, and that loudness whips our attention back to where we are.

She starts to get up, but I put my hand in the air and quietly get up from my chair. I put my ear against the door and listen. I expect to hear voices and footsteps down the hallway getting closer to us. Any minute now, we should be getting busted. But we don't. As I stand here trying to hear anything other than the breathing in this room, I hear nothing. Stepping back from the door with a relieved sigh, I turn around and she's back to huddling her body. "I don't hear anyone out there. I'm going to go check it out and I'll be right back."

Her entire body is trembling and her voice is shaky. "Please don't leave me."

I make the couple of strides across the room that it takes to get to her, and I kneel down in front of her. I wrap my arms around her body and she quickly melts into me. Letting my warmth dissolve all of her fear and panic, I whisper in her ear, "I'm not leaving you. If someone is still out there, I can distract them and get them out of the building so you can slip out. If no one is out there, we both can leave and everything will be fine. Trust me. I would never leave you."

I lean back to look up into her eyes, and she slowly nods her head. Reluctantly, I let go of her body and stand back up. I stare at her face for a beat longer before turning around and heading out the door. I quietly shut the door behind me and lean against the door. I shake the fogginess from my brain and start heading back down the narrow hallway. I don't hear any voices or movement, so that's a good sign.

I make it onto the stage and pause a moment to listen again. I don't hear anyone, so I peek out from behind the curtain and breathe a sigh of relief when I don't see anyone standing out there. That relief only lasts for so long before it hits me. I jump off the stage and run down the aisle, only to be met with exactly what I knew was coming. Oh no no no no. Shit.

Reluctantly, I head back up the aisle. I'm dragging my feet the entire way back to Chloe, absolutely dreading this conversation. I reach my sweaty palm out to the cold brass doorknob and turn it achingly slowly. Pushing open the door, I'm met with Chloe's expectant face and I say the only thing I can think of. "So, there's good news and bad news."

CHAPTER ELEVEN

Chloe

As Hudson walks out of the room, I hug my bag to myself again. I peek over at the vanity and can't help but think of Mom. This one is beat up and old, but I'm sure back when it was new or at least in good condition it looked a lot like the one she had. She had one of those cool vintage old Hollywood ones, with the globe light bulbs that surround the mirror. Every time I sat down at that thing and pretended to put my makeup on, I always felt so glamorous. Just like a movie star. I always hoped that one day she would give it to me. Maybe on the set of my first movie.

But now it's long gone. Along with anything else we had in our house in Santa Barbara. I wish I at least knew what happened to everything in our house. It's my own fault, really. If I had responded more and actually talked to someone, anyone, then maybe I would know what happened. I could have gone to my parents' funeral and gotten my goodbye. Not like that would have been a substitute for the fact that I will never truly get to say anything to my parents ever again. They're gone and never coming back.

My eyes start welling up with tears when I hear footsteps coming down the hallway. I straighten up in the chair and wipe at my eyes. Taking in a deep breath, I hold it in while the doorknob slowly turns. When the door is pushed open and Hudson is standing there, I finally let myself release it. His face is blank as he steps into the room and says, "So, there's good news and bad news. Which do you want to hear first?"

Frowning, I shrug my shoulders and he continues. "The good news is there's nobody out there." I get up out of my chair and start moving toward the door when he puts his hands up. "The bad news is they locked the door on their way out."

I cock my head to the side and ask, "Okay, what's the big deal? Even though the door is locked, we should be able to go, right? Unless…is there an alarm?"

"No, there isn't an alarm. But the doors are chained shut on the outside. There's a lot of expensive equipment in here and they take that very seriously. Especially if they're borrowing stuff from the Shakespeare Festival."

I slump back down in the chair. So we're locked in. What does that even mean? Someone has to come in here eventually, right? I look at Hudson's face and notice the slouch in his posture. Moving up his body and landing on his face, I let out a gasp. No one is coming in here. Tomorrow is Thanksgiving, and the school will be locked up tight for the next four days. We are trapped in here all weekend. This can't be possible.

I get up from the chair as my heart starts racing and my entire body flushes with heat. My breathing quickens and I can't catch my breath. I need to get out of here. I need air. I'm gasping for anything at all, but it won't come. My head starts pounding as I hear my heartbeat throbbing. This can't be happening. This can't be happening.

Hudson wraps his arms around my body and whispers into my ear, "Chloe, focus on me. Breathe." I shift uncomfortably and he lets up on the tightness of his arms around my body. "Just keep breathing and listening to my voice. It will be okay, I promise you." He continues whispering into my ears, but I focus on his heartbeat against my own as I close my eyes. Slowing my breathing down, I try to match my beat to his, and slowly the pace starts coming down. The pounding in my head fades and my entire body tingles as it slowly starts cooling down.

I'm aware of my body moving, but I don't open my eyes until we suddenly stop and Hudson sits me down. I peer over at him as we sit front row in the theater. Taking a deep breath, I ask the only thing I can think to ask right now. "What the hell just happened?"

He shrugs his shoulder. "I have no idea. But if I had to guess, you just had a panic attack."

"Shit." He nods his head. "I need another drink."

He chuckles but then becomes serious. "Yeah, well, that's kind of what started this problem in the first place."

I blush slightly. I know he's right. What the fuck was I thinking? Oh, right, I wasn't thinking. Plus, that bitch Potter fucked with my day. Somebody needs to put her in her place one of these days. That will show her. Speaking of drinks, I'm suddenly aware of how badly I need to pee. With all of the adrenaline coursing through my body the past hour, I wasn't even thinking about it. Oh, but man, I need to pee. Hudson's spacing and not paying attention to anything. I'd love to leave him to his thoughts, but man, I need to go. If I weren't sitting, I'd start hopping and dancing around. "Please tell me there's a bathroom in here somewhere and I don't have to go find a bucket or something to pee in."

Leaning his head back on the chair, he lets out the best laugh ever. It's completely uninhibited and one hundred percent real. "No, you don't have to go scavenge for a bucket to pee in. We passed the bathroom while we were backstage. There's running water and a vending machine back there too. Although it's not in the bathroom. Fortunately, even though we're stuck in here, we should be fine."

"Wait. Can't we call someone?"

"Nope. Phones don't work in here. I don't know the specifics, but they have an electronic device that jams signals or something."

My head falls in defeat when I remember something. "I watched an episode of one of those crime shows one time, and they said you can make emergency calls on your phone with no service. Is that true?"

Hudson nods his head and his grim expression

transforms into a huge smile. "I think you can! Pull out your phone and try it."

In my excitement, I forget that I killed the battery blasting Good Charlotte earlier. I turn it around and show the phone to him. "My battery is dead. Try yours."

His smile vanishes. "I left it out in my Jeep."

"What are we going to do? Won't your parents worry? I can't believe I got us into this situation. I'm so fucked up right now."

He crosses the room and pulls me into a hug. "Hey, stop right there. You're not fucked up. Maybe a little sad, but we'll work through this. My parents are so off in their own issues right now they probably won't even worry about me. We'll be fine."

"Yeah, except for the boredom."

He smirks and replies, "Well, I guess we'll have to figure out something to do, then."

Heat covers my body from head to toe at that thought. I can be okay with figuring out something to do with Hudson. I know both of our minds are thinking about the same thing, and my body is more than ready for that. Breaking the tension, he clears his throat and says, "Well, why don't you go to the bathroom and I'll go scrounge up a feast from the vending machines. We can meet back here in five minutes."

I nod my head and follow him backstage. After pointing out the bathrooms, he continues walking to where I assume the vending machines are.

I flip the switch, and luckily the bathroom lights turn on. In a teeny room like this with no windows, I would have been mortified if I had to leave the door open for light and

Hudson walked by. After going to the bathroom, I get a good look at myself in the mirror while washing my hands. While I don't look hideous by anyone's standards, I don't look good either. My makeup is partially melted off and my hair is a disaster. I quickly wash my face, choosing to ignore what kind of harsh soap I'm currently slathering on my face. After I'm satisfied with the squeaky cleanness of my skin, I shake out my hair and pull it up into a messy bun. It's not the best, but an improvement to what I looked like a few minutes ago.

I head back out and find Hudson sitting back in the front row. I stifle a giggle when I see all of the snacks sitting in his lap. "I wasn't sure what you would want, so I grabbed a bunch of stuff. It's all crap, but it can hold us over while we're stuck in here." I sit down next to him and grab a water bottle and a bag of Gardetto's.

Yum.

We eat in silence and take in our situation. Worst case scenario, someone won't come and find us until Monday morning when everyone is back at school. That means including today, we'll be stuck here five days. I'm not sure I can last on vending machine food alone for that long. I hope this won't be the worst case scenario and someone will come in sooner. Although it might be hard to explain what we're doing in here. With that being said, I'd much rather get in trouble for being in here and go home sooner.

After finishing our feast of vending machine snacks, my eyes start drooping. I'm not sure how long we've been in here, but it must be late. Or maybe I'm just bored. I reach down for my bag and it's gone. Frantically, I stand up and turn around in a circle. Did I leave it in the dressing room? The bathroom? I can't remember the last time I had it. "Chloe, what are you doing?"

I ignore him as I drop to the floor and check underneath the chairs. Not finding anything, I start to hop on the chair when he grabs my arm. I lean back and hesitate slightly. "I can't find my purse. I thought I left it out here when I went to the bathroom. But—"

Letting go of my arm, he smiles and brings his hand up to my face, pushing some stray hairs behind my ear. "Why didn't you say something? I moved all of our stuff."

"You…you moved it?" He nods his head and I let out a breath of air. "Where?"

He points over to the stage, but there isn't anything there. Cocking my head to the side, I open my mouth to ask, but he replies first. "Are you done here or was there anything else you wanted to do?"

I shake my head, and he grabs my hand and stands up, pulling me with him. I open my mouth but immediately shut it. I let him drag me wherever he's heading. It's not like I have anything better to do anyway. He drags me backstage, and we stop in front of a different room than we were in earlier. I wasn't paying attention, but it looks like we're on the opposite side of the stage from the dressing rooms. He pushes the door open, and situated in the middle of the room is a bed.

An actual bed.

Without even thinking, I take off running and fling my body across it. It's not the most comfortable bed in the world, but it's much better than sleeping on the floor or the chairs like I thought we would have to. I sigh and let my body relax into the mattress, ignoring the musty smell of it.

"I take it you like the bed?"

I giggle deliriously. "It's perfect. Thank you." He's beaming, and I put that smile there. My body warms at the thought.

"Your purse is on the floor on your side of the bed."

I fling my body across the bed and look down, and sure enough, my bag is sitting right there. Wait. My side of the bed? I don't know why I never thought of it before, but we have our own sides of the bed. We've been sharing a bed together for months, and every night we go to sleep on the same sides. I'm always on the left side of the bed. Clearing those thoughts, I reach down and grab my purse to hunt for my phone. How the heck is it already ten o'clock? Have we been here that long?

Noticing my shock, he says, "Yeah, it's late. I thought time was dragging, but we were in the dressing room a lot longer than I thought."

I nod my head and drop my bag back onto the floor. No wonder I'm so tired. I clear my throat, and for some reason he hasn't moved from his position near the doorway. "So…you ready for bed, then?" He doesn't say anything. He shuts the door and starts moving toward the bed. Why is this so awkward? It shouldn't be. We've slept in the same bed together for months now and it's never been like this before. But we've never been this alone together either. We could do anything right now. I swallow the lump that has built in my throat and my palms start to sweat. That thought terrifies and excites me at the same time.

Sliding onto the bed, Hudson stays as close to the edge on his side as he possibly can. We're both lying on our backs, and there's an invisible line that goes right down the middle of the bed. Yep, awkward. I peek over at him, and he has his eyes closed so tight. With a groan, he rolls over with his back to me and grumbles goodnight. I guess that's what kind of night it's going to be. I say my goodnight and roll over, facing away from him. How is it that I was barely able to stay awake a few moments ago, and now that we're in bed I'm wide awake? I guess I'm in for a long night.

Yippee.

CHAPTER TWELVE

Hudson

My stomach growls for the millionth time today, and it has nothing to do with being hungry. It's like my body knows it's Thanksgiving today and I'm withholding. I wish it were something that simple. Unfortunately, I will be missing out on all of it. No delicious roast turkey that has been soaking in a brine for twenty-four hours. A turkey that is so incredibly moist my mouth is salivating just thinking about it. Then there's the cranberry sauce. We don't have the can-shaped gelatinous mess on our table. Nope, it's real, fresh cranberries with a hint of orange zest. Jax always pigs out on the mashed potatoes, but me, my absolute favorite part of Thanksgiving dinner is the green bean casserole. Fresh green beans that still have a crunch to them, smothered in mushrooms, caramelized onions, and Mom's homemade mushroom soup. She doesn't sleep and spends hours in the kitchen. Everything is always homemade and we eat like kings. I just hope my bastard bother leaves me some leftovers.

"What do you think about me auditioning for the play?"

We've been lounging around all day. After spending most of the day in bed, we moved to the theater and have been sitting in the chairs out here ever since. Opening my eyes, I expect to find her sitting on the other side of me. Did I fall asleep? Sitting up, I find her in the middle of the aisle, sitting and looking up toward the stage. "I think you should do whatever you want to do. But what brought that on?"

She turns her head to look over at me and sighs. "For one, we're trapped in the theater. But it's what my mom would have wanted me to do. Plus, it'd piss Brooke off if I got the part she wants."

I don't know what it is with girls always being mean to each other. I wouldn't purposely go out of my way to make someone else's day worse. It seems like a waste of time and energy. But what do I know? I'm just a guy. "If we put the whole Brooke thing aside, I get why you would want to do it for your mom, but...is it something that you want to do?"

She shrugs her shoulders and turns back around to face the stage. She pulls her legs up toward her chest and hugs them to her body. "Being in here has pretty much sucked, no offense, but it's brought me back to what I used to love. I forgot how much just being around this environment makes me feel alive. But do I think I'm ready to go up on stage again?" She looks back over at me and I nod my head. "I don't know. And if I'm not one hundred percent sure I can do it, it's not a good idea."

"Then I guess you have your answer."

With a small sigh, she replies, "Yeah…I guess I do." She's quiet after that, and I wait for her to say something more. After a few minutes of her silence, I peek over and watch as her chest slowly rises and falls. She looks so content and I don't want to wake her, but I know I need to do something to cheer her up. I hate the constant state of unhappiness that she's been in, and being stuck in here isn't helping anything.

Quietly, I get up and pick her up. I pause, but she doesn't stir, so I continue walking her backstage to the storage room. Placing her on the bed, I pull a blanket on top of her and watch her contentment for a moment. With an idea in mind, I walk back out onto the stage. It might not be perfect, but I can make her day a little bit better, I hope.

After double-checking everything in front of me, I head back to where Chloe is lying down. I go back into the storage room and find her right where I left her. She looks so peaceful, and I'm hesitant to wake her. She rarely gets a peaceful rest like this, and she needs it. I can't even count how many times I've been woken up from her stirring and mumbling. On the nights when she gets wasted, she sleeps like a rock, but it's not quite the same. That's partly why she does it. That, and she gets to forget while she's awake too. Neither one of us slept much last night—not from her nightmares, just from the ridiculousness of this whole situation.

We've been trapped in this giant theater, yet the walls feel like they're closing in on me. My chest tightens with the thought of not getting out of here, and I worry that my fear is written all over my face. Claustrophobia is a real bitch, and you never know you have it until you're experiencing it. I get chills just thinking about it and shake those thoughts off. I know I told Chloe that my parents probably haven't even noticed I'm gone, but I'm freaking out that they just might have. I don't want to add any more problems to their plate.

"Chloe." I wait to see if she'll stir, and when she doesn't I gently reach out and shake her arm a little. "Hey, Chloe, it's time to get up." She rolls over and grumbles while pushing my hand away. I chuckle and shake her again. "Hey, c'mon, I've got a surprise for you."

She stirs slightly and opens her eyes. "A surprise?" I lean back and laugh. I should have led off with that and saved myself some trouble. "Yeah, a surprise. Now get up and come with me." She smiles sleepily and I pull her up from the bed.

I lead her out onto the stage, and when she sees everything I set up, she stops dead in her tracks and gasps. I didn't have much to work with, but I did the best I could.

I rummaged through the other storage room and pulled some old props out. On the center of the stage I laid out an artificial grass rug. On top of that I put out a blanket, and I found an old picnic basket that I filled with our vending machine feast. While scavenging for other props, I came across an unopened bottle of wine. I'm not much of a fan, but anything to make our time a little more fun works for me. The fake moon was already hanging from the ceiling for A Midsummer Night's Dream and all I needed to top it off were some white Christmas lights. That and of course some music. I used to run the sound system for every play before we started getting serious about the band, so I know my way around the equipment.

There's sniffling behind me, and I drop her hand to turn around. Her right hand is across her mouth and tears are pouring down her face. Oh no no no. I did something wrong. What did I do wrong? I reach for her and she backs away and shakes her head. I take a step back and hold my breath.

Wiping away her tears and clearing her throat, she smiles up at me. "I can't believe you did all of this." I open my mouth, but she puts her hand up to stop me. "We're trapped in here, and instead of freaking out like I am, you did this amazingly sweet thing. How did you even do all of this?"

Moving forward, I grab her hand, forcing her focus on me. "I'm freaking out just as much as you are right now. I'm trying to be strong for the both of us because I know you need me. I wanted to do something special for you since we're missing both of our families today. And I'm very familiar with the storage rooms here, so I knew what I was looking for. I didn't go to any extra trouble."

"Thank you. Everything has gone to shit, but you're still trying to make me feel better."

I nod my head and pull her toward the picnic I have set up. As we take a seat, she looks around expectantly and I pull out the picnic basket. "I know it's not Thanksgiving dinner, but I grabbed a little of everything." I start laying everything out on the blanket and put out a couple of bags of Funyuns, Cheez-Its, Lays potato chips, some meat sticks, Famous Amos chocolate chip cookies, and M&M's. Chloe's nose curls up at the M&M's. More for me, then. "And I can't guarantee this will be any good since it's a few years old, but I found this in the prop room and apparently it's never been opened."

She cocks her head to the side, and her eyes light up when I pull out the bottle of wine. It's a pear wine from RoxyAnn Winery, so it has to at least be sweet, right? Her grabby hands swipe the bottle from me and attempt to open it up. When she spots the cork, she hands the bottle back to me and bounces back to the other storage room.

That was weird.

When she comes skipping back out with her bag in hand, I have no idea what she's going to do. She plops herself back down on the blanket next to me and starts digging through her bag. She motions for me to hand her the bottle and pulls out her keys. "Chloe, I don't think—"

Waving me off with her hand, she lifts the keys and I finally spot it. She has a freakin' Swiss Army Knife keychain. She quickly maneuvers out the corkscrew and pops the bottle open. I'm so impressed I can't even say anything. I look like an idiot with my mouth hanging open, but I'm pretty sure I just fell even more in love with this girl. She takes a long chug from the bottle and looks up at me. "What?"

Closing my mouth and wiping away the invisible drool, I say, "Nothing. You're like a Boy Scout. Except you know…a girl…and freakin' hot. And…uh…not a Boy Scout 'cause you're not a boy, but you're awesome, and did I mention hot? And I'm shutting up now before I ramble on a little more."

She laughs and nods her head. "My dad got this for me a few years back before I started high school. He told me, 'Chloe, I always want you to be prepared for anything. Worst case scenario, you shank a boy that doesn't know the meaning of the word no, and best case scenario, you'll always be able to open a good bottle of wine.' At the time I thought he was crazy, but I can't tell you how many times this little thing has come in handy."

She hands over the bottle and I chug it. The fruity liquid slides down easily and actually tastes pretty good. Must be those Oregon pears. I don't know anything about wine, but I wouldn't mind drinking a few more bottles of this stuff. I hand the bottle back over and start digging into our feast of snacks. I'm used to a food coma on Thanksgiving from stuffing myself so full of delicious food. I just hope I don't go into one this year from all of the junk we're consuming. My body isn't used to eating like this.

We eat our snacks in silence and pass the bottle back and forth. It empties a lot quicker than the packages of food sitting in front of us. I'm feeling a slight buzz, but there wasn't enough wine to make it last very long. It's going to be a very long night and an even longer weekend. I just hope someone comes in here sooner rather than later. I don't think we can handle being stuck in here all weekend. I guess we'll just have to make the most of our situation and hope for the best.

CHAPTER THIRTEEN

Chloe

We've been trapped in this damn building for a day now. Thanksgiving came and we missed all of it. I don't necessarily miss the festivities, but oh how I miss the food. Instead we're sitting here snacking on our delicious vending machine feast yet again. Yes, Hudson made an amazing picnic, and I appreciate all of the trouble he went to. It's super sweet and I can't thank him enough. But when we finally get out of here, I'm going to figure out how to roast a damn turkey. I will make an entire fucking Thanksgiving spread and devour all of it. My body will rebel against me if it doesn't get all of the fixings this year.

Since there's no liquor in sight and there isn't anything better to do, I figure we might as well get to know each other a little better. Our relationship or friendship, whatever you call this, has been pretty surface so far. I contemplate the perfect first question.

With a smirk, I ask, "Who's your favorite celebrity crush?"

Hudson's mouth falls open and he shakes his head. "Are you kidding me? We're locked up in here, most likely not leaving until Monday morning, and you want to play twenty questions?"

Crossing my arms across my chest, I nod my head as I reply, "That's not how you play twenty questions; that's a different game. All we have right now is time, Hudson. I'm out of alcohol, so I can't numb my mind right now. I need to think about anything other than my parents being dead. Do you have a problem with that?"

"Nope," he says.

"Okay. So answer the question. Who is your favorite celebrity crush?"

He hesitates slightly and taps his forefinger against his chin. A wide smile breaks out on his face and he answers, "Umm, I guess Miranda Kerr."

Throwing my head back, I let out an uncontrollable giggle. "Are you kidding me?"

"What, do you have something against former Victoria's Secret supermodels?"

"No. It's just mine is Orlando Bloom. If they were still together we could have made quite the team breaking them up and sweeping them off their feet."

"That's kind of twisted."

With a smirk, I add, "Whatever. You like it."

"If it gets me Miranda Kerr, then hell yeah I like it."

Boys and their supermodel dream girls. Maybe a little bit of the arrogance that Jax struts around with rubbed off on Hudson. At least it's just a little. "Ha-ha, you're so funny. Your question."

He studies my face and I'm terrified how deep he's going to go. This was a dumb idea. Of course, for every question I ask him, he gets to ask me one in return, and I'm not sure I'm ready for him to ask me anything personal. "Favorite color?"

I let out a small sigh of relief. That is one question I can answer. "You could ask me anything right now and you want to know my favorite color?"

"Why not? A person's favorite color tells you a lot about their personality."

"Well then, Mr. Smartypants, my favorite color is pink. What does that say about me?"

"The color pink. People who choose pink as their favorite color are typically feminine, romantic, and generous. You seek love, protection, and nurturing from others."

"You know that off the top of your head?"

"What can I say, I know all kinds of useless information."

Rather than contemplating how close to home some of that hits, especially now, I choose to brush off his analysis and switch the spotlight back onto him. "Okay, so what's your favorite color and what does it mean?"

Without even pausing, he blurts out, "My favorite color is green, and that means I'm a stable person who enjoys nature. I'm also caring, compassionate, and I love to take care of others."

I don't know if he just made that up or if he's being truthful. I'm going to ignore it and move on to my next question. He's looking at me, expecting a response, but I just wave it off.

"Have you ever had sex?"

His mouth is hanging wide open, and I know he wasn't expecting that at all. Bluntness is my favorite quality in myself. He snaps his mouth shut and recovers quickly. "It's my turn."

I shake my head at him. I won't let him pull a fast one on me like that. "No it's not. How do you figure?"

He smirks and replies, "You asked me my favorite color?"

Shit.

I did do that. I didn't even mean that as one of my questions. It was more of a response to him asking me what mine was. Oh well, I guess.

"Okay, smarty pants, ask me a question then."

He doesn't even contemplate before asking me, "What do you want to be when you grow up?"

I open my mouth to respond but then shut it. Now it's my turn to be shocked. If this were a few short months ago, my answer would roll right off my tongue, and it almost does. But I can't give that answer anymore. Honestly, I don't even know how to answer that question anymore. Do I even want to grow up?

"I don't know. Why plan for something if I don't even know I'll be alive tomorrow?"

Shaking his head, he says, "I don't believe you. You almost answered and then stopped. Why don't you want me to know?"

Ugh, he's being annoying. If he wants the truth, I'll give him the fucking truth.

"I don't know what I want to do with my life and that's the truth. I almost told you what I used to want to do, but I don't want to do that anymore."

Tilting his head to the side, he asks, "Why not?"

Is he seriously not going to drop this?

"Because my mom died, Hudson."

"I don't mean to sound insensitive, but what does your mom have to do with it?"

"My mom and Ashtyn's mom, Audrey, were best friends. When Audrey was just starting out, she was Flynn's dad's assistant. She met my mom on the set of a music video, where my mom was one of the extras. She originally wanted to be an actress, but you have to start out somewhere."

He nods his head and waves his hand like he wants me to continue.

"Anyway, Audrey made sure my mom always got cast in a part no matter how small or large. They were inseparable. She never made it past bit parts in music videos, but she loved every minute of it."

"Is that why you've been avoiding Ashtyn?"

I slowly nod my head. Being around Ashtyn and her family is too painful right now. It just reminds me of Mom and how I no longer have her. I pause as I remember how proud she was of all of those music videos. She had a copy of each one on tape and constantly played them for me. I remember telling her I wanted to be glamorous just like her when I grew up. She beamed with pride, and that's when it all started. I started acting lessons and going on audition after audition. Most kids would have hated it, but I loved every minute of it. This was something we had together. Our way to bond. Plus…the spotlight.

I tell him how much it meant to me. That acting had always been my true passion in life, but that's connected to my mom. I'm so lost without her, and I feel like it would be horrible for me to continue it without her. Like it was our thing, but it can't be my thing. That sounds silly. We were in it for my future. My mom loved acting, but she loved being a mom more. Me? I had the drive and desire to go all the way.

Whenever I saw my future, I was standing up on that stage in the Dolby Theatre, accepting my own Oscar. The one person at the top of my thank-you speech was always my mom. I know, we always practiced it. Hudson is hanging on every word I'm giving him. I feel this strong compulsion to lean over and kiss him, so I do. It's light and sweet and he pulls away first.

"What was that for?"

I shake my head before answering, "I felt like it. You were sitting there truly listening to me like you actually cared about what I had to say. Nobody ever cares about what I say."

"I always care about what you have to say, Chloe."

"Exactly. Now that was a zillion questions and you never answered mine. Have you ever had sex?"

With a growl, he says, "If I answer this question can we be done with this game?"

"Yes." My voice comes out all breathy and a lot sexier

than I intended. I lean back over and this time he leans with me. My breath starts to quicken as he brings his hand up and caresses my face. I lean into his touch and melt a little inside. Turning my head slightly, I see the same desire in his eyes that I'm currently feeling. I lean forward slightly and he matches my movement.

"Hudson—"

He puts his finger over my mouth and says, "The answer to your question is yes. Now stop talking."

He doesn't need to tell me twice. I throw my arms around his neck and kiss him with everything I've got. His kisses start out distant, like he's trying to figure out if this is what I want, so I throw everything into it. Our lips glide together and I slightly part my mouth. He takes that as an invitation and runs with it. His tongue tangles with mine and I can't get enough of him. It's like electricity shooting through my body as our tongues caress one another. This is actually happening. We're actually doing this right now. My entire body is on fire.

Like some dumb teenage girl, all I can think is, OMG, I'm actually kissing Hudson. But his lips are amazing. They're smooth and they slide right alongside my own. His arms wrap around me and I melt even further into his touch.

If this were Jax right now, it would be over with quickly. With Hudson, all of his focus is on me. He's focused on making sure every moment is worth it for me. Our lips move together and all I can focus on is everything he is making me feel. He keeps running his arms along my own, and I involuntarily shiver at his touch. He leans back to look at me and I shake my head, pulling him back to me.

While his kisses were slow and exploratory, mine are rushed and intense. I pull him toward me and straddle his lap with a strong need to get as close to him as I can. I don't even hesitate when I break the kiss to rip my shirt off and then slam our lips back together. My body is charged with electricity that's flowing back and forth between our bodies where our skin is touching.

There's a loud pop, and suddenly we're sitting in darkness. I scream at the top of my lungs like a girl, and Hudson hugs me tighter. "It's okay."

My entire body is shaking. "How can you say that? What if there's a serial killer in here? We could be waiting to get murdered."

Hudson is shaking worse than I am. Then the laughs come out. We're unprotected in the dark and he finds this hilarious. "I'm sorry, that was too much. The lights are on a timer. They're super expensive to stay lit so they go off on their own. They must have forgotten about the long holiday weekend or else they would have gone off yesterday. We got so carried away, I kind of forgot to say something."

That makes a little more sense than what I was thinking. Okay, it makes a lot more sense. "What are we going to do, then? I can't even see you."

He shuffles next to me and says, "Stand up and grab your bag. I'll take you somewhere."

"If I didn't trust you, I'd think you just want to take me away so you can have your way with me."

Chuckling, he says, "What makes you so sure I won't do that anyway?"

"I'm counting on it."

He laughs again and takes my hand. He's pulling me across the stage, and suddenly the floor in front of us is lit up. I jump a foot in the air. He shows me the flashlight on his keychain. Oops. He leads me back to the room where we slept last night and starts rummaging through boxes. "What are you doing?" I ask.

He continues searching and ignores my question. "Aha! I found it."

"What did you—" I start to ask, but he turns around with a pillar candle already lit. It's one of those flameless kinds, and he slowly starts setting out more around the room. After a few minutes, there's a soft glow to the room and I can see more than a few inches in front of my face.

"Chloe?"

I look up to respond, and my words get caught on my tongue. Hudson is slowly working his way across the room to me, and everything on his face says pure lust. My heart rate speeds up and my chest quickly rises and falls with each breath. I start backing up slowly with each step he takes until the back of my legs hit the bed. Coming up to me, he brings his hand up and cups my face while placing his forehead against mine. His heart is rapidly beating in his chest, almost as fast as mine. "Chloe," he repeats again before gently placing his lips against mine.

I wrap my arms around his neck and run my fingers through his hair there. I gently tug on the ends, causing him to release a groan. He breaks the kiss long enough to toss me onto the bed. I can't stop giggling as I bounce slightly, but it quickly gets caught in my throat as he puts his hands on the hem of his t-shirt and slowly pulls it up and over his head. I lick my lips as I devour every inch of his muscular torso with my eyes. Playing the drums does a body good. Feeling bold, I get up from the bed and make my way to him. He sucks in a breath of air as I run my hands along his front. They settle on the waistband of his jeans, and he releases a groan when I open the button.

I start to tug down his pants, but he places a hand over mine. "Wait. I'm not going to be the only naked one in the room."

I quickly rip of my bra and haphazardly throw it over my shoulder as Hudson chuckles. "Somebody's eager." I step away from his grasp and look into his eyes.

"And you're not?" I ask as I gently run my fingers down the front of his jeans. He lets out a deep groan and then everything becomes a blur. Suddenly we're both on the bed with a lot less clothing. The only barrier between us is the thin material of our underwear. Hudson runs his hand up my body, leaving kisses behind everywhere he touches me. I'm on fire and my heart is going to beat out of my chest any minute now.

After what feels like hours of torturous teasing, Hudson holds up the little foil packet that seems to have appeared out of nowhere. And I'm fully aware that the rest of our clothing disappeared at some point. He starts to open it, but I take it from his hand and say, "Let me do it."

He gulps down the invisible lump in his throat and nods his head slowly, never taking his eyes off mine. I make quick work of opening the package, and I return the favor of his teasing and slowly slide it onto him. It doesn't take long before he settles himself between my legs and I gasp, waiting for the first push. Our bodies move together in sync, like this is right where they belong. Our two halves found the other to make ourselves whole. I look up into his eyes and see nothing but love. I tremble underneath him and get lost in our connection. I never realized that something could feel so right. So perfect.

We quickly find our releases and stay there, looking into each other's eyes. Even though we haven't said the words yet, I can feel all of the love he is radiating to me, and I'm returning the same. Hudson jumps up from the bed and cleans himself up before hopping back into bed. Coming up behind me, he wraps his arms around me and kisses me lightly on the back of my neck. I settle myself back into him, and quickly his breathing starts to even out. I take a peek over my shoulder, and sure enough, he has fallen sleep. I kiss him lightly and say, "I love you, Hudson," before joining him in a peaceful slumber.

CHAPTER FOURTEEN

Hudson

Opening my eyes, I'm aware of the cute little blonde breathing deeply into my neck. Everything from the night before comes crashing back to me and I squeeze Chloe tightly to me as she curls into me even more. I'm on cloud nine right now, and I can't believe we did that last night. Part of me is in complete shock that it happened, but the other part of me, the one winning right now, is ready for round two. I run my fingers through her hair as her body relaxes even more.

Her eyes flutter open and the biggest smile is plastered on her face before it falters slightly. "What's going to happen with us now?"

Now? Definitely a few more rounds. What else are we going to do while we are trapped in here? I don't say that to Chloe, though. "What do you mean?"

Untangling herself from my arms, she sits up and gazes off before bringing her attention back to me. She's nibbling on her bottom lip, and I pull it out from between her teeth. She has something to say, and if she keeps doing that, I won't give her the chance. "Everything can't go back to normal, Hudson. We changed things. It's different now."

I bring my hand up and rub the back of my neck. I don't know why she wants to hash all of this out right now, but I guess we have nothing but time. Although we should have had this conversation before we got started. "What do you want to happen, Chloe?"

Barely above a whisper, she replies, "I don't know."

After everything, she doesn't know? I stand up and hunt for my clothes. Finding my boxer briefs, I forcefully pull them on. I have to attempt two times before I actually get them on. I throw my t-shirt on and start pacing. My fists clench and unclench multiple times before I turn back to her. "Seriously? You don't know. That's not good enough for me."

Apparently, during my rant she got dressed as well. I feel like a complete ass. She's tugging on her hair and nibbling that damn bottom lip again. There are unshed tears in her eyes and she says, "I'm sorry."

I take a deep breath and bring my heart rate down. Sure, she's come a long way, but she's still not healed. Treading lightly, I take a few steps toward her. She lets go of her hair but stands her ground. I make my way to her and wrap my arms around her petite body. "We've been skating around this, Chloe. I know my feelings for you and I'm hoping you feel something similar. Let's do something about it."

She nods her head and gently lays it against my chest. She wraps her arms around my waist and says, "What do you want from me?"

Leaning down, I kiss the top of her head and squeeze her to me more tightly. "You. I just want you."

Pulling back slightly, her gaze zeroes in on me, and the room becomes incredibly silent as I wait for her reply. I'll either get everything I want or nothing at all with the next words to leave her mouth. My heart rate spikes back up, and all I can hear is the loud beating.

Her tongue darts out and slides along her lips. I'm torn between leaning down and pulling it into my own mouth or waiting to hear what she has to say. Luckily, the voice of reason beats out the caveman in me and I move my gaze away from her mouth.

"You have me, Hudson. You have all of me…if you want me."

I don't even hesitate before leaning down and slamming my lips to hers. She lets out a slight moan as I massage my fingers through her hair. Before I can let my inner caveman truly come out, I break the kiss. She lets out a small whimper and I say, "I want all of you. There is nothing I want more."

She lets her head fall back down to my chest and sighs. "So we're doing this?"

"Hell yeah, we're doing this."

"What do we do now?"

"Oh, I can think of something we could do now."

She giggles and pulls herself from my embrace. "That's not what I meant. When we leave here. Do we tell everyone? How does all of that work?"

I chuckle. "You know everyone already assumes we're together, right?"

She narrows her eyes and states, "I don't give a shit what Brooke and her damn posse assume."

There's a little bit of the fiery girl I know and love. I guess part of her is coming back. "Do I sense a little animosity there?"

In a clipped tone she says, "No."

Yep, definitely a little anger toward the supposed queen bee of the school. I have no doubt in my mind Chloe held a similar role at her old school. "I wasn't talking about Brooke anyway. I was referring to our friends. My brother…"

I end with that to see what kind of reaction she has. I don't know if I should pump my fist in the air or jump around like a crazy person when she doesn't react at all. I never thought it was possible, but she wants me and not him.

"Hudson, there's never been anything between Jax and me. Not like it is between us. Especially not now."

After everything that's happened between us, I shouldn't need to know what has actually gone on between Jax and Chloe. But some sick twisted part of me needs a confirmation. I need to know whether or not she was ever with him. I know we all made assumptions, but that was it. "I need to ask you a question."

Her entire face breaks out into the biggest smile, and

I'm struck by how gorgeous she is. How did I ever get so lucky to find an amazing girl like Chloe? She's the best thing that has ever happened to me and she doesn't even know it. I plan on making sure she knows it. "You can ask me anything."

Taking in a deep breath and then letting it out, I ask, "Did you and Jax ever sleep together?" Jeez, real smooth there Hudson. I couldn't lead up to it. Just had to throw it out there and be super blunt about it.

She doesn't even look shocked that I asked her. Almost like she was expecting me to ask her eventually. "Nothing ever happened between Jax and me. We spent hours talking to each other, but it was never anything more than that."

What the fuck? "Seriously? What could Jax have to say for hours?"

She lets out a small giggle and says, "We talked about lots of stuff. Mostly the band, our futures. He talked a lot about Erin too. You should have let me beat the shit out of her at the Halloween party."

"I can't believe you two never slept together."

She rolls her eyes. "Because I'm some big slut that sleeps with any willing guy?"

Shit, I walked myself right into that one. "No, nothing like that. That's how Jax is. But honestly, I just meant because all of the time you spent together. Don't get me wrong, I'm fucking ecstatic. Just a little shocked, too."

"Well, Mr. Ecstatic, why don't I show you how much you're the right Hartley brother for me."

And then she does, until we pass back out blissfully in

each other's arms. I'm pretty sure life can't get any better than it is for me right now.

"What the hell? Who's in there? You better open this door!"

What is going on? I peel my eyes open to a glorious sight. Chloe's hair is partially falling in her face, but she's sleeping so peacefully. In fact, I've never seen her sleep so still in the months we've been sharing a bed.

Bang. Bang. Bang.

Oh shit! That must have been what woke me up. Fortunately, we both got redressed last night. Peeking again at Chloe, she's still sleeping like a rock. I hate to wake her while she's so peaceful, but I do it anyway.

Shaking her shoulder slightly, I say, "Hey, Chloe." She grumbles nonsense and rolls away from me. A little louder, I say, "Babe. C'mon, you need to get up."

That causes her to stir a little more, and her eyes peel open. Of course the dude outside the door chooses right then and there to jiggle the doorknob, which sends Chloe into panic mode. She goes from dead asleep to wide awake in five seconds flat. She flies up and away from me, attempting to straighten her clothes with her hands. Getting up, I reach for the doorknob and open it.

Standing in front of me is a very red-faced janitor. "What the hell are you kids doing in here? I could have you arrested for trespassing."

Chloe's eyes go wide with panic. I hold my hand up to

her to appease her and turn my attention back to the janitor. "Excuse me…" I look down at his name tag like I'm inspecting it. "Bud, is it? I would have you know that we have been trapped in here all weekend. Chloe and I had an after school project to take care of before the holiday weekend. Unfortunately we got locked in. As you should be well aware, you cannot get any cell reception while you're in here. I guarantee you our parents have sent out search parties for us and my father could have you arrested for being negligent about the safety of two students. Fortunately for you, there are bathrooms, running water, and vending machines in here. If there hadn't been, you could have walked in on a very different scene this morning and faced some very serious charges. Now you can let us go and I can drop it. Or you can make more empty threats, and I'm sure my father would be very happy to press charges."

He stumbles over his words and finally spits out, "Get out of here, the both of you. I don't want to ever walk in on this again. You hear me?"

Still scared shitless, Chloe nods her head and quickly gathers up her belongings. I take my time grabbing my things and stroll right out of there. It isn't until we make it out to my Range Rover that I let out a shaky laugh. "Holy fuck. Motherfucking fuck! Oh, fucking shit balls."

I calm down enough for Chloe to squeak out, "What just happened?"

I start laughing again and motion for Chloe to get into the SUV. "I didn't think that would fucking work."

"What do you mean?"

"I was blowing shit out of my ass the entire time. I have

no idea if anyone was worried about us or what's happening back at home. But all of that other shit…fuck. I guess I am my father's son."

Shaking her head, Chloe says, "Okay, now you've lost me."

"What just happened in there is one hundred percent Jacob Hartley. My dad can bullshit a bullshitter, and apparently so can I. When we were in there…it was weird, but I didn't even have to think about it. I just channeled my dad and said whatever I thought he would say."

"Huh."

"That's it? Huh."

Her eyes blaze. Shit, she's pissed.

"I almost peed my pants. I thought we were getting arrested back there."

"I never would have let that happen. Besides, even if I couldn't talk our way out of it, my dad would have. Trust me. Neither one of us would have seen the inside of a jail cell."

She doesn't look like she believes me, but I pull the car out of the lot anyway. I need to get out of here and into a shower, like yesterday.

CHAPTER FIFTEEN

Chloe

My heart is still racing. I can't believe how calm and collected Hudson acted back there. I thought for sure we would both be hauled off to jail. If the cops had been called in and searched us, there's no question I could have been arrested for the empty rum bottle in my bag. I don't know much about the law, but having anything on your record is bad, no matter what it is.

I'm so lost in my head that I don't even realize we're already at his house. Was I stuck in my head for an hour? "Sorry for speeding. I just wanted to get as far away from there as soon as possible," he says, answering the question I had in my head. Without a second glance my way, he gets out of the SUV. Well, that was weird. I'm pulled out of my thoughts when the passenger door is opened and Hudson unbuckles me and envelops me in the biggest hug. A few minutes pass while we stay in our embrace until he pulls back slightly. Bringing his hands up to cup my face, he looks into my eyes and asks, "Are you okay? I know I said back there that we were fine, but I can tell you're not fine."

Leaning into his hands, I close my eyes with a sigh. He's always being my prince charming, coming to my rescue. "I'm fine. A little shaken up, but I'll be okay. You handled the situation perfectly, and because of you, we're sitting here right now."

"I don't know if I would say that."

"Well, I would. So let's drop it before we get into a stupid argument over this."

He nods his head and steps back from me, holding out his hand. I grab it and step out into the cold November air. As I let out a small breath, I can see it float away in front of me. I zip up my flimsy jacket and hug my arms to myself. When did it get so cold out?

We step foot in the door and Jax is waiting for us. Without hesitation, he says, "Downstairs right now."

I'm not sure if I should laugh right now or be scared. I never thought I would see a serious side of Jax come out like this. Especially not a pissed off side. I look over at Hudson as we walk down the stairs to their practice room, and his face is blank. He's staring straight ahead and I'm freaking out because I don't know what he's thinking. We all file into the room one by one, and Jax shuts the door behind us. The room is eerily quiet as we stand in a circle looking at one another, waiting for the first one to talk. Normally that would be me, but I have no idea where to even start. Fortunately, Jax is just like me and can't stay silent for long.

"Where the fuck have you two been the last couple of days? You got out of school on Wednesday and today's Friday. Dad's been working nonstop and Mom is who knows where. I covered for you when Dad asked, but a little fucking heads-up would have been cool. I was quick on my feet and said you were spending Thanksgiving at Ashtyn's parents' house."

I breathe a sigh of relief. I know Hudson said Jax would make up a story, but he was extremely believable when he told that janitor our parents had sent out search parties. That's obviously impossible for my parents to do, but Hudson's parents are very much alive. And he missed Thanksgiving, which is a big fucking deal. My parents would have flipped even if there were some story of where I was.

Hudson has a huge grin on his face as he says, "Thanks for that, bro. If you could believe it, we were actually trapped at the school."

"Whatever, bro. I don't buy it. Where were you really?"

"We were—"

I don't even let him finish before I cut him off. "Hudson is telling the truth, Jax. I had a shitty day at school on Wednesday. Did you ever have Potter for English?"

Reluctantly, he replies, "Yeah, what about her?"

"So then you know she's a complete bitch. Well, Wednesday was no different, but she chose me as her victim for the day. I took off and Hudson found me getting drunk in the theater. Not my finest moment, but long story short we were locked in the theater all weekend until just a little bit ago when a janitor found us in there."

His mouth is wide open. "Shit, you're serious. I can't believe that fucking happened. Are…are you guys okay?"

My jaw locks up as I try to respond. I start shaking and I can feel tears start to well up. Jax's eyes go wide as he takes a step toward me, but Hudson brings his arm up and possessively pulls me toward him. I can't look up and see his face, so I take the coward's way out and turn my head into Hudson's chest. He clears his throat and says, "Yeah, we're fine. Chloe's still a little shaken up, but we'll be okay. I think we just need to clean up and take it easy for the rest of the day."

"Yeah, you guys do that. I'll…uh…leave you to it, then." The door opens and closes behind us, and I know Jax is gone. I peek up at Hudson through my hair and his jaw is clenched tightly. Without a word, he pulls me behind him and we head upstairs toward his bedroom.

"I'm going to go take a shower and wash the last couple of days off of me."

I take a seat on his bed and say, "Okay, I'll just be here."

"Or you could join me."

"With your parents downstairs right now? I think I'll pass." I don't actually know if his parents are downstairs, but he doesn't think twice about it when he responds, "Yeah, that's a good idea."

"I know. I'm pretty smart like that. Now go take your shower before I jump in there instead and lock you out."

"Alright, alright. I'm going."

Once he starts up the shower, I wait a few minutes before I leave his room. I check to make sure no one is around before heading down the hallway to Jax's bedroom. Standing outside his door, I contemplate turning back around, but instead I raise my hand and knock. My fist is still raised when his door swings open and he pulls me inside. He envelops me in a giant hug and holds on tight. Whispering into my hair, he says, "I was freaking the fuck out the entire time you were gone. I couldn't get ahold of either one of you."

I don't know what to say, so I respond simply with, "I'm sorry."

He holds on to me for a minute longer before letting go and taking a step back. His face is blank of emotion and it's killing me to not know what he's thinking. "So?" he asks me.

"So what?" I ask dumbly. I don't want to have this conversation, and I'd rather delay the inevitable.

"What happened this weekend, Chloe? Between you and my bother?"

I know what he's asking, but I don't think he wants to know the answer to that question. Instead I answer with. "I…I love him, Jax."

"More than you love me?" His voice is broken when he asks me, and I just about fall apart right then and there.

"It's not like that."

His voice rises slightly when he clips out, "Then what's it like? Please enlighten me."

"What I feel for Hudson and what I feel for you are different. With Hudson it's all-consuming. My body is hyper-aware whenever he's near. I become breathless and my heartbeat speeds up. Every time I look into his eyes, I can see everything I'm feeling mirrored back at me."

"And with me?"

"With you I'm always happy. We laugh and have a good time, but it's all very surface. You're one of my best friends, Jax, but your eyes don't light up around me like Hudson's do. Underneath all of that hatred you hold for her are layers and layers of love. Can you honestly say the way you feel for me even holds a candle to the way you felt for Erin? Or still feel?"

His shoulders slump down and I know I have my answer. "So that's it? You've made your choice?"

"I don't think there ever was a choice. But yes, I choose Hudson. He's the one for me. I will always love you, Jax, but it's not the same." I turn to walk away and he doesn't stop me. I'm tempted to turn around, but I don't. If he's broken up right now, I don't think I could take it. But if he's not broken up about it, I think that would be worse.

When I open the door back up to Hudson's room, he's sitting on his bed quietly, waiting for me. The only indicator that he actually took a shower is his dripping hair. I take my time stepping into his room and shutting the door. The expression on his face is blank, and I'm scared to find out whether or not that's a good thing or bad.

"Did you take care of what you needed to?"

I open my mouth, but I'm not sure what to say. "I don't know what you're talking about."

He gets up from his bed and starts pacing his room. He keeps clenching and unclenching his fists at his side. "I'm not an idiot, Chloe. What were you talking to Jax about?"

I open up my mouth to talk, but my words get caught in my throat. He's so angry, and I know I caused that.

Clearing my throat, I say, "I never said you were an idiot. I was telling him that we're together now. That you and I are together now."

"So why did you have to wait until I was in the shower to do that?" he asks as he moves to stand directly in front of me.

I look down at the floor for a moment then move my eyes back up to his. "I didn't think it would be nice to have that conversation with the three of us."

"Why is that?"

"Because that would be like rubbing it in his face."

"So what's the big deal?"

I start pacing now. I don't understand how he can be like this. Either he's that dense or just doesn't care about hurting his brother. I guess it's possible that any anger he has is clouding his judgment, but still, the guy I fell in love with would never intentionally hurt someone else. "Are you being serious right now, Hudson?"

"I don't know. How should I be feeling right now, Chloe? We're locked in the theater for almost forty-eight hours together and have sex for the first time. As soon as we get out you immediately go running to him. That's kind of fucked up."

I stop and look him straight in the eyes. "It's not like that, Hudson. I don't want to be with Jax. I want to be with you. I thought the considerate thing to do would be to let him know that."

"I just wish you would have said something to me rather than sneaking behind my back."

His voice is quiet as he talks, and I know that I was wrong. "You're right. I went about it the wrong way. I'm sorry for that."

"No, I'm sorry. I'm being such a jerk right now."

I walk forward and wrap my arms around his neck and tell him, "I love you, Hudson. I want to be with you."

I can feel his head nod against me when he says, "I know that. I do. I'm insecure when it comes to you, Chloe. I love you so much and I still can't understand why you'd choose me over him."

"There was never a choice, Hudson." I squeeze him tighter and hope he never lets me go. Wordlessly, we move to the bed and spend the rest of the night showing each other just how much we love one another.

CHAPTER SIXTEEN

Hudson

One of the things that make being with Chloe so easy is our downtime. We can be sitting in a room not talking or doing anything but be one hundred percent comfortable. It's like no matter what is going on, if we're together, that makes everything better. Like right now, for example. We're lying in my bed watching an old Marilyn Monroe movie, Chloe's idol, and we're comfortable. It's been a few weeks since we were trapped in the theater, and things are better than ever. It's the best feeling in the world, aside from Chloe currently being in my arms. Suddenly she pops up on the bed and pauses the movie. "Don't laugh at me."

I look around the room and back at her. Where did that just come from? I tread lightly when I ask, "Why would I laugh at you?"

"You might. Just promise me you won't."

I bring up my hand and cross my finger over my heart. "Okay. I won't laugh at you. Now what's going on?"

"Will you show me how to make coffee?" A big grin covers my face. She's so cute, and I love that she wants me to teach her something.

"You said you wouldn't laugh," she says as she puts her face into her hands. I reach up and pull her hands away. She looks absolutely beautiful with a hint of redness to her cheeks. She's not worrying about anything and looks so carefree right now. If I could keep this lightheartedness with her forever, I would. "I'm not laughing."

"No, but you are smiling."

"I am. But I'm not making fun of you."

She cocks her head to the side and asks, "Then why are you smiling?"

I poke her lightly on the nose. "Because you're so cute. Now why do you want me to show you how to make coffee?"

"I've never done it before. Plus, wouldn't you love to be woken up by a naked me and a steamy cup of coffee in the morning?" I don't even hesitate before grabbing her hand and dragging her to the kitchen behind me. She's giggling incessantly. She knows exactly what she just did, and she's getting just what she wanted. Not that I wouldn't have shown her how to do it anyway. But this way she knew I couldn't turn her down.

When we reach the kitchen, I grab the tea kettle, fill it up with water, and set it on the stove. I turn the burner on and pull the French press out of the cupboard. I go to grab the coffee beans when Chloe asks me, "What are you doing?"

I look down at my hand on the pantry door and look back up at her. "What do you mean?"

She picks up the French press and looks at me again. "Well, what is this?" She points toward the coffee maker on the counter in the corner of the kitchen. "Are we not using the coffee maker?"

I chuckle and grab the ceramic container of coffee beans as well as the grinder out of the pantry and place them on counter. "When I'm in a rush in the mornings for school, I use that to make my coffee. But if you want a perfect cup of coffee, you use the French press. So I started out by putting the tea kettle on the stove to heat the water up, and I grabbed everything out of the pantry I would need. Are you following so far?"

Her eyes are slightly glazed as she takes everything in and she slowly nods her head. So I take that as my cue to continue. I open the container of coffee and the aroma immediately fills the air around us.

I take a big whiff and hold it in front of Chloe to do the same. "Wow, that smells amazing."

I place the canister back on the counter and add, "Wait until you drink a mug of this. You'll never want one of your frou-frou drinks again." She laughs lightly and I grab a measuring cup out of the drawer.

"I usually only fill the container half full, but since I want you to try some and I know Jax will come running once it starts steeping, I'll fill it all the way up. Since we're filling it up, you want to measure out half a cup of beans."

I hand her the measuring cup and she scoops them up. "Next you want to put them into the grinder. Jax will tell you it was fancy schmancy and a waste of money, but to get the beans perfectly ground up, you want to use a burr grinder." I hold that up and she dumps the beans in and gets the grinder going. While she's doing that, the tea kettle starts whistling and I remove it from the burner.

Holding up the grinder in her hand, she asks, "Okay, what now?"

"Now you put the ground beans into the French press. After you get all of that coffee goodness poured in, you want to add the water from the tea kettle." Very gently, she pours the coffee and slowly adds the water. She's treating it like a delicate science, which is kind of hot.

"So what do we do with this thingy?" she asks while holding up the press.

"You're very technical with your terminology. I'll remember to call it a thingy in the future. That part is actually the press part of the French press. After the water and grounds steep for sixty seconds, you'll slowly press it down into the coffee."

She diligently presses the coffee down and unknowingly brings her body down with it so her eyes are perfectly level with the counter. She studies the coffee for thirty seconds before bringing her attention back to me. "And then?"

Handing her a mug, I pour her and myself a cup. "And now we drink." She takes a sip and her eyes light up. "Wow, that's the best cup of coffee I've ever had."

I give her a wink and ask, "No more frou-frou drinks?"

"Hell no. Not anymore."

Not even a minute later, Jax comes wandering into the kitchen. "Are we having coffee?"

"Told you he'd come running once he smelled the coffee. I was just showing Chloe how to use the French press."

Mid-reach to a coffee mug in the cupboard, he stops and turns around. "Should I trust it? Maybe I'll pass this time."

Chloe playfully smacks Jax on the arm and says, "Of course you should trust it. This coffee is delicious."

Shrugging his shoulders, he grabs the mug and fills it up. He sniffs it and hesitantly takes a sip. With a thumbs-up, he turns and heads backs upstairs.

"Hudson, your mother and I would like to have a conversation with you for a minute, alone."

I glance over at Chloe, and she smiles at me and nods her head before heading upstairs with her mug of coffee to my bedroom. They aren't oblivious to the fact that she's been staying here, but they also haven't felt the need prior to right now to say anything. It's not like either one of them spends much time here themselves anyway. Mom's been gone, which I'm not supposed to know, and Dad's always working. I've never complained because I've got Jax. "Yeah, what's going on?"

Mom plasters on a fake smile and steps forward. "Sweetie, we know that this band of yours is fun and all, but we wanted to talk to you about all of your options."

Oh, so this conversation has nothing to do with Chloe. Maybe they don't even care that she's been staying here? But I'm not sure where this conversation is even going.

"What other options? We signed a contract." I turn my attention to Dad and my heart drops a little. "Dad, what is she talking about?"

He clears his throat a little and has the gall to look uncomfortable. "Son, you need a backup plan in case—"

My entire body is shaking and I clench and unclench my fists repeatedly. Standing up, I shout, "In case what, Dad? There is no backup plan. Why the fuck aren't you having this same conversation with Jax?"

Calmly and without emotion, my mother says, "Honey, watch your language please. You could do anything in the world. You can go to college and become a doctor or a lawyer—"

"If you truly knew me, you'd know I have no interest in anything like that. This isn't about the money and never has been. If I spend the rest of my life in the band but never make money, then I'll truly be happy. I don't even understand where this conversation is even coming from. Dad, you went over the contract with us."

Leaning back in his chair, he runs his hand over his face. His eyes are sunken in and he looks defeated. "We just want what's best for you. I have an old friend that works at the university up in Eugene. Your mother and I are going up there for a weekend trip and we want you to come with us. Tour the campus. Meet some people. You never know, you might love it there."

I open my mouth, but Mom cuts me off before I even have the chance to get a word out. "This isn't a debate, Hudson. You will be coming with us tomorrow. And you will be coming alone. Don't even think you can bring that little girlfriend of yours. I'm well aware that she's been staying with us, but I haven't said anything. It's just a little high school relationship that will fizzle out just like your little band. Take your future seriously, Hudson."

"You have got to be kidding me. My little band? You can't force me to come with you."

Coldly, she says, "You're still a minor. We can and we will. You will be coming with us tomorrow, so stop trying to get out of it."

"Fine, Mother, if you want me to go on your stupid trip, then I'll go. But I guarantee you I will not be going to school next year. That isn't where my future is headed and that is a fact."

"Hudson, I just want you to take your future seriously. You're making a lot of bad decisions right now, and that little girl upstairs is one of them.

Never in my life has the thought of hitting my mother ever crossed my mind until now. If she continues talking this way about Chloe, then I can't control what I may or may not do. "You don't know anything about her. And stop calling her a little girl. She has a name, and it's Chloe."

"I know a lot more than you think. But it doesn't change the fact that she's toxic and I don't like her for you."

"I don't care what you think. I'll go on your stupid trip this weekend, but after this, no more talk of college. This is my life, not yours.

She purses her lips and crosses her arms over her chest. "Hudson—"

I don't even let her finish before cutting her off. "No. I'm ending the discussion now. Like you said, this isn't up for debate. I'm compromising for you and whether you like it or not, that's my final decision. In a few months I'll be eighteen and you'll have no say in this anyway."

"I'll have a say if you want to keep your trust fund."

"First of all, I don't care about money. And second of all, you and I both know you can't touch my money. Grandpa left us that and you have no way of accessing it."

"He's right, Barbara," Dad says. He's been pretty quiet this entire time, but I guess he chose now to speak up and put Mom in her place. I know what it took for him to do that and I know it wasn't any easy choice to make.

She doesn't even let him finish before storming out of the house. The tires on her Mercedes squeal out of the driveway and Dad cringes beside me. "Well, that went well."

"Dad, you need to get your marriage shit under control. Your problems are starting to bleed over into my life and that's not okay. I'll be down here bright and early for this dumb trip, but it's pointless. I won't be going to college next year."

"I know that, son."

"As long as you know that."

I head upstairs to my room and find Chloe passed out in my bed with a different Marilyn Monroe movie playing on the TV. I must have been gone a lot longer than I thought. I won't be going to bed anytime soon, so I settle in to spend the rest of my night with Marilyn and next to my girl. No matter what Mom says, this is not something that will ever fizzle out. Chloe's the one for me, and that won't be changing anytime soon.

CHAPTER SEVENTEEN

Chloe

Rolling over, my hand runs along the coldness of the bed beside me. Where is Hudson? I open my eyes and see him quietly packing a small bag at the foot of the bed. Is he leaving?

"Hey, where are you going?"

Startled, he looks up at me. "Shit. I'm sorry. I didn't mean to wake you up. I thought I was being quiet enough."

I let out a little yawn before replying, "You didn't wake me. I rolled over and didn't feel you beside me. What's going on?"

He sighs heavily as he zips up the backpack he was just packing. "My dad has a client meeting up in Eugene. My mom and him want me to go with them."

"Okay. I don't get it."

"They're not one hundred percent sold on the band. They still think of it as a hobby."

Well, that sucks that they aren't more supportive. If my parents were still here, they would support me no matter what I chose to do. I guess I can see from a parent's perspective that a band isn't the most lucrative career aspiration. Especially when you have such a successful lawyer for a father. That still doesn't answer why he's going on the trip.

"So what's in Eugene?"

He looks out the window as he answers me. "I'm supposed to be looking at colleges."

Just hearing that makes me crumble inside. That makes sense for any normal senior in high school. Hell, if I were still normal, I'd be doing the college weekend thing too. But the word normal can no longer be used to describe me. I'm so far from normal, I don't even remember what that looks like anymore.

"From your parents' perspective, I get it, but why didn't you just tell me?"

"You were asleep and I didn't want to wake you up to make you feel any worse than you already do. But now that I say that out loud it just sounds dumb. I made you feel worse by not telling you."

"Well, I wouldn't have been very excited waking up in an empty bed and you gone."

He looks sheepish when he tells me, "They didn't give me a choice. We'll only be gone for two days max. I swear."

I plaster a fake smile on so that he can't see what I'm feeling. Two days shouldn't feel that long, but it feels like an eternity to me. So much can happen in such a short amount of time, and I'm terrified of one thought. What if he doesn't come back to me? I'm not even thinking extremes here, but what if he meets some great college girl and realizes my drama is too much for him?

"Two days is no big deal. I'll just stay holed up in your room the entire time."

He cringes before stating the obvious. "So it looks like it's going to be you and Jax for the next couple of days. Since my mom is coming too."

Leaning up in bed, I motion him over to me with my finger. When he makes his way over, I pull him down onto the bed with me. I run my fingers through his hair before pulling his face down to look at me.

"You have absolutely nothing to worry about between your brother and me. I want to be here with you. I spend my nights in your bed, not his. You should know by now that this is where I want to be."

He nods his head and his cheeks heat up a little with redness. My mouth is incredibly dry, so I run my tongue along my lips to create some moisture. Hudson's eyes zero in on them and darken with desire.

"You're right. I know that, I do. I'm still baffled by the fact that I got the girl."

"Well, you better get used to it. This girl isn't going anywhere."

I pull his head down and lightly press our lips together. I flick my tongue out and tease his bottom lip as he releases a deep groan. We tangle our tongues together like we're devouring one another's mouths.

Moving his body in between my legs, he grinds his

hardness into me, causing me to moan his name. Trying to add a little more pressure to me, I wrap my legs around him as he continues his tortuous grinding.

Who knew that dry humping could feel so good?

I'm panting and I can feel both of our hearts racing. I want nothing more than to feel him inside me. I reach for the button on his jeans and he quickly gets the idea. Swiftly removing his pants, he settles back between my legs. The only barrier between us now is the thin fabric of our underwear.

Slowly and lightly, he runs his fingers across my stomach. Back and forth. Over and over again. Each time his fingers drop a little lower, teasingly playing with the top of my underwear. Unable to handle the torture any longer, I push up from the bed, forcing us closer together. Looking into my eyes, he smirks and continues his torture.

Throwing my head back, I groan in frustration and look back over at him. "Please, Hudson."

"Please what, babe?"

"I can't take it anymore. I need you to touch me. You're leaving for two days and I want you so bad."

That's all it takes and he slips his hand inside my panties.

He lets out a tortured groan and says, "You're already soaked. How am I supposed to leave you for two days?"

I give him my own smirk right back and say, "And to think you were going to just leave and not get a proper goodbye."

"Obviously I'm a fucking idiot."

I let out a small laugh that turns into a moan, causing

me to lose all train of thought. My whole body is on fire as he continues bringing me closer and closer to what I need.

"Hey, bro, Mom and Dad are—shit, sorry."

Hudson jerks the blankets over us and attempts to cover me.

"What the fuck, Jax? Don't you know how to knock?"

Jax just looks annoyed when he responds, "I stood there knocking for a solid minute. You obviously couldn't hear me."

Jax looks over at me and winks. I feel my face heat up with legit embarrassment. I slink under the covers even more, successfully covering my face.

"What do you need?"

"Mom and Dad are waiting for you in the car."

"Shit. Already? Tell them I'll be down in a minute."

"Sorry, Chlo, is that all he's good for?"

I don't even understand Jax. He can be a sweet guy when he wants to be. I think that's why I originally liked him. He showed me his softer side. His real side. Ironically, the side that makes him more like Hudson. But for some reason he never shows it to anyone else. At least from what I've seen.

"You've officially killed the mood. And not that it's any of your business, Jax, but your brother is a fucking rockstar in bed. So trust me, your apologies are not necessary."

If it's possible, I think I actually shocked the silence into Jax. He stands there dumbfounded for a minute before saying, "Well, I'll tell them you're just finishing up and will be right down."

Before either one of us can say anything, he turns around and leaves, closing the door behind him. We both sit there staring at the door a little longer than necessary before turning our attention back toward each other. Looking into my eyes, Hudson leans down and sweetly pecks me on the lips before getting up from the bed.

"I'm sorry for that. I wish I had more time, but if I don't get down there soon, the next person through that door will be my dad, and I don't think either one of us wants that."

I cringe just thinking of that. It's one thing for Jax to walk in on us, but their dad? No way. Not a conversation I want to ever be a part of.

"It's okay, I know you have to go. Besides, I wasn't lying when I told Jax the mood was killed." I nod down at Hudson's boxer briefs and the lack of fullness that was just there. "It was obviously killed for the both of us."

Angrily pulling his jeans up, Hudson says, "I'm seriously going to kill Jax when I get back."

I let out a small laugh, get up from the bed, and saunter over to where Hudson is still struggling with his jeans. I reach forward and put my hands on top of his, and they still with the contact. I move his hands away to zip and button his jeans for him.

Leaning up on my toes, I plant my mouth on his and softly whisper into his mouth, "I get you first, then you can kill him. Just make sure you make it back to me."

Shit. Did I just say that? If I keep letting all this needy shit come out, he's going to run far, far away from me. I can't lose him too. Fuck! When did I turn into this kind of girl? I never used to care or form attachments with guys. Things were so much easier then.

Pushing back from me, Hudson looks into my eyes and

I close them up tight. I don't want to see whatever he's feeling.

"Chloe, open your eyes."

I look like a two-year-old as I shake my head no.

"Please, just open your eyes for me. I need to say something and I want you looking at me when I say it."

"Don't break my heart, Hudson."

"Never. Now please open your eyes."

Reluctantly, I open them. I can't tell what he's thinking, so I mentally prepare for the worst.

"I will always come back to you, Chloe. Nothing could ever keep me from you. You're my girlfriend and I'm the luckiest guy in the world because you chose me." He kisses me on the forehead and looks back into my eyes. "I love you and I'm never letting you go."

My heart warms with so much happiness, I don't even know how that's possible. I stand there looking up into his eyes and I feel like I found my home. No matter where I go, as long as it's with Hudson, I'll be home.

"Babe, why are you crying?"

Am I? How is it possible to be crying and not even know it?

"I'm so incredibly happy right now. I know I have so much baggage in my life right now, but you've stuck by my side through all of it. I love you so much, Hudson. You're healing me and have been since you walked into my life. Or at least since I let you in."

He wraps me up into his arms and I never want to let go. I'm engulfed in a smell that can only be described as Hudson. I don't know if it's his soap or cologne, but he always has a very fresh woodsy smell with just a hint of citrus. He kisses me on top of my head and I relax into him even more. I think my new favorite place is in Hudson's arms. If I could spend all day with his arms wrapped around me, I think I could die happy.

"I hate to do this now, but I have to go."

"I know. Text me when you get there."

"I'm going to be blowing up your phone with so many texts, you're going to get sick of me."

"Not even possible."

Giving me one more kiss goodbye, he walks out the door, closing it behind him. Wrapping my arms around myself, I climb back into bed and cuddle up on his side of the bed. I hear my phone ding with a text message, so I grab it off the nightstand.

Hudson: I love you. And I'm already missing you like crazy.

Me: I love you too! <3

Hudson: Go back to bed. It's early.

Me: I'm already way ahead of you.

Hudson: See you in two days.

This is going to be the longest two days of my life.

CHAPTER EIGHTEEN

Hudson

My parents mean well with this whole college visit thing. Yeah, they're just looking out for my future, but this morning it was a major cock block. All I want to do is go back home and spend all day in bed with Chloe.

Even worse than that, they wanted to drive up here rather than fly. Being stuck in a car with your parents for any length of time sucks, but a road trip is the worst. Mom has to stop all the freakin' time to pee and Dad likes to listen to news radio.

Who does that?

Luckily, I brought my earbuds with me and I have my newest playlist on repeat. If I can't change my location, I can drown out everything around me and just get lost in the music. I'd like to say that has helped the trip fly by even faster, but no such luck. I feel like this entire day has just been one big waiting game.

Unfortunately, I've been wandering around a college campus that I'll never attend since I got here. A big waste of fucking time. On top of that, my tour guide has been MIA. I've been pacing the same area for thirty minutes now, and I'm about ready to throw in the towel.

Tired of pacing, I sit down on a bench and pull out my phone. Apparently it's been forty-five minutes. It's a good thing I don't plan on going to college. This visit alone would be crossing this school off my list. How the fuck is the tour guide late? Don't they live for this shit? I haven't sent Chloe a text since I got here, so I go ahead and do that now.

Me: Hey, I'm finally here.

Chloe: I'm glad you made it. Are you having fun?

Me: Not even a little bit. My tour guide is almost an hour late.

Chloe: I'm sorry, that sucks.

I'm suddenly aware that the sun is being blocked and look up to see a girl staring down at me. She's cute in that nerdy kind of way: glasses, hair pulled back, and a little button nose. All of that aside, the thing I notice the most is her red-rimmed puffy eyes.

Before I get the chance to ask her if she's okay, she asks me, "Are you Hudson Hartley?"

So this must be the tour guide. "Yeah I am. Are you okay?"

Holding back, she just nods her head and looks away. I grab her arm to focus her attention back on me and she loses it. Slumping down on the bench next to me, I barely make out her saying, "My boyfriend just broke up with me."

I did not come here to deal with some girl's boyfriend drama. I didn't even want to come to this thing in the first place. I get up from the bench and try not to make it obvious how uncomfortable I am.

"That sucks. Why don't we just skip the tour? I'm sure you aren't in the mood for this. I can just walk around by myself."

She quickly wipes away her tears and composes herself. "No. I'm supposed to be giving you a tour, and that's just what you're going to get."

Standing up, she starts walking away from me. What the fuck just happened?

"Are you coming? I was late showing up, so we're already behind."

Shaking my head, I take off after her. This chick is serious business. She may be cute and little, but I don't want to get on her bad side. When I finally catch up to her, I notice she's headed off toward a cluster of buildings. Great. Classrooms.

"Hey, what's your name?"

She stops and looks over at me, a little confused. Then she smiles. "Sorry, I guess I didn't introduce myself." She reaches her hand out to me, and I shake it as she says, "I'm Clare Quinn."

"Nice to meet you, Clare. Look, I don't want to sound rude, but this whole tour is unnecessary. I'm not even planning on going to college, but my parents made me come here."

She opens her mouth and looks like I spoke a foreign language. "What do you mean you aren't going to college? Who doesn't want to go to college?"

"My band just signed with a record label—"

"My boyfriend was in a band."

Um, okay? I don't even know what to do with this girl anymore. This whole situation is getting a little uncomfortable, even for me, and I can usually handle a plethora of drama.

"Seriously, we can just stop this thing right now. I get the feeling neither one of us wants to be here right now."

She nods her head and says, "You're right. Jeez, Hudson, you're a nice guy. I bet you think I'm just a disaster right now."

Yep, just a little bit. "No I don't. You're going through a breakup. Everyone gets a little messed up when that happens."

"This is un-tour-guide like, but I know there's a party getting started that we can go crash if you want?"

I look around me and up at the sun before switching my focus back to Clare. "A party…now?"

She nods her head and sighs. "Yeah, it's a lame frat party. It's beach themed."

"It's December."

"They're frat guys."

"Fair enough."

I contemplate that for a minute. My parents dropped me off here this morning, and I have nowhere to go until they pick me up tomorrow. They planned this whole trip without me knowing and even arranged for me to stay in the dorms. If I can't be with Chloe right now, I might as well make the most of this trip and go to a party. Couldn't be any worse than my current fun times.

I nod my head and say, "Why the hell not. Lead the way."

Her entire face lights up and I feel like I just made her day. If anything, maybe I can help her relax a bit and not worry about the obvious broken heart she has. I'm just lucky I have Chloe back home waiting for me. What I wouldn't give to have her wrapped around me right now. I hope these two days fucking fly by.

I don't know how I always get myself into these predicaments. Clare is hammered, and being the noble person that I am, I'm taking care of her. I barely know this chick, but there's no way I'd let something happen to her. I'm not some dick who would just ditch her to take care of herself. Right about now, I wish I was.

When we got here earlier, the party was just getting started. Although the house is off campus, I can tell it's all students who live here. They have beer pong set up in the garage and they're playing some variation of truth or dare in the kitchen. I didn't stick around long enough to get pulled in.

As soon as we walked in, Clare headed straight for the keg and has been drinking heavily ever since. I get that she's going through a breakup, but why do girls always have to get uncontrollably wasted? It's not fun for anyone else around them. I stopped paying attention to her when she decided to do a keg stand. If this is what college is going to be like, then I know I don't want to be here. I can do all the partying I want and not waste my parents' money on an education that I'll never use. What a waste.

"Hudson!"

I turn my attention to where she is now. She's grinding up against two other girls, and there's a bunch of guys standing around them, leering. All three girls look like they've lost a few items of clothing in the process of dancing. Done with the whole situation, I walk over to her and fling her over my back. I start heading toward the front door when she starts hitting me on the back. It doesn't hurt, but it is getting annoying. Like little pin pricks all over my back.

Placing her down on the ground, I see her entire face has turned green, and she takes off to where I hope there is a bathroom. Following behind her, I watch as she runs in and slams the door. I don't know her well enough to help her out, so I just stand guard outside the bathroom and wait.

Eventually she comes stumbling out, and I figure now is the best time to leave. Her eyes are half closed and she's using the doorjamb to hold her up.

"Where do you live?"

She's staring off into space, not paying attention to me, when she suddenly stiffens beside me. I follow her line of vision to some nerdy dude who's all over a busty blonde. This must be the ex-boyfriend. I turn to say something to her, but she immediately grabs my face and slams her lips to mine. She must have found some toothpaste or mouth wash because her breath is luckily minty. Out of the corner of my eye, I can see nerd boy looking over at her, so I don't make it obvious when I push her away.

I move my forehead to hers and whisper to her, "While I understand you want to make your boyfriend jealous, I have a girlfriend at home that I love very much. Why don't you tell me where you live so I can take you home."

She nods her head and I can see the start of tears in her eyes. I wipe away the single tear that drops and pull her into me for a hug.

"Your girlfriend is seriously so lucky. Why can't all guys be like you."

I sigh. I'm the lucky one who gets to call Chloe mine. I'm still in shock over how my day started out, and I can't wait to get back home.

We start walking away from the bathroom and Clare stumbles all over herself. Knowing there's no way she's going to be able to walk all the way home, I pick her up and carry her toward the door. Surprisingly, no one stops me, and that just pisses me off. Her ex-boyfriend is somewhere at this party, and I'm a stranger carrying her out the door. Even if they broke up, that's still pretty fucked up.

I start walking down the street and realize I have no

idea where I'm going.

"Hey, so where do you live?"

I'm met with silence and look down to see a very crashed out Clare in my arms. Great. My only option now is to take her back to the room I'm staying in. Luckily I'm there by myself. Unluckily, there's only one bed, so it looks like I'll be crashing on the floor tonight.

The house was off campus, but it's not a very long walk back to the dorms. We reach the room quickly and I lay her down on the bed. I remove her shoes and lay a blanket on top of her. Hopefully she'll have a more comfortable night's sleep than I do. I plug my phone into the charger and get ready to lie down on the floor.

I hear moaning coming from the bed and I jump up to check on her. Sitting up quickly, she leans over the bed and throws up right on top of me. She lets out a little sigh before she lies back down and shortly starts snoring.

What the fuck?

Did she even wake up? Never again am I helping another drunk girl besides Chloe. I fucking reek. Walking to the en-suite bathroom, I crank the shower up and strip my clothes off. I'm just going to throw that shit away. No point in trying to clean it up.

This day started out amazing and went from bad to worse. I don't care if I have to catch a bus back home. There's no way I'm staying another day. This time tomorrow, I will be holding Chloe in my arms.

CHAPTER NINETEEN

Chloe

I don't know how it happened, but it did. Hudson broke down all my pain and somehow gave me the ability to find happiness. I'm not healed in any way, but my rocky road is turning a little less rocky and I'm a little less broken now. Hudson is the light in my darkness and I'm slowly working my way out.

It's hard for me to even imagine the feelings I thought I had for Jax. What I had with Jax was one hundred percent pure lust. To put it lightly, Jax is sex on a stick. I'm sure the sex would have been mind-blowing, and sure, he's still great to hang out with and share a laugh with, but he isn't Hudson.

We share such a deep connection, and I don't think we would have ever figured that out if it weren't for the weekend in the theater. And then this morning. This morning he told me the one thing I needed to hear. The one thing that truly broke through the walls I didn't even know I had put up. The timing pretty much sucks though. Why did his parents make him go on that stupid college visit?

I'm not super into the same music that Ashtyn is, but Marlowe has quickly become my new favorite band. I know I won't be the last person to say that either. They're music is good, like really good, and the moment their music gets spread around, they're going to take off.

I'm not sure how I feel about being a rock star's girlfriend. Sure, rock stars are fun to hook up with and have fun with, but I've never thought past that. Then again, I never wanted a boyfriend either, yet here I am. Hopelessly in love with a soon-to-be rock star. I guess we'll just have to cross that bridge when we come to it.

He's been busy all day with touring the college, but if his tour guide ever showed up, that should have been done with hours ago. He's been pretty radio silent, so I decide to give him a call. I would much rather hear his voice than text him. The phone rings a few times and then he answers.

"Hello?" On the other end is what sounds like a drunken girl I just woke up. I pull the phone away from my face and look to make sure I called the right number. Sure enough, there's the picture we took the day in the theater staring right back at me.

What the fuck.

There's a bit of an edge to my voice as I bark out, "Hi,

who's this?"

Drunkey says, "This is Clare, who's this?"

Who the fuck is Clare? And where does she get off questioning who I am?

I'm over this bullshit and I go straight to what I should have asked in the first place. "Where's Hudson?"

She lets out a heavy sigh and I hear some shuffling. Are they in bed together? Why would he profess his love to me this morning if the first thing he was going to do is go off and have sex with some random girl? How could I be so stupid to fall for him?

"I think he's in the shower. I can tell him—"

I don't even let her finish that sentence. I chuck the phone across the room and watch it shatter into a million pieces. I don't even recognize the feral scream that I release, but it comes out. It hurt when my parents died. It hurt like hell. But this, this feels like I'm literally dying inside. I'm in complete agony and I can't even comprehend how excruciating this is. I trusted him, and the first chance he got, he cheated. And I thought Jax was the bad one. Speaking of Jax, he comes barreling through the bedroom door.

"What the fuck, Chloe? What's going on in here?"

His anger quickly slips away and turns to concern when he sees my face. I'm sure it looks horrible with snot and tears running down. I feel like I can't even breathe, and I can't stop the sobs that are wracking my body.

How could he do this?

Why would he do this?

He said he loved me.

Jax doesn't say anything more. He picks me up and

carries me back to his room and lays me down on his bed. I'm still sobbing as he gets in the bed with me and pulls me close. I don't know how long we lie like that before I finally fall asleep, clutching him and just wanting this entire day to start all over again.

I'm not sure what time it is, but when I open my eyes it's still dark outside. My throat is scratchy and my lids are heavy. I feel Hudson next to me and I snuggle in closer. He pulls me tighter, but something doesn't feel right. His body feels different and he smells different too. Not bad. Just different.

"Are you awake?"

That's because this isn't Hudson, it's Jax. The entire night comes crashing back to me and I feel like breaking down all over again. I have to tell him something, but if those words leave my mouth, they become real. They become the truth. I can't handle what he did to me, but I have to say it anyway.

My tongue feels heavy as the words fall from it. "He cheated, Jax."

He stiffens beside me and I feel him press a kiss to the top of my head. I curl up into him even more and wish it were Hudson comforting me right now, not his brother. But I wouldn't need comforting right now if Hudson were here.

Talking into my hair, he asks, "How do you know

that?"

I start breaking down again, but I take a deep breath and swallow those emotions. If I let myself fall apart again, I'll never get this out. And after everything Jax did last night, he deserves an explanation.

"I called him last night and a drunk girl answered his phone."

"That doesn't necessarily mean anything."

"When I asked her where he was, she told…she told me…he was in the shower."

"I'm going to kill him."

I can't hold back the sobs any longer and I just let it go. That's the last thing I want. I can't shut off my emotions and I'm still so in love with Hudson. Why can't I just stop loving him? He healed me and stayed by my side through everything these past few months. None of this makes sense to me. Why would he go to all the effort if he was just going to throw it all away?

Jax hugs me tighter and tells me everything will be okay. I'm clutching him so tightly that I feel like I could crawl up inside of him. He's running his hands up and down my back and continually kissing me on the top of my head. I wish everything could be okay. But it's not going to be. My life is a giant shit storm, and everything is not going to be okay. Nothing will be okay ever again.

I accidentally rock my body against him while squeezing him tighter, and I can't help the moan that leaves my mouth. His hands are still on my back, and neither one of us does anything. The room becomes eerily quiet.

I should get up from his bed right now and walk out of here before anything else happens. I should go back to

Hudson's room and pack my things. What I shouldn't do is stay here and do something I might regret. But my voice of reason went out the window when some random bitch answered Hudson's phone. No, it went out the window the minute he fucking cheated and ruined us.

I rock myself against Jax again and this time he groans right along with me. I lean back slightly and look up into his eyes. They're dark with desire, and I know he's feeling everything I'm feeling right now. But he's also fighting an internal battle, and I know it. He wants me, but I belong to his brother. Or I used to.

Forcing the decision for him, I slam my mouth to his as I continue rocking against him. His hands continue running along my back, but they're rougher this time. He breaks the kisses and tries to push me away. I let out a whimper and try to pull him back to me.

"No. We can't do this."

I pepper kisses up and down his face and hook my leg around his waist.

"Please, Jax. Please help me forget."

I know I sound desperate and needy, but at this point I don't even care. The old Chloe would never have begged a guy for sex. Shit, they were always the ones begging me. But the old Chloe died a long time ago, and the shell of her is all that is left.

"Shit, Chloe. I can't do this. He's my brother."

I can tell it won't take much to push him over the edge, so I tell him the one thing I know will push him over with me.

"My year has been nothing but hell, Jax. My parents

died and Hudson helped me out of that dark place. He told me this morning that he loved me, and then he turned around and cheated on me. He single-handedly pushed me back into that dark place, and I just want to feel good for a little bit and not think about it. Is that so wrong?"

As he bows his head, I have no idea what he's thinking. When he looks back up at me, I know he's going to give in. "I told you when you were in the hospital that I'd be there for you in any way that you need me. I wasn't lying to you."

"I do need you, Jax."

"I never thought my brother would royally fuck things up like this. I'm holding on by a thread right now, but if this is what you want, I'll make you feel good. Even if it's just for a little bit."

"Please, Jax."

That's all he needs. Flipping me onto my back, he looks deep into my eyes, and I know he's right there with me. He pushes his hardness into me and I let out a moan.

"Don't worry, Chloe. I'll make you forget."

I nod my head as he leans down and kisses me deeply. He's running his fingers through my hair and being so incredibly sweet with his gentle caresses. He leaves feather-light kisses down my face and over my jaw. When he reaches the top of my shirt, he pulls me up to lift it off of me. His hands are on the hem when I stop him. He's attempting to take Hudson's shirt off of me.

My hands are shaking as I push his away. I'm on an emotional overload and the tears start pouring. I'm trying to put my all into this, but I can't. He runs his hand down my face and feels the tears, causing him to break away from my kiss.

Pressing his forehead to mine, he asks, "Do you want me to stop? We don't need to do this."

I'm bawling and I'm finally able to get out, "I'm sorry, Jax. I can't do this. I want to so bad. I want to hurt him like he's hurting me, but I can't…I can't fucking do it."

Hugging me tightly, he whispers in my hair, "You have nothing to be sorry about."

I let out a harsh laugh. "I'm such a fucking mess. You think I'm crazy right now. Your brother cheats on me and the first thing I do is throw myself at you."

"You're heartbroken. I could never think you're crazy."

"Just for the record, Erin's a fucking moron."

He's quiet beside me and I know he's lost in thought. I don't know her side of the story, but I don't understand what the fuck she was thinking. Jax obviously worships the ground she walks on and she dumped him. Who does that?

"I wish I could be what you need, Chloe. That I was the right one for you and not so screwed up."

"Me too, Jax. Me too."

Groaning, he rolls over and says, "Why don't we go back to sleep? It's late and that's the best for right now."

I nod my head and realize he can't see me because it's still dark in here. "Okay. Can we just forget about this whole thing?"

"What whole thing?"

"What we—oh, I see what you did there. Goodnight, Jax."

"Night, Chloe."

He pulls me in tight and I lie there, softly crying myself to sleep. I try to be quiet, but he squeezes me more tightly, so I'm guessing I wasn't as quiet as I thought. How did things get so fucked up? I went from being absolutely in love to being heartbroken to almost having sex with Jax. This has been a fucked up year for me. I don't see how things could get worse, but then again, things can always get worse.

CHAPTER TWENTY

Hudson

After getting out of the shower last night, I knew I wasn't going to be able to sleep, so I pulled up the bus schedule on my phone to find out when the next one was leaving. After calling a taxi to come pick me up, I packed my shit up, left a note for Clare, and got myself out of there. It's still early, but I'm going through Chloe withdrawals. I call her up and it goes straight to voicemail. That's strange. Maybe she forgot to charge her phone. I leave her a quick message telling her to call me when she gets it and hang up.

I want nothing more than to go home and crawl into bed with her. I've been absolutely miserable without her, and I don't want to feel this way ever again. After finding a seat on the bus and settling in, I try calling her again and it still goes straight to voicemail.

Knowing I have a long-ass bus ride ahead of me, I lean my head against the window to get a little sleep.

I wake up a few hours later and notice we aren't that far away. I actually slept almost the entire drive down. I try calling Chloe again, and her phone is still going straight to voicemail. I hope everything is okay. It's starting to worry me that her phone isn't turned on. I contemplate calling Jax, but if something were wrong, he would have called me.

I decide to call Flynn since he doesn't live that far from my parents' house. The phone rings a few times before he finally picks up.

"Hello?"

"Sorry, dude. I know it's early, but I was hoping you could pick me up at the bus stop."

"What are you talking about?"

"It's a long story, but I was up in Eugene and I took a bus back down. Can you pick me up when I get to Ashland?"

"Hold on."

I can hear muffled voices and I'm guessing Ashtyn is there with him. I feel like an ass for waking both of them up, but I figured if anyone would understand my wanting to get back to Chloe, it would be Flynn.

He comes back on the line and asks, "Hey, you still there?"

"Yeah, I'm here."

"What time are you coming in?"

I pull my phone back and check out the time. I'm guessing about an hour, so I tell him, "I should be in town around eight."

"Yeah, we'll be there."

"Thanks, man. I appreciate it."

"No problem."

He hangs up and I lay my head back against the seat. If only Chloe knew what I was going through to make it back to her. The first thing I'm going to do after kissing her senseless is pull her into the shower with me. I need to wash this bus off of me, and I don't plan on doing that alone. Then I'll pull her into bed with me and not leave.

Unfortunately, the next hour doesn't go as quickly as I would like it to, but we finally reach our destination and I'm seriously itching to get off this bus. It sucks stopping along the way and watching people get off, knowing that I have a longer trip to go.

Running my fingers through my hair, I stand up and see Flynn and Ashtyn standing by her Jeep. That would have fucking sucked to ride on the back of his bike. I'm guessing Ashtyn wanted to come too in hopes that Chloe would finally talk to her.

"Hey, you guys. Thanks again for picking me up. I know it's early."

"Dude, don't even worry about it. I'll just find some way for you to return the favor later."

Ashtyn playfully slaps him on the arm and turns to me. "He will do no such thing. We were happy to help." She hands me a coffee and I just now realize they both have them in their hands. "Here, I had us stop. I figured you might need one."

I greedily take the coffee from her and take a giant gulp. Other than the small nap I took on the bus, I haven't slept since I woke up yesterday morning. This coffee could taste like shit, but it tastes like heaven right now.

"If I didn't love Chloe, I might be tempted to steal Ashtyn from you, buddy."

I'd be terrified of Flynn wanting to beat my ass for the comment, but Ashtyn steps in front of him, jumping up and down.

"You love Chloe? When did this happen? Are you two together?"

If I didn't know any better, I'd think Ashtyn were Chloe right now. Or at least the old Chloe.

"We are together, although it's a recent development. We told each other yesterday for the first time but we've both felt it for awhile. But I had to go on a stupid college visit and all I want to do is get back to her. So can we get going?"

That halts the conversation, and we hop into Ashtyn's SUV. I'm so antsy I'm sure my anxiety is rolling off of me. Nobody in the car talks, which is just fine with me. I can't keep my body still and my hands are shaking. It's either a result of my anxiousness or the fact that I drank coffee on an empty stomach. Probably a little bit of both.

Fortunately, Ashtyn drives a little faster than normal, and soon enough we're parking in my driveway. I don't say anything to either one of them as I hop out of the car and start toward the front door. I hear the car doors slam behind me, so I guess they're coming inside too.

I walk up the stairs and go straight for my bedroom. I know it's still pretty early, so I'm sure Chloe is still asleep in our bed. My heart is racing at the idea of finally getting to pull her into my arms and just hold her. I know it's only been a little over twenty-four hours, but that was twenty-four too many. Quietly opening the door, as to not wake her, I slip inside. I'm shocked when I don't find her in bed.

I drop my bag on my bed and walk over to my bathroom. I find it empty, and when I come out, I find a shattered cell phone on the floor.

What the fuck?

Where is she?

You know that feeling you get deep in the pit of your stomach when you know something is wrong? As I get closer and closer to Jax's bedroom door, that clench gets tighter and tighter. My entire arm is shaking as I reach for the doorknob, and the cold metal is scorching under my touch.

I know what's behind that door, but the sick masochist inside of me has to confirm it. I'm so fucking naïve, but I thought she was finally mine. I guess "I love you" doesn't mean the same thing to her as it does to me.

I should have guessed she'd go running back to his bed the first chance she got. The miserable bastard can have anyone he wants. Why did he have to take Chloe from me?

I finally work up the nerve to turn the knob. Entering the room, my worst nightmares come true. There she is, looking so innocent snuggled under his blankets with her hair fanned over his pillow.

Just the sight of her makes my entire heart crack wide open. I never understood what Jax went through when Erin left him, but I get it now. I just never knew my own brother would cause me that same pain.

It's ridiculous, but even now I can't stop loving her. I

wish I could just shut it off and feel nothing. Being numb and lifeless would be so much better compared to the excruciating brokenness I'm feeling right now.

I'm frozen to the spot and can't seem to get out of there. I'm so focused on Chloe. How could she do this to us? Why would she do this to us? My trance is broken when Jax comes walking out of his bathroom. He's strutting out wearing nothing but a towel. I don't know whether I want to vomit or hit him, so I go with the latter.

I start walking toward him and Jax's attention switches from Chloe to me. "Hey, little brother. What's going—"

I don't even let him finish before my fist connects with his face. I catch him off guard, so I get one good punch in before he comes back after me. We're rolling around on the ground beating the shit out of each other, and I can faintly hear Chloe yelling in the background. I'm guessing Flynn and Ashtyn heard the fighting, because suddenly Jax is being pulled off of me.

Flynn looks back and forth between both of us before asking, "What the fuck is going on in here?"

Shaking out of Flynn's grip, Jax responds with, "Why don't you ask this dipshit? I just came out of the bathroom and he attacked me out of nowhere."

I'm furious and fuming. My entire body is shaking and I know it's not the coffee this time. Is he fucking kidding me? I attacked him out of nowhere?

"That fucking asshole slept with Chloe."

Ashtyn gasps, and everyone turns their attention to Chloe, who is still in his bed, wearing nothing but one of my t-shirts. Are you fucking kidding me? She fucked my brother and then put my shirt back on? Who does that shit?

She starts to talk, but I don't even let her. "I don't want to fucking hear it. I want you and your shit out of my house right now. As of this minute we are done."

She shuts her mouth and nods her head. I don't even wait for a response. I walk out of that room and head downstairs. I can't fucking look at anybody right now. I head down to the studio to beat the shit out of my drums for the rest of the day. What a fucking awesome way to be welcomed home.

CHAPTER TWENTY-ONE

Chloe

I'm stunned and in shock. I understand why Hudson thought I cheated on him. The situation didn't look the best, but what about him? He had another girl answer his phone in the middle of the night while he was in the shower. Why is it okay for him? Double fucking standards.

After he stormed out of the room, I finally notice that both Ashtyn and Flynn are here. I know I've been a horrible friend to Ashtyn lately, but she's still here. I truly don't deserve her, but I'm glad that I have her anyway. Rather than stand here and have everyone gawk at me, I walk back to Hudson's room and pack up all of my shit. Not that there is much to pack up anyway.

I don't even have to turn around to know that Ashtyn

followed me in here.

"Are you okay?"

And that's all it takes. I turn around and run into her arms. I have the best, best friend in the world, and after what just happened, I need her now more than ever. I can't stop the tears that flood out of me, and my entire body is shaking with my sobs. She wraps her arms around me and rubs my back. No matter what I do, I know I will always have Ashtyn to turn to. She is my rock. My person.

"I'm so sorry, Ash. I've been such a horrible friend."

"Seriously, don't even worry about that right now. You've been through one giant shit storm. My only concern is making sure you're okay."

"I just want to get out of here. Can we talk about everything once we're gone?"

She nods her head, and we silently move around Hudson's room, packing up my stuff. The majority of my belongings are still back at Ashtyn's house. I don't even know what happened to all of my stuff from Santa Barbara. I guess it's a little late to be thinking about that now. It's for the best anyway. Most of that stuff would just remind me of my parents, and they're the last people I want to think about right now.

We make our way downstairs and I spot Jax standing with Flynn near the front door. I drop my bag and run into his arms.

"I'm so sorry. I didn't mean for any of this to happen."

He rubs my back and tells me, "It's okay."

Shaking my head, I pull back from him. "No, Jax, it's

not okay. He hit you and he thinks you did something horrible."

He lets go and backs away. "Don't worry, sweetheart. I'll have a chat with him and get it all fixed. He just needs time to calm down. Go take care of yourself. I've got it covered. Don't worry about a thing."

I've got nothing to say to that, so I nod my head and pick my bag back up. We get into Ashtyn's Jeep and I force myself to look out the window and focus on something, anything. I don't even know what just happened, so I'm not ready to talk about it. I know the minute this car stops and we get settled in Ashtyn's bedroom, she'll want to talk.

How do I tell her that the man I love cheated on me and instead of owning up to it, blamed me instead? I know the situation I was in looked compromising, and technically what Jax and I did would be considered cheating, but it's nothing like what he did. How could he do that to us? It sounds bad, but I expected something like this from Jax, but never Hudson. No, he was supposed to be the good brother. The better brother. He's the one I fell in love with.

I never loved Jax. I never knew what love was until Hudson. Jax was unattainable. A good chase, nothing more. Hudson and I are deeply connected. I thought he understood me. I thought we understood each other. I guess I was wrong. Very wrong. How could I be so wrong?

The car comes to a stop and I look up. The trip was a lot shorter than it should be, and I realize it's because we've stopped at a different house. This isn't where Ashtyn lives. Where are we?

Even though we haven't been around each other for a few months, we still have that best friend ESP, and Ashtyn answers my question without me even asking. "I wasn't sure if you wanted to deal with my parents just yet, so I figured I would bring you back to Flynn's place in case you wanted to shower, cry, talk, or just stare at the wall."

"Flynn's place?"

"Yeah, it's a long story, but he bought this place shortly after our accident."

Where the fuck have I been? Oh yeah, that's right. Fucking wasted off my ass. God, I'm such a bitch. What is my problem? I pulled myself inside and only opened up to Hudson since the accident. I guess I'm lucky Ashtyn is even still talking to me.

I follow the two of them inside. It's not massive like the Hartleys' house, but it's not something a normal twenty-one-year-old would be able to afford. I'll have to get the story about Flynn later from Ashtyn, after I pull my head out of my ass and actually have a real conversation with her. After everything she just did for me, it's time.

Maybe she'll let me have a drink first. I could use a drink right about now. Or a cigarette. Not that I even smoke, but I hear those are good for stress. What am I thinking? Just trading one vice for another. One step from being a fucking addict. Or maybe I'm already there. Who knows?

I look around me, and we're standing in the living room. Shit, I need a minute to pull myself together. My breathing becomes labored and my palms are sweaty. What is wrong? This is Ashtyn. She's been my best friend my entire life. "Hey, where's the bathroom?"

She looks over at me and smiles. "Oh, sorry. It's just down the hallway and the first door on your right. Do you need anything?"

I lift up my bag and look at it. Do I need anything? I don't even know what I need right now. "No, I think I'm good. I think I'm just going to take a shower real quick. Clear my head a little."

She just nods her head. "Okay, sounds good. There are some towels in the closet in there. Just help yourself."

She sounds so domestic. When the hell did she get married? Cause it certainly sounds like she is. I just nod my head and speed walk to the bathroom. Once inside, I lock the door behind me and finally breathe evenly. How did things get so awkward between us?

Tossing my bag onto the floor, I turn the shower on as hot as it will go and step in. I look at the shampoo and start to reach for it but change my mind. Collapsing into myself, I sink to the floor and let everything out. My chest aches with the heaviness of the world crashing down around me. The malice in Hudson's voice hurt more than the act of him cheating on me. I get it. I was in a pretty compromising position when he found me, but that's pretty fucking funny coming from him after he just cheated on me. My body wracks with the sobs leaving me, and I pull my legs up against my chest.

How could he do this to us? My tears are pouring out of me so quickly that I can no longer tell the difference between them and the water flowing over my body. It physically feels like my heart is breaking in two. I can't handle the pain that is breaking open inside of me, and I just want it to go away. The intensity is killing me, and I don't think I can handle it any longer. I'm rocking over and over as my body shivers. The blistering water is pouring over me, but it does nothing to warm the coldness that's swept over my body. I want the numbness to sink in and I don't want to feel anything ever again.

As my agony takes over, I remember that last pint of 151 sitting in my bag. After our weekend in the theater, I hid it away, thinking I wouldn't need it again. Picking my body up, I throw myself out of the shower and go hunt that bottle down. Rummaging through my very full duffel bag, I find the hidden prize and hug it to my chest. My body shakes uncontrollably in the cold and I slam myself down onto the shower floor.

I crack open the bottle and toss the lid—I won't be needing that. Taking a swig, the familiar burn slides down my throat and coats my belly. The bite in my mouth catches me off guard, but I fight right through it and continue chugging until I can't feel it anymore. Feeling much lighter and happier, I savor the tingling of my skin and the heat coming from the water pouring over my body. I throw my head back and enjoy the wonderfully warm waterfall.

I peek one eye open and spot the half-empty bottle in my outstretched hand. I chug the rest of it down and get lost in the euphoric feeling I'm currently in. Tossing the bottle to the side, I'm suddenly tired and lean down to take a quick nap. I can't remember where I'm at, but I'm sure Hudson knows.

He'll come find me.

"Oh shit! Flynn, come quick!"

What is going on and why is there yelling? Some people can be so rude. I roll over, or try to, and my body is screaming at me.

"What the fuck?"

"Is she going to be okay?"

"I don't know, Ashtyn. Let's get her to the bedroom. She's freezing and we need to get her warm. Then we'll figure out if she's hurt."

There's all kinds of commotion around me, and suddenly I feel my body being lifted. Or maybe I'm floating? Either way, I'm fighting it and trying to roll over. I just want to go back to sleep. Rolling over, I inhale the warm body that's carrying me. I hug the very firm chest, but something is wrong. This isn't Hudson. Opening one eye, I peek up and see Flynn's familiar face. I breathe a sigh of relief until I look down and notice I'm naked. What the fuck is going on? Why am I naked and why is Flynn carrying me while I'm naked?

I start struggling and try to push myself out of Flynn's arms. I accidentally elbow him in the face and he groans. Through clenched teeth, he says, "Will you fucking stop that? I'm trying to get you into my bed."

Are you fucking kidding me? He drugged me, stripped me naked, and now he's going to rape me? Where the hell is Ashtyn? Adrenaline starts coursing through my body and I twist and kick Flynn right in the family jewels. Catching him off guard, he drops me, and my shoulder slams to the wood floor below me. I realize I didn't think that through as I struggle to catch my breath and get up.

Ashtyn comes running and asks, "What just happened? Chloe…oh my god, Flynn, are you okay?"

In an unfamiliar tone, most likely due to the agonizing pain, Flynn replies, "Ask your friend. She woke up while I was carrying her and kicked me in the balls."

Ashtyn leans down and helps me get up. If I thought I was in pain a little bit ago, my pain has reached a ridiculous level. It's shooting throughout my body and I can no longer pinpoint one location that it's coming from. Ashtyn tilts her head to the side, and in a concerned tone, she asks, "Why did you kick Flynn?"

I sputter as the words leave my mouth. "He wa…was trying to…to…to rape me."

Her mouth falls open with a gasp as she turns toward Flynn. "I don't know what the fuck she's talking about."

Pulling myself up, I attempt the best I can to cover myself up and clench my jaw. "He was carrying me naked to his bed. He drugged me and he was going to rape me."

The tension leaves Ashtyn's body as she puts her hand on my shoulder. "Chloe, honey, nobody drugged you. You drank an entire bottle of 151 in the shower. You shattered the bottle and passed out. I came in to check on you and found you. You have cuts all over your legs from the broken glass, and Flynn was carrying you to his bed because the water had run cold."

As the adrenaline starts leaving my body, I'm vaguely aware of the shivers wracking me. Looking down, I notice the cuts up and down both legs. I turn my attention back up to Ashtyn's face and it starts shifting around me. First there's one Ashtyn, then two, then four. What the hell is going on? I turn away and the room moves around me. Or am I moving?

Oh shit.

CHAPTER TWENTY-TWO

Hudson

"What the fuck is your problem, dude?"

I turn my head slightly to see Jax standing in the doorway, then I turn my focus back to my phone.

> Clare: Sorry I got so drunk over the weekend. I don't even know what happened. And that is so unlike me. I hope you got home okay. Thanks again <3 Clare

Part of me is tempted to text her back because I'm so pissed at Chloe and my brother. How could they do that to me? Instead, I throw my phone down on my bed. Brothers don't do shit like this to each other. My hands are shaking as I get up and turn my attention to Jax. I clench and unclench my fists as I contemplate punching him in the face again. I've never been one to have a temper; I've always been the calm collected one out of the two of us. But this. This changes everything.

"What's my problem? Are you fucking kidding me, Jax?"

I reach out to shut the door in his face. It's better to just shut him out than deal with all of this stupid shit right now. Jax pushes his way into my room before I can stop him, and I'm fuming. This asshole shouldn't even be looking at me right now, let alone in my room. He has a lot of fucking nerve.

"Why are you ruining the best thing that's ever happened to you? Are you that fucking stupid, Hudson?"

I let out a disgusting, menacing laugh. "That's real funny coming from you, Jax. I didn't ruin shit. You and Chloe did that."

He shakes his head and looks down at the floor before looking back up at me. His eyes are filled with rage and anger. "If you really think that, she's better off without you. Just think about it. Would she do that to you?"

I don't even get another word out when he turns around and leaves my room. I walk behind him and slam the door shut. Asshole couldn't even be bother to shut my door. I'm still so pissed. Normally I get my rage out on my drums, but even that didn't help me. I throw myself across my bed and lie there, looking at the ceiling. How the fuck did all of this happen?

Turning over, I notice my phone still lying there. I pick it up and re-read the text from Clare. I don't even hesitate before shooting off a quick text to her.

Me: Don't even worry about it. Shit happens. I'll be drowning my sorrows in a bottle of something this weekend myself.

Clare: Oh no! What happened?

Me: Apparently me leaving town is a good time for my brother and girlfriend to hook up.

Clare: Oh, that's awful, Hudson. I'm so sorry.

Me: Yeah well, like I said. Shit happens.

Clare: I don't know either one of them, but that's pretty messed up. Who does something like that to their own brother?

Me: Mine, apparently.

Clare: Do you want some company?

Do I want some company? I'm not sure whether or not that's a good idea. Clare seems cool and all, but I don't think either one of us is ready for something like that. On the other hand, it would stick it to those other fuckers for the shit they pulled. I toss my phone to the side and ignore it. I don't feel like starting up extra drama right now.

We haven't seen much of Oliver since we signed our contract during the summer—well, minus Jude. I think the accident probably has a lot to do with that. Things were pretty crazy for a bit, and I think he's waiting for everything to really calm down. We've been trying to practice like crazy, but I know I've been playing pretty shitty lately. My concern is always Chloe, but not anymore.

I'm throwing all of my anger toward my drum set. I can't tell you how many sets of sticks I've busted, so that's either a good thing or a bad thing. Not sure at this point. I know the guys have noticed the difference in me, and it's a giant ugly elephant in the room. The tension is haywire and not very good for us as a band.

Why the fuck did he do it?

We finish up the song that Flynn wrote for Ashtyn before he speaks up. "Well, we're sounding better, but we're still not all the way there. I talked to Oliver on the phone before I came over and he said he's going to be down visiting for the weekend."

Jax looks over at me before looking back over toward

Flynn. "I hope he isn't planning on getting us in the studio. Dude, we are so not ready for that yet."

Flynn nods his head. "Yeah, I know. Maybe a different environment will help. We don't have to pay for the studio time, so it won't hurt to at least try."

What is with these guys? "Whatever, I'm sure we'll kick ass."

"Hudson—"

"No, don't even talk to me right now, Jax."

"You know what? Fuck it."

He gets up and walks out of the room and slams the door behind him. I'm not even sure how this whole band is going to work anymore. I can't even stand to be in the same room as the guy, let alone the same band. He fucking screwed us and he doesn't even care. I wonder if he even thought about how this would affect the entire band when he was screwing her brains out.

Fucking dick.

"Hey, Jude, do you want to give us a minute? Go check on Jax for me?" Flynn asks.

Check on Jax? Are you fucking kidding me? I guess nobody gives a shit that I'm the one who got fucked in this whole situation. But like his little errand boy, Jude gets up and follows the same way Jax just left.

Flynn turns his attention back toward me and runs his hands through his hair. Looks like he's been doing that a shit ton lately because his hair is sticking up all over the place. He appears to be contemplating what he's going to say, but I don't expect what he actually says.

"What the fuck are you doing, Hudson? Do you want

the whole band to fall apart? Because that's what's going to happen."

Is he fucking kidding me right now? I hold back the desire to punch him in the face. "Seriously, Flynn? How is any of this my fault?"

"Fucking around on Chloe was messed up, dude. Just own up to your shit. I expected something like this from Jax, which is why I'm glad they never hooked up, but never from you. Why did you do it, man?"

"What are you talking about? I didn't do shit. I got home and walked in on Chloe half naked in Jax's bed and him coming out of his bathroom with nothing but a towel on. What else am I supposed to think here? Chloe cheated, not me."

Skeptically, he asks, "Are you so sure of that?"

I shake my head and turn away. "What the fuck am I supposed to think, Flynn? How can I walk in on that and think otherwise?"

"I don't know, but somebody needs to own up to something. I had to rescue Chloe from the shower yesterday."

My nostrils flare and I clench my fists. My body moves forward involuntarily, and I try to hold myself back. "What the fuck are you talking about? You rescued her from the shower?"

Matching my stance, he moves up toward me and says, "Shut the fuck up, Hudson. It wasn't like that and you should know that. She drank an entire bottle of 151 and passed out in the shower. She shattered the bottle and cut up her legs a little, but they were scratches. I don't think she was trying to kill herself or anything like that. But she's fucked up right now."

My lips flatten as I glare at him and snap out, "Yeah, I'm sure she's pretty fucked up."

"You're both playing innocent and blaming the other guy. I'm sick of this shit and we don't need this drama right now. I want you to know I'm not above kicking you out of the band. I don't want it to come to that, but this shit isn't working."

"Yeah, and who made you the king of the fucking world? Why do you think that you can make a decision like that?"

"I don't want you out. I'm just telling you like it is. Get your shit together or you're out. It sucks, but that's how it has to be."

"You know what, Flynn? Fuck you. I don't need this bullshit right now."

Kick me out of the fucking band? Are you serious? Who the hell do these guys think they are? Oh, that's right, Flynn and Jax are best friends, so they'll obviously take each other's sides. Even though I brought Jude into the band, he's so far up Flynn's ass it's not even funny. Fucking bullshit.

Fortunately or unfortunately, Jax chooses that time to walk back into the room. "Fuck that bullshit, Flynn. Nobody is getting kicked out of the band. Let's deal with this man to man." He brings his fists up like he wants to fight me, and the entire room erupts into laughter and tears. The sad thing is, I think he's being serious and not trying to be the comic relief.

"What the fuck is so funny? Why are you all

laughing?"

I compose myself long enough to say, "There's no way you could beat me, man. Your workouts include lifting a beer to your mouth or having sex. Have you ever tried playing the drums for hours on end? I hate to break it to you, but in a fight between you and me, I'd break you. Don't worry, I won't mess up your pretty little face."

He lunges toward me, but Flynn holds him back and replies, "I hate to agree with him, but he's right, Jax. Sure, you're in great shape, but you're toned and skinny. Hudson is pretty ripped compared to you."

Looking around the room at all of us, Jax says, "No fucking way." We all nod, and his shoulders slump down.

Uncomfortable silence starts to ensue, but Flynn's phone saves us from that quickly. He's getting a booty call from Ashtyn. I wish I could say the same thing right about now, but with Chloe, not Ashtyn. I'm pretty sure Flynn would kick my ass if that were the case.

His brow furrows and he answers the call, "Hello?"

The room is silent as we wait and we can only hear the answers on Flynn's end. "You've got to be fucking kidding me."

Jax is bouncing around like a little kid and asks, "What? What? What?"

"Excuse me for a minute." He pulls the phone back and looks at Jax and says, "Will you shut the fuck up for five minutes? I'm talking to Oliver. I'll let you all in on it in a minute."

Pulling the phone back to his ear, he asks, "When?" And then, "You're fucking kidding me, right? There's no way. Okay. I'll let the guys know and we'll be there as soon as we can. I'll see you tomorrow."

See him tomorrow? Is Oliver coming here? Doesn't he have family shit to do? Or are we supposed to be going to Portland? Flynn hangs up the phone and I think Jax waits approximately five seconds before jumping on him. "What the fuck is going on? What did Oliver say? Why are you seeing him tomorrow? Are we seeing him tomorrow?"

Turning around, Flynn has a death glare that pretty much shuts Jax up. "Give me five fucking minutes to explain and you'll know everything that is going on. I can't damn well answer your questions if you keep throwing them at me. Got it?"

Jax plasters a giant grin on his face and pulls his fingers across his lips. Yeah right, like he could ever zip his lips.

"Okay, so like you already know, that was Oliver. He's got the four of us booked on a flight to LA in the morning. Apparently, while we've been dealing with shit drama and trying throw our EP together, he's been working miracles. I guess there's some big benefit concert in LA on Christmas Eve and he got us on the line-up."

That causes shouts from all of us. A fucking concert in L.A. There's no way we could've done something like that on our own.

"That's not all. Dudes, we're fucking playing Vegas for New Year's."

At that point he can't stop the chaos that erupts in the room. Screw getting all of the details. That's what our flight will be for tomorrow. Oliver hasn't been with us that long, but he is fucking moving mountains. And fucking fast. You can't fake the kind of exposure we'll be getting this week.

Fucking ridiculous.

Insane.

"I think we should call it a night. I know I need to go tell Ashtyn the good news, and Jax needs to get his beauty sleep because four a.m. is going to come bright and early."

We all laugh at Jax's expense but head off in our separate ways. L.A. on Christmas Eve and Vegas on New Year's. This is insane. I rush up to my room to tell Chloe the good news, but when I get there I remember she's gone. She isn't here for me to share this with. Lying down on my bed, I throw on "Medicine" by Sunset Sons. I wish Chloe were my Katie. My medicine.

CHAPTER TWENTY-THREE

Chloe

I hate when you wake up and don't remember the night before. I know I drink too much, but it always feels so much better to just numb myself rather than feel anything at all. I peek my eyes open and panic sets in. I have no idea where I am, but fortunately I'm alone in this giant bed. Slowly, I raise my body as the room starts spinning around me. I peel back the sheet that's clutched against me and let out a sigh of relief. I'm not naked, but I'm only wearing an oversized t-shirt and panties. My head is screaming at me and I notice a bottle of ibuprofen and a glass of water on the nightstand next to me. I contemplate taking it, but since I don't know where the fuck I am, I pass.

Next to the pills is a piece of paper with my name at the top. I grab it and unfold it to find Ashtyn's familiar handwriting.

Chloe,

I'm not sure how much you remember from last night, but just in case you couldn't remember anything I figured it would be a good idea to leave you a note. You're sleeping in Flynn's bed right now and I left the water and ibuprofen for you. There's also a brand new phone for you to replace the one that was apparently shattered. Come find me when you're ready.

Love Ashtyn

I crumple up the note but swallow the pills and chug

the water right along with it. I still get that lump-in-your-throat feeling after taking any pills, and I try to swallow it back down. I swing my legs over the edge of the bed and they scream at me in pain as soon as I put any pressure on them. Glancing down, I see cuts up and down my legs.

What the fuck?

I spot my bag near the foot of the bed. I scrounge up a pair of yoga pants and a hoodie and go on a hunt for Ashtyn. Flynn's house isn't too large, not like Hudson's, so it doesn't take me long to find the two of them sitting at his kitchen table and quietly talking. Most likely about me, but I don't care. I'm a fucking mess right now.

Ashtyn whips her head up when I come in and grimaces. "Hey. How are you feeling?"

"Like I got hit by a fucking bus."

She gets up and pours another cup of coffee and places it on the kitchen table. Assuming it's for me, I take a seat in front of it and take a sip of the bitter beverage. No doubt I cringe as it hits my throat, because Ashtyn says, "Sorry. I know you usually like it a lot sweeter. I can get you some sugar." I wave her off. No use in making her go to extra trouble after everything she's already done for me. "So what do you remember from last night?"

I knew this was coming, but I guess I didn't expect it to start off my morning. Maybe I've gotten my body so used to alcohol lately that it doesn't affect me the same way as it used to. I close my eyes and I seem to remember every damn one of yesterday's horrible events. I cringe slightly at that thought. Opening my eyes, I look up at Ashtyn and say, "I remember everything." I turn to Flynn. "I'm sorry for what I said last night. Or what I accused you of. I know you would never do something like that ever."

He sadly nods his head and says, "You weren't in the right mindset last night. But thank you for apologizing."

I turn back to Ashtyn and ask her the inevitable. "So, what's next?"

"After you finish your cup of coffee, we're going home. And you don't have any say in that."

I nod my head and take my precious time savoring the horrible cup of coffee sitting in front of me.

Being back at Ashtyn's house has been strange to say the least. Everyone has been walking on eggshells around me like I'm going to crack. Shit, I wish someone would be real around me. Yeah, I feel like shit and I'm broken in two, but the way everyone is acting is making me feel a million times worse. Why can't everyone just act normal? I've been pacing the room since I got back to her house, and I feel like I'm going to start climbing the fucking walls. I'm suffocating and I don't know how I'm supposed to just stay here. I can't. I throw on my Uggs and a hoodie and head downstairs to leave.

"Chloe, honey. Can I talk to you for a minute?"

I stop in my tracks, cringing at what this conversation will be about. I have a pretty good idea since I've been MIA for the past few months, and there's no way she hasn't noticed. I turn around, and Ashtyn's mom motions for me to follow her into the kitchen. I drag my feet behind me and take a seat at the breakfast bar next to her. She's sipping on a mug of coffee. After a few sips, she places it down in front of her and turns her attention toward me. "You're mother was my best friend and I miss her every single day. I don't understand why this happened, but I have to believe it happened for a reason. We don't have to know what that reason is today, but I'd like to think we'll figure it all out one day. That's not the point of why I want to talk to you though."

"It isn't?"

She picks up her mug and takes another sip before placing it back on the counter. With a shake of her head, she says, "No. Even though things have been hard for me, they've been tremendously harder for you. And I don't have to see you to know that; I just know it. I know you haven't been staying here since you left the hospital." I open my mouth, but she lifts her hand and shakes her head. "There's no reason for excuses right now, and I'm not upset with you. I could imagine it hurt worse to be around us and I get that. But things are going to be different now."

"How so?"

"For starters, you live here. If your mom had known you were shacking up with your boyfriend she'd have fried me up. Don't get me wrong. I know Hudson is a sweet boy, but that needs to stop. You need to focus on yourself right now, and I intend to help you with that."

"What makes you think I was staying with Hudson? It could have been Jax."

"Just because I'm a mom doesn't mean I'm blind. Jax is

a nice boy, a little wild, but he's nice. I also know you're not in love with him. Even if you were out of it in the hospital, I saw the way you looked at Jax and the way you looked at Hudson."

"And how was that?"

She smiles and replies, "The same way Ashtyn looks at Flynn."

If only she knew how much things have changed. I wish I could look at Hudson that way, but I don't think that will ever happen again. There's too much pain and anger between the two of us, and I'm not sure either one of us can be forgiven. "So how are you going to help me?"

"I want you to talk to someone."

I cock my head to the side and ask, "Aren't we talking right now?"

"No, I mean a professional."

"What, like a therapist? Where some person with too many degrees can make me lie on a couch and spill my guts while they silently judge me? No thank you," I say as I get up and start to walk away from this ridiculous conversation.

"You sound just like your mom right now." That stops me and I turn around and look at her. Really look at her. I see a bit of the sadness that I've been feeling lately through her own eyes.

"Well, she was a smart lady."

Nodding her head, she says, "She was, but I think she would agree with me on this. Holding in all of your anger and sadness is not helping you right now, and talking to someone will help."

"I don't like it. But I don't have a choice, do I?"

She gets a big smile on her face and says, "No, you don't."

Dryly, I say, "Well, when you put it that way. I'm so excited."

"And you have your father's sarcasm."

I laugh because it's true. If there's one thing Mom always hated, it was the sarcastic conversations Dad and I could have together. She would get so frustrated and we would laugh our asses off. Of course she would always end up laughing right along with us. That's just how we were. No, our lives weren't perfect, but they were pretty damn close. I had a good life and I recognize that. It fucking sucks to realize it only now that it's gone. Life can be a real bitch like that sometimes. You only truly appreciate things once you no longer have them. I give Ashtyn's mom a hug before leaving the kitchen.

I start heading back upstairs when I hear hushed voices coming from Ashtyn's bedroom. Her bedroom door is wide open, so if they wanted to keep whatever they're talking about a secret, they should have done a better job. Pausing just outside her door, I eavesdrop on their conversation.

"So what happened, Ashtyn?" Abbie asks her.

I hear sniffles and a pause before Ashtyn asks, "Did you not talk to Jude yet?"

Pausing slightly and in a hesitant tone, she answers, "No, he was supposed to come by later today. We were going to go Christmas shopping."

More sniffles, and Ashtyn replies, "Well, you should expect a text at some point today. He won't be coming over."

What the hell is going on? Ashtyn is breaking down and I'm guessing this is something band related because that would be the only explanation for why Ashtyn is talking to Abbie about Jude. Of course, whatever it is, they didn't feel the need to include me in this little conversation.

"What are you talking about? What's going on?"

Ashtyn is full-blown sobbing now, and the majority of her words are muffled by her sobs, but I clearly hear her say, "They left us."

I can't even be bothered to eavesdrop anymore before I take the few steps to storm into her room. Both girls look up at me, shocked. Ashtyn's face is drenched with tears and Abbie just looks confused. I guess I'm not the only one here not in on whatever Ashtyn is talking about. "What's going on? Who left who?"

Ashtyn continues sobbing and I'm starting to get pissed off. I open my mouth to say something when Abbie holds up her phone. I guess she was texting Jude. "It looks like they're heading down to L.A . for a concert. I'm not sure what's going on, but they aren't leaving us, just leaving for a bit."

I've heard enough. I storm out of there and head back to my room for my phone. One of them calls my name behind me, but I don't stop until I'm back in my room and have shut the door behind me. Picking up my phone, I send off a quick text to Jax.

Me: Were you planning on telling me that you were leaving?

Jax: Shit has been crazy, Chloe. Sorry.

Me: So are you not talking to me either?

He starts to write something back but then the three blinking dots disappear. I sit there staring daggers at my phone for five minutes. When he doesn't respond to me, I call him instead. "Getting a little impatient now?" he asks on a chuckle.

I don't have time for his playfulness right now. "Don't give me that. Are you mad at me?"

"Of course I'm not mad at you. I just didn't know what you wanted to do about this whole situation. I figured it would be best to lie low for a bit. Until everything blows over."

What the fuck is he even talking about? "Lie low for a bit? You make it sound like we have something to hide."

I can just picture him running his hands through his hair and tugging on the ends when he says, "We didn't have sex, Chloe, but we came pretty damn close to it."

"So? Hudson did have sex," I add as I start pacing my room. I don't see how what we almost did even compares to what Hudson did to me. Did to us.

"Are you so sure of that?"

Is he kidding me right now? "What are you talking about? You were there. Why else would a random drunk girl answer his phone in the middle of the night and let me know that he was in the shower?"

He lets out an exasperated sigh. "I don't know, Chloe." He pauses before continuing. "Maybe there's a perfectly good reason for it? I can't believe my brother would cheat on you."

"Yeah, well, you were all for it the other night."

"Fuck, Chloe. I'm an asshole and I was thinking with my dick."

"There's more to it than that and you know it, Jax." He can't honestly think there's nothing more between us. I've felt it and I know he feels it too.

"Yeah, maybe. But you're Hudson's girl, not mine."

I don't even believe my own words when I say, "But I could be."

"You don't mean that. We've gone over this. I'm way too screwed up for that and it would never work out between us anyway."

"Yeah, I know. Why the fuck did I have to let my heart get involved? I never do that, Jax, and this right here is why I don't."

"I get it, babe. I do. That's why I refuse to ever let my heart get involved again."

I let out a harsh laugh. "We're both just a couple of fucking cynics. Love sucks and all of that bullshit."

"Fuck love."

"I second that one." I pause and let the silence surround me for a moment. "So you're leaving?"

"Yeah." He sighs. "We're heading down to L.A. for a benefit concert. There was a last minute opening, so we're heading out tomorrow. We'll be playing a show there for Christmas Eve and then off to Vegas to play a New Year's Eve show."

"That's amazing," I say as I ungracefully flop onto my bed.

"Yeah, I'm pretty fucking stoked right now." I can hear the smile in his voice as he talks about their amazing news. If there's one thing that stands true for all of the guys in the band, it's their equal love and passion for the band.

I angrily laugh into my phone. "At least one of us will have a fucking merry Christmas and happy New Year."

"Don't be like that. I'll work on Hudson. You'll get your guy back. Trust me. Have a little faith."

"And if I don't want him back?" I'm fucking lying to myself if I say I don't want him back, because that's the complete opposite of what I want. But if he did cheat on me, what does that say about me? Am I just going to be one of those girls who are always the victim? I'm not sure how I feel about that.

"I know you, Chloe. You do want him and you'll get him back."

"What did I ever do to deserve a guy like you?"

"Fuck if I know. But you're stuck with me. I gotta go pack, babe, but trust everything will turn out okay."

"I'll let you do that for the both of us. I'm all out of trust for the time being. Go pack, I'll talk to you later."

"Try to be happy. Bye, Chloe."

I hang up and toss my phone on the bed. This fucking sucks.

CHAPTER TWENTY-FOUR

Hudson

This whole trip is starting out shitty. Everyone, myself included, is so fucking mopey it's not even funny. Flynn misses Ashtyn, I'm all screwed up over Chloe, Jude is silent as always, but he's missing Abbie, and well, I'm not sure what to say about Jax. Erin's on the plane with us, so I can't tell if they're going to rip each other apart or rip each other's clothes off. Possibly a little bit of both. If it's the latter, I hope they at least have the decency to join the mile-high club in the back. Apparently there is a bedroom back there.

When Flynn talked to his dad about this weekend, he

made sure to have his company jet waiting for us at the airport. I guess it pays to know people in high places, like having a dad who owns one of the most successful record labels, for one. We didn't sign a contract with his label, but apparently we still get access to the perks, which I am just fine with. One of the perks includes a very busty flight attendant who is trying her damnedest to join the club with anyone aboard. It's pathetic, so much so that not even Jax is biting. Although he might just to spite Erin, which would actually be pretty funny to see go down.

After shoving her tits in my face for the millionth time, I think she finally got the hint that I wasn't into it and moved on. The ridiculous thing is she's moved onto Flynn, and he isn't interested. Stupid girl. Maybe she'll take the hint eventually. Either that or she's just so used to rock stars taking her up on her offer. She's not ugly and she has a nice rack, she just doesn't look like a certain blonde who's back home without me.

I don't even know what fucking happened between us. One minute things are perfect and the next she's in Jax's bed, half naked. How does that even happen? Maybe I shouldn't have come home early. I would still be ignorant to the situation and Chloe and I would still be together. His ears must be burning because across the plane Jax says, "Dude, we need to talk."

I force myself to look up and see the determination in his eyes. "I don't think I need to talk to you about anything." With a grunt he gets up and walks to the back of the plane. I'd rather not get kicked out of the band, so I follow him back there. If we can deal with our shit and remove some of our excess drama, it'll be better for everyone. I find him pacing in the small bedroom when I walk in and he's mumbling something to himself. "So talk."

He must not have heard me come in because his head whips up and he takes a couple steps backward. He's pulling the shit out of his hair and it looks like he's done that a few hundred times since he's been back here. "Nothing happened between Chloe and me."

I don't buy that for a minute and I tell him just that. "Bullshit. There's no way you can even pull that over on me. I saw it with my own eyes."

"Okay, dumbass. What did you see?"

I don't even hesitate before spitting out my response. "I saw a half-naked Chloe sleeping in your bed, and you came out of your bathroom only wearing a towel."

"Precisely," he says as he throws his arms down to his sides.

"What does that even fucking mean?"

"It means nothing happened."

I clench and unclench my fists. If his whole point of this conversation is to rub this shit in my face I will hit him. I don't care how high in the sky we are right now. "You're going to need a better explanation than that, dude."

He starts pacing the room again and he's starting to make me dizzy. "I had a rude awakening when I heard something shatter against the wall in your bedroom. I came in and found Chloe's phone smashed against the wall and she was curled up in a ball, crying her eyes out."

"Okay. And?"

Stopping and turning toward me, I can see the hurt and intensity in his eyes. "She was a fucking mess. I wasn't going to leave her like that. So I picked her up and brought her back to my room. To sleep. Nothing more."

"And that's it?" Did I jump to conclusions over nothing? Is it possible that this whole thing is just one giant misunderstanding and we could put this behind us?

"Not quite."

I guess it couldn't be that easy. Where is he even going with this? I move to take a hit at him like the morning I found her, but I pause instead. I'm not usually one to hit first and ask questions later. "Not quite what?"

"Apparently the chick you were with answered your phone drunk and told Chloe you were in the shower and couldn't come to the phone."

Fucking Clare. How did I not know she answered my phone? I can just imagine everything that went through Chloe's mind when she heard another girl's voice on the other end. I felt every single one of those emotions when I saw her lying in Jax's bed.

"Shit."

"Yeah, shit. Chloe was hysterical and things escalated a little." He bows his head and has the nerve to look a little sheepish.

Raising an eyebrow, I ask, "What do you mean they escalated a little?"

"I'm not going to lie to you. We made out. We almost had sex, but it never got that far."

The anger is pouring off of me and my heart rate rises. My hands clench into fists at my sides. I'm so ready to hit Jax in the face right now. "What the fuck does that mean? How do you almost have sex?"

Throwing his hands out, he says, "It means she wanted to forget you and use me to do it. I know that, and it feels like shit to know that, but I was willing to do it for her."

Oh fuck. It can't be. "Do you love her?"

"You know I can't fucking love anyone, dude. That ship has sailed for me."

I hesitate before asking my next question. Do I want to know? This is a pretty fucked up situation to be in. One I never thought was possible, but I ask it anyway. "But if it hadn't?"

"Maybe. Probably." He stops and stares off for a minute before shaking his head out of the daze he was lost in. "But it doesn't matter. She loves you and you're the better man for her."

"Clearly she doesn't think that."

"Prove it to her, dude. Make this shit right, because she's the best thing that's ever happened to you, and I'll beat the shit out of you if you mess this up."

I hang my head. I don't even know how we got here. One minute I want to beat the shit out of him and now? "How do I fix this?"

"You're supposed to be the romantic one here, not me. Why don't you ask Flynn? He's whipped now. He could give you a few pointers."

"I still want to beat the shit out of you. You know that, right?"

He nods his head sadly. "Yeah, I do."

"I'm not going to though."

Whipping his head back up, he cocks it to the side. "Why not?"

"Because you were taking care of her. I can't fault you

for that." And I can't. He's different with Chloe and he truly cares about her. I can tell. If it were any other girl, he wouldn't have thought twice about just going for it and forgetting about her later. Shit, he wouldn't have even been in a situation like that with any other girl. But he was willing to put whatever he feels for her aside to make her feel better. Does it suck that they almost had sex together? Hell yeah it does. But I get it.

He steps toward me like he's going to give me a hug and says with a big grin on his face, "Did we just have a moment?"

"Shut the fuck up." I push his arms away and step out of his potential grasp with a goofy grin on my face.

He still reaches out to pat me on the back. "Get your girl back."

"I will," I say with a small chuckle. This conversation has reached a ridiculous level, and I don't even know what to think. One minute I wanted to beat the shit out of Jax for stealing Chloe from me, and now we're talking about me winning her back. I won't question it. Anything that gets me Chloe back and everything back to normal is fine by me.

We make our way back out of the room and Oliver stands up to greet us. "Okay, glad you're back. I have a few business things to go over before we land."

Jax looks over at me and I shrug my shoulders as we both take a seat. Flynn and Jude both share similar expressions to Jax's and mine, so they must not know what this is about either. Pausing just long enough for us to get comfortable, Oliver jumps back in. "I want you all to know that even though your show isn't until the twenty-fourth, you're going to be non-stop busy until then. After we land, we're heading straight to the Forum for your first round of rehearsals. You've never performed on a stage that size before or for a venue of that size. After rehearsal, we'll break for a quick lunch before you start up interviews for a few different online music media outlets. Then you'll go back to rehearsals again with a break for dinner somewhere in there. Then we'll go to the hotel for the evening."

"Oh, so you're going to let us sleep? Good thing you wrote it into the schedule," Jax says sarcastically.

He didn't say it in the nicest way, but he is right. Our schedule is ridiculously packed. Will it always be like this? Or is it just because we're new and we have to work on publicity right now? "He's right, Oliver, that kind of seems like a lot," I add.

The energy in the room changes as tension rolls off Oliver. "Are you guys even serious about this? Because if you aren't interested in busting your asses for this, then we can turn the plane around right now. I thought you were willing to do whatever it takes, but if that's not the case—"

Flynn moves faster than I've ever seen him move before when he gets up to stand in front of Oliver. "No way. We are all for this. No reason to turn the plane around. Right guys?" He turns his attention toward Jax and me, shooting daggers at us. We both nod our heads, and the conversation turns back to our schedule. I tune it out and instead focus on how I can win Chloe back. Something as small as a Christmas present isn't going to cut it, no matter how extravagant the gift is.

Getting her back is my only priority right now. I'd quit

the band right now if she asked me to. That's how much she means to me. Everything will always come second to Chloe. But I know Chloe, and she'd never make me do something like that. She knows how much this band means to me and she knows what it's like to have dreams and aspirations. I saw it in her the entire time we were trapped in the theater. It might be too painful for her right now, but I will make sure she gets back to her own dreams and follows through. I will not let her sit on the sidelines, watching me get mine while she doesn't get hers.

CHAPTER TWENTY-FIVE

Chloe

If it's possible, I think Ashtyn is more of a wreck right now than I am. Of course, she's always got a fake smile plastered on her face while I'm around. It's getting fucking old and I wish she would just be herself around me. Sure, I'm going through shit, but that doesn't mean she can't be sad too. Her parents left for Colorado to rekindle the romance in their marriage, and Flynn is gone too. Yeah, she has Abbie and me, but we are a very sorry replacement. I'm a complete clusterfuck, and Abbie is a perky little gymnast, bouncing all over the place. Although it's way over the top, like she's trying to overcompensate. If I weren't so fucked, I might try to figure out what's going on with her.

Her ears must be burning, because my door creaks

open and she peeks her head in. When she sees I'm awake, her chipper ass comes running in and hops onto my bed. I haven't had anything to drink since that horrible night at Flynn's house, so thankfully I'm not hungover, but still.

"Abbie, stop jumping."

Being all bright and shiny, she says, "Come on, Chloe. Don't waste the day away in bed. You and Ashtyn need to stop being so grumpy. Be happy."

I reach out and grab her ankle, pulling her down to the bed. She lands with a thud, knocking the wind out of me as half of her covers my body. "It's 8:00 a.m. You can't honestly be this awake."

She hops up from the bed and turns around. "Oh, I've been up for hours searching for stuff for us to do. I have a plan. Now get up and get ready for the day."

I roll over with a muffled groan. "Fine, at least let me take a shower first."

She doesn't respond, and I look up to see her walking out the door and shutting it behind her. I contemplate rolling over and going back to sleep, but I know she'll be back in here in half an hour if I do that. Instead, I push myself up and head over to my en suite bathroom. A long hot shower is just what I need this morning.

After I hop in, though, everything from the other night comes slamming back to me and I finish up quickly. I haven't really unpacked anything, so I grab some jeans and a thermal out of my duffel bag and quickly get dressed. After putting on my Uggs, I grab my hoodie and throw it on. I'm torn between wanting to punch something or cry as Hudson's scent wraps around me. I know I shouldn't be wearing his hoodie, but it's the only thing I have of his and I still love him so much. No matter how fucking bad it hurts, I won't take it off.

Since I'm refusing to drown my sorrows in liquor, I go off to the kitchen for the next best thing: coffee. I foresee a lot of coffee in my near future.

Finally, a little past noon, Ashtyn comes waltzing out of her room. The fakeness is written all over her face and down to her toes. She looks incredible, of course, in her sweater dress and boots. But no matter how good she makes her outside look, it won't cover up what I know is going on inside. She's dying a little inside, and she's not okay with any of this. Maybe she just needs a good blow-up to finally accept what she's feeling. I don't know. "So, ladies, where are we off to today?"

I'm half listening to their conversation as I Google Marlowe yet again. I find the usual, their Facebook page, Twitter, website, etc. But what I'm searching for is anything about this Christmas Eve show. It seems to be a big deal, and while I don't know most of the bands playing, I know Ashtyn has mentioned all of them a time or two. Although Christmas Eve seems like a bad time to have a concert, they nailed down Thirty Seconds to Mars, All Time Low, and Black Veil Brides, just to name a few. It appears to be a benefit concert with all of the proceeds going to Christmas presents for kids with fatal diseases. So it's a fucking good cause. I can't even be a little upset that they're doing this.

After looking at the same sites that I've been trolling since yesterday, I let out a small sigh. Part of me keeps thinking I'll stumble upon a TMZ post or something. "Hudson Hartley is spotted getting cozy with Miranda Kerr." Okay, maybe not quite that, but close enough. He's down in L.A., the land of fake boobs and gold-digging ho-bags. If someone thinks they can snag an upcoming musician before they make it huge, then they've hit gold. Unfortunately, all four of the Marlowe members are prime pickings for that gold because even I can admit they're going to be huge.

"C'mon, Chloe, let's go see what Abbie is up to." Ashtyn is still beaming with that fake smile. I feel like smacking her and telling her to snap out of it. Why pretend?

Standing up, I lock my phone and shove it into my hoodie pocket. I guess they decided we're heading out somewhere today. "Fine, whatever." I can't wait to see what kinds of fun and adventure are planned for today. Not. I just want to spend all day, or week for that matter, in bed and obsessing over my damn Internet search. In true stalker fashion, I put a notification on my search. Whenever something new pops up referring to "Marlowe," my phone dings and I know. I didn't even know you could do something like that. I had to Google it.

I'm dragging my ass behind, and after we shut the front door, I continue following. Unfortunately, we continue walking past Ashtyn's Jeep. Oh joy, we're walking to wherever the hell we're going. This day just can't seem to get any better.

As we arrive at our destination, my lungs feel like they're going to burst from my chest. It's only a couple miles from Ashtyn's parents' house to the center of town, but it's fucking freezing out here. I'm a California girl through and through. Anything less than sixty degrees is not natural, and it has to be at least forty out here. I feel like I'm walking around naked even though I'm fully clothed. I take a few shallow gasps of air when we stop in front of a decorated Christmas tree. In her overly cheery Christmas tone, Ashtyn asks, "What's this?"

I ignore her and decide to send Jax a text and see how everything is going.

`Me: How's the trip going?`

`Jax: Oh it's fanfuckingtastic.`

`Me: Rub it in why don't you.`

They're still talking about the tree when I choose to look over and read some sign they are both fixated on. It's a little plaque that's placed near the front of the tree, and it says:

Everyone can always use a Christmas wish. Grab a gift tag off the tree and fill it out. You can write your name or leave it anonymous. The only requirement is to make a wish. Make a wish for yourself, a friend, a family member, or anyone you choose. On Christmas Eve, all of the wishes will be gathered off the tree for a celebratory bonfire. By burning the wishes, we'll release them into the universe, and come Christmas morning your wish may just come true. So fill out the tag and join us back here on Christmas Eve for the wish burning party.

That's actually a pretty neat idea, and I would like it if I cared right now. But I don't. I look back down at my phone and notice a waiting text from Jax.

Jax: It's not, trust me. Yeah, it's fucking awesome that we're here, but I'm surrounded by a bunch of mopey bitches.

Me: Oh, you have such a way with words…maybe you should write the next song? ;)

Jax: Maybe I will…

Me: Please don't. I was kidding.

"Wow, that's an awesome idea. I think we should all make a wish."

Ugh, I can't take the fake anymore. "Of course you think it's awesome. Your life is awesome."

I glance up at Ashtyn, and I can tell she's fighting to bring her real emotions out. Her face cracks and a scowl comes out before she brings that stupid smile back. "It couldn't hurt to make a wish, Chloe. Why don't you make a wish? Isn't there something you want?"

That's pretty fucking low. She might not realize what she just said, but of course I want lots of things. I can't hold back what I'm thinking or hoping for when I say, "Oh, I don't know, like my parents back?"

She unhinges her locked jaw and softens slightly. "You're right, Chloe, that was super insensitive of me. I'm sorry."

She doesn't get it, does she? Why can't she just be herself? I'd much rather her be an insensitive bitch, although she isn't one, instead of this fake person she's pretending to be. "Why are you sorry? It's not like you killed them. And why are you being so nice to me? Stop walking on fucking eggshells and say what you want to say."

I look back down at my phone and see another waiting text from Jax.

Jax: Gotta go, babe. All work and no play around here.

Me: Bye.

Ugh, I wish he were here right now. At least I know that if Jax were here, he'd be real with me. Yeah, I'm going through shit, but I can't stand when people are fake. It fucking grates on my nerves. There's a difference between being sensitive and being absolutely fake. A big fucking difference. My phone is suddenly ripped out of my hands and I look up. I don't even get the chance to open my mouth before Ashtyn starts spewing. "I'm sorry you've got shit going on and you feel like curling up into a ball. I'm sorry things are fucked up between you and Hudson. But I'm not sorry you're acting like a bitch right now."

Abbie tries to stop her and says, "Ash—"

I'm a little shocked that Ashtyn is finally getting the balls to say something, but I'm letting her have her moment. She needs to finally let her emotions free a little bit. "No, Abbie, she needs to hear this." She takes a few deep breaths and I wonder if she's going to back out. "Chloe, we're trying to help you out right now. Stop wallowing in your self-pity and make a fucking wish."

I can't help the smirk that slips onto my face. "Jeez, what crawled up your ass and died?" And then it happens. A little giggle bubbles out of Ashtyn, and soon the three of us are full-blown laughing right in the middle of town. I don't even care if people are stopping to stare at the crazy girls. This is the first time since I left Hudson's house that I feel like I'm heading back into normal territory rather than a downward spiral. After a good five minutes of non-stop laughing, we finally calm down enough for Ashtyn to turn toward us and say, "Well, let's make some fuckin' awesome wishes! We could all use a little holiday cheer."

I grab the tag that Abbie is still dangling and we all start filling them in. Or at least Ashtyn and Abbie start filling out theirs. I honestly don't know what I should wish for. Even if some of these wishes do come true, I know my parents will never come back. It seems silly to waste a wish on the impossible when I can dream for the possible. I'm not the only one having a sucky Christmas, so I'd rather not waste my wish on myself. I decide instead to simply put:

I hope my friends have a very merry Christmas.

I fold up my tag, and when I look up, both Abbie and Ashtyn are hanging theirs up on the tree. I circle the tree a couple of times before I find a perfectly open spot on the backside, right underneath the angel on top. If a wish is going to come true, it's got to be the one in that spot. I admire the angel for a moment and then join Ashtyn and Abbie in front of the tree. While zoning out in admiration, Abbie breaks the silence and asks, "So, what did you all wish for?"

Silly Abbie, doesn't she know how wishes work? "I'm not sharing my wish. If I do, it won't come true."

Ashtyn pipes in with, "Same here."

Abbie lets out a small giggle and says, "Jeez, you guys are no fun." I'm sure she wouldn't answer if we asked her. I open my mouth to do just that, but Ashtyn beats me to it. "Oh yeah, then what did you wish for?"

Her face gets pink and she turns away. "You're right. If we want our wishes to come true, we can't share."

Both Ashtyn and I don't even pause before laughter erupts from us. By the shade of pink she turned, my guess is her wish had something to do with Jude. And I'm pretty sure Ashtyn's was something Flynn related. Just a bunch of sappy girls lovesick for our rockstar boys. Right about now I'd rather not be in love with Hudson anymore. Before I get the chance to go down that road, Ashtyn breaks me out of my thoughts. "What else did you have in mind for the day, Abbie?"

Shrugging her shoulders, she replies, "I didn't have much in mind other than the tree. We could do some shopping. A little retail therapy never hurt anybody."

If there is one thing I could never pass up, no matter what my mood, it's always been shopping. Mom and I would make a weekend trip at least once a month to do major shopping. My favorites were always South Coast Plaza and The Grove. But any time hanging out with Mom was always a good time. That's what's hardest about all of this—besides Ashtyn, she was my best friend. And Ashtyn knows what that's like because it's the same with her mom. Sometimes they would come with us on our trips and it would be one giant girls' weekend.

I pull myself out of my head as we turn away from the tree and head down Main Street. Maybe someday I'll let myself fully deal with my parents, but right now it's too hard and I'd rather not think about it. Instead, I fall into step with the girls and allow myself to get dragged from store to store.

CHAPTER TWENTY-SIX

Hudson

Hanging out backstage is insane, but hanging out backstage for your own show is ridiculous. We've been hanging out with dudes we have the utmost respect for. These are guys we grew up listening to, and now we're playing at the same show as them. Never in a million years did I think we'd be hanging out with, let alone performing alongside All Time Low, Sleeping with Sirens, and Black Veil Brides.

So epic.

To say it's unreal is an understatement. I don't even know how they got so many of these bands to agree to a Christmas Eve show. I bet a lot of it had to do with the charity aspect of it. Instead of everyone getting a paycheck, all of that money is going toward a local children's hospital that provides Christmas presents to the children and their families. Exposure for us aside, I think it's a great cause, and I'm glad we get to take part.

I've been texting with Clare a lot since we've been down here, which I thought would be weird. She's actually really funny and we've kept the conversations to lighter topics like school, music, etc. Neither one of us wants to think about our breakups, so it's been a nice distraction to focus on making a new friend instead. If Chloe and I were still together, I could see them becoming really good friends. I look down at her last text to me and shoot off a reply before putting my phone back into my pocket.

"Wow, you guys were absolutely amazing tonight." A high-pitched, whiny voice screeches at me. This chick needs to tone it down a notch. I turn my attention to the offending voice and I'm met with not one but three scantily clad girls. None of them look even close to legal, which means even Jax won't touch them with a ten-foot pole.

"Yeah, you're totally my new favorite band," the second chick says. I can't differentiate between the three of them other than the fact that they all three have a different colored streak in their hair. It looks like they all went shopping at Hot Topic for pre-teens, bleached the shit out of their hair, and grabbed three different tubs of Manic Panic. We have Pink, Purple, and Blue.

"And you guys are so hot!" Blue says. Obviously this one doesn't believe in filtering herself.

I look over at Jax, and he nods his head as he goes between two of the girls, Pink and Purple, and wraps his arms over their shoulders. "I love meeting new fans. Which song of ours was your favorite tonight? Maybe we can perform it again. A private show this time." He winks at the girl on his right as she pushes her boobs up against him even more. These chicks are shameless. They ignore his question, so I ask again. "Yeah, which of our songs did you like the most?"

They all look at each other and Blue says, "Oh, I think it was the third song you guys played."

I nod my head at Jax and reply, "You mean the one about running away to Neverland?"

Pink vigorously nods her head and says, "Yes! That song was absolutely amazing."

Jax lets out a small chuckle. "You're right, that song is good. Those dudes in All Time Low have some amazing songs."

All three of the girls show similar looks of confusion that quickly turn to scowls when I say, "It's too bad we haven't even played our set yet and neither have they."

"You guys are just assholes. We're going to go find some real musicians," Purple says with a huff as all three walk away. When they're gone, Jax and I share a glance before throwing our heads back and laughing our asses off. How dumb do they think we are?

Once we stop laughing, I feel a pang of guilt deep in my gut. Jax opened up to me and cleared everything up on the plane ride here, and I feel like a douche by keeping secrets from him. I know I'm not supposed to say anything, but it needs to be said. It isn't right that everyone in our family except Jax knows what's going on. "So there's something I need to talk to you about."

"Oh? Sounds serious," he says as he cocks his head to

the side and raises an eyebrow.

"It is. I feel like shit that I've been keeping this from you, but I can't do it anymore."

"Okay. Just tell me, then."

I take a deep breath and slowly let it out. "It's about Mom and Dad."

"What about them?" he asks and waves his hand for me to continue.

"Mom doesn't know that Dad told me, but they've been having problems. Apparently Dad cheated and Mom moved out a while ago."

"I know."

I do a double-take before asking him, "What do you mean you know?"

"I mean Mom told me about it. But Dad doesn't know she told me."

I bring my hand up and rub the back of my neck. "Are you kidding me? So Dad told me and Mom told you and neither one knows that they told us?"

"Sounds like it."

"Fuck. Maybe this separation is for the best if they still can't communicate properly."

"You're telling me," he adds, ending the conversation. Maybe those two should be getting a divorce. I don't have the chance to contemplate it further before Flynn and Jude show up, and we're suddenly heading out onstage. This is fucking happening right now. My entire body starts humming and I forget about any of the drama in my life as I settle behind the drum set and pick up my sticks. This right here is what we've been working for, and it feels fucking amazing.

"How's everyone doing tonight?" The crowd goes wild with cheers, and it feels fucking amazing. The lights are pretty bright, so I can't see most of them. Plus, I'm at the back of the stage, so it helps my nerves calm down a bit. Flynn continues his little speech and gets the crowd riled up. "You've never heard of us and that's fine with me, but I'm hoping after tonight's show you'll love us. We're Marlowe, and we traveled down here from Ashland, Oregon." That gets a few more hollers from the crowd. "Great, some of you have heard of it! We've been putting our blood, sweat, and tears into rehearsals this week, but we're so fucking excited to be here that our bodies are going on pure adrenaline right now. So how about we play some music for you now. I know you didn't come here to listen to me talk."

With that, I start in with the first song on our set list. I close my eyes and get lost in the music. I forget where I am and pretend we're back home in our basement just having fun. My body comes alive with energy every time I bring a stick down to my drums. The vibrations pass through the sticks and travel up my arms. Time passes by so quickly that before I even notice it, we've already played half of our set. Yeah, we're only playing six songs tonight, but time is flying by.

"I've been told this whole thing is being televised tonight, which is awesome. When we got offered a chance to do this show, we jumped at the chance. Sure, it's great exposure for us, but even better is that it's a charity show. And the ones benefiting tonight are kids. If anyone should have a kickass Christmas, it's kids, and I'm glad we're helping make that happen tonight." That releases a huge round of cheers from the audience and I can feel their energy being directed toward us. We're feeding off of each other tonight and it's amazing.

"I hope you're enjoying what we've been playing so far, but I thought I would give you all a chance to get to know us real quick. I'm Flynn, and obviously I'm the lead singer. Off to my right is Jax, my best friend and a ridiculously awesome guitar player. How's it going tonight, Jax?"

Jax grabs his mic and says, "Well, it's fanfuckingtastic tonight, buddy. We're playing an awesome show and there are a lot of fucking babes here tonight." That gets a lot of squeals from the audience, and from the smirk on Jax's face, I'm sure a few chicks flashed him.

"Alright, well I'm pretty sure your night is officially made now. And to my right we have our baby bass player, Jude. How are you doing tonight?"

"You know, I'm typically a pretty quiet guy, but I'm having fun tonight. Best night of my life and I'm glad I could spend it with you guys."

"We all feel the same, dude. And last but certainly not least, behind me we have our drummer, Hudson. You doing okay back there, buddy?" Flynn asks as he turns around and faces me.

"I'm doing better than okay. We're living the dream right now and I'm loving every minute of it."

Flynn turns back around and faces the audience again. "Hell yeah we are! Well, I'll shut up now and finish up the rest of our set. Again, we're Marlowe and I hope you've enjoyed our show tonight. Come find us on Facebook to get all of our latest news."

The crowd eats it up and starts going wild. I'm not sure what this night will bring for us in the future, but I have to believe it will be nothing but good things. It's our weekend right now, and we've finally arrived. Without even realizing it, we've blown through our last three songs, and roadies start shuffling us off the stage to prep for the next band coming up. We weren't up there for longer than thirty minutes, but it was still the fastest and best thirty minutes of my life. I'm so ready to do that again and never want this feeling to go away.

"Holy shit, did we just do that? Did we fucking just do that?" Jax is laughing and bouncing around like a crazy person, but I can't even blame him. Somebody hands us all shot glasses, and I look up to see Oliver standing there.

"I don't fucking care that you aren't all legal. That just happened and you need a celebratory drink. This is the start for you guys. It's only up from here. I can guarantee it."

The six of us, including Erin, pound back our shots of Patrón, and I welcome the familiar burn as it slides down my throat. We're short a few more Marlowe girls, but I push that to the back of my mind. Tonight is a celebration and I'm not letting anything bring me down. I will remember this night for the rest of my life, and I intend to make it a memorable one.

Jax starts singing that song "Shots" by Lil Jon and I know it's going to be a night to remember. Well, maybe the majority of us will remember. I'm not so sure about Jax. But he's a big boy and can take care of himself.

I hope.

CHAPTER TWENTY-SEVEN

Chloe

Surprisingly, I had fun the other day with Ashtyn and Abbie. I can't remember the last time I was sober and smiling. It felt good, but it felt wrong at the same time. How can I be happy with everything else that's going on around me? Is there something against that? I should be sad and depressed right now. I should be grieving for my parents and depressed over what happened between Hudson and me. I shouldn't be allowed to be happy right now. It just isn't right.

I got my one happy day and now I need to go back to

reality and realize that everything is still exactly the same. My parents are still gone and it kills me. And Hudson hates me and I don't even blame him a little bit. Even if I didn't have sex with Jax, I almost did, and that's still cheating. Rather than sit here and contemplate all of the shit in my life, I throw my legs over the edge of my bed and get up. Waddling out to the kitchen, I get the coffee going and scrounge up something to eat. As I'm pouring my cup, Abbie comes out and we both get our breakfast and sit down at the table. Shortly after, Ashtyn follows, and we continue eating our breakfast in silence.

It's weird to think today is Christmas Eve. Nothing in my life has turned out the way I thought it would, and I never thought I would be spending Christmas Eve alone with my best friend and her little sister and be depressed about it. If we were back in Santa Barbara, I would be stoked about no parents and planning an epic party. Instead, we're here, going to some lame tree wish burning thing. "So are we actually going to this thing tonight?"

Ashtyn actually smiles when she says, "I know you want to be all kinds of Grinchy this holiday season, but yes, I want to go to the bonfire."

I roll my eyes and reply, "I'm not being Grinchy. Besides, come tomorrow morning we'll just have even more broken hearts. Those wishes aren't coming true."

"Both of us? What did you wish for?"

I open my mouth to throw something back at her, but it's not even worth my time or energy. "Never mind. It doesn't matter."

Her jaw clenches as she throws her hands in the air.

"Fine. You don't have to come with us tonight if you don't want to, Chloe. I'm not going to force you." With a huff, she gets up from the table and tosses her garbage before heading from the kitchen. Right before she steps out of the kitchen, Abbie says, "Ashtyn, wait."

She turns around and folds her arms in front of her body. She's closed off and impatiently tapping her toe on the ground. Ashtyn is throwing her best bitch mode out there, and Abbie falters slightly before saying, "This isn't the Christmas any of us wanted, but it's the one we're getting. Ashtyn, stop being a bitch, and Chloe, please meet us halfway. Let's try to have at least a little fun."

With a huff, she replies, "I'm going to go spend the day with my Kindle. How about we plan on leaving here by six?"

Abbie nods her head in agreement and turns her focus to me. "Chloe, are you coming with us?"

I'm so caught up in the conversation going on around me that she catches me off guard. I open my mouth and my voice comes out in a weird monotone sound when I say, "Fine, whatever."

With that, Ashtyn turns toward her precious Kindle. Abbie only stays long enough to clean up her breakfast mess and head off to wherever she plans on spending the day. I suddenly find myself alone in the kitchen, and I have no idea what to do. After cleaning up my mess and heading toward my bedroom, I pull out my phone and do yet another round of Marlowe- and Hudson-related Google searches. It's going to be a very long day.

I felt silly getting dressed tonight when I kept pulling layer upon layer on. I'm wearing an extra-thick pair of tights underneath my sweater leggings. I put a couple pairs of thick socks on underneath my Uggs, and I'm wearing a couple of long camis underneath my thermal tunic. Of course I added a hat, scarf, gloves, and a jacket. Fortunately, when I came walking out of my room, both Ashtyn and Abbie looked like variations of that big marshmallow guy from the Ghostbusters movie.

Abbie decided there would be traffic and it would be better to walk rather than worry about parking. I can see where she's coming from, but by the time we make it to the center of town where the bonfire is being held, all three of us are shivering like crazy. Trying to make some conversation, I ask, "So, Abbie, you're the one that looked into all of this. What exactly is going to happen?"

Her face lights up in a cute little grin and she answers, "Well, there's wish burning, of course. But I think there's going to be some performances from the Shakespeare Festival and hot cocoa, which is necessary."

I can just feel the hot liquid sliding down my throat and warming me up. I need to get a cup of cocoa like five minutes ago. I start looking around for any signs of cocoa when Ashtyn says, "Of course. I think I would be more than happy with some cocoa right about now."

I spot the cocoa vendor less than twenty feet away from us once a large crowd moves away. I don't even hesitate before venturing in that direction. If the girls want cocoa, they'll follow right behind me. I was right in that assumption. We get up to the cart and each buy the largest size they carry. We bring the cups to our lips and take a drink. The cocoa burns my tongue, but I don't even care as I feel the warmth slowly spread through my body. Rather than risk more injury to my tongue, I bring the cup up to my face and let the steam wash over me. Taking a peek over the top of my cup, I notice Ashtyn and Abbie doing the same thing. This wintery Oregon weather is just a little too much for a few California girls like us.

We're standing around facing the stage, and as some performers that were up there before start stepping down, a woman with a microphone comes up. Clearing her throat, she says, "Good evening, everyone, and thank you for being here."

The crowd tightens up around the stage and goes wild with cheers. With the mass of people and the small space they're cramming us into, it doesn't take long to forget about the cold all around us. The crowd slowly dies down and quiets so that the woman on stage can continue her speech. "Thank you again for being here. Every year I feel like our Christmas Eve event gets bigger and bigger. This year is no exception. For those of you who don't know who I am, my name is Margaret Holden and I'm the mayor of our lovely town. As is always the tradition here in Ashland, we placed the tree in our town square so that everyone could fill out the tags to make their own Christmas wishes. All of the tags have been placed into Santa's sleigh, and here in a minute we'll be lighting the tags on fire to release your wishes into the universe. Maybe some of you will be the lucky ones who find tomorrow your Christmas wish came true."

She turns around and grabs the last tag off the tree, and it's only now that I notice the tree is empty. She holds up the tag in her hand above the Santa sleigh that is set up on stage and any mumbles going on around us stop. The whole center of town is eerily quiet as everyone is focused on what's about to happen. She holds up a lighter in her other hand and says, "We had a record-breaking number of tags this year coming in at seven thousand two hundred and fifty-three. That's a lot of wishes we have right here. I hope you all have a very merry Christmas, even if your wishes don't come true." And with that she lights the tag and drops it into the bin.

I'm so focused on that bin and the magic that seems to have filled the air all around us. Abbie's voice breaks me out of my concentration when I hear her say, "Oh my gosh, it's snowing. Ashtyn, look, it's snowing."

Sure enough, it is snowing. Living in Southern California, we always had to travel to see snow. I've never experienced an unexpected snowfall before. The energy around us changes as people spin around underneath the falling snow. There's laughing and joy all around us. "Even if our wishes don't come true, looks like we'll at least have a white Christmas this year, ladies," Ashtyn says.

As I lay my head down later on that night, I keep going over the wishes we all wrote down. I don't know what the girls wished for, but I hope we can all find a little bit of happiness tomorrow. I open the floodgates as I finally let myself mourn the loss of both my parents and Hudson. Sobs wrack my body, and I only hope that I'm not separated from Hudson for too much longer.

"I love you guys both so much. Don't worry about me and have fun on your trip. You both deserve it." I wrap both of my parents into one giant bear hug as tears are streaming down all of our faces. "We love you too, Chloe." The terminal is packed, and the people behind us in the security line are getting impatient.

"Hurry up with the goodbyes. Some of us have places to be!" the clean-cut, cold business man spits out. His eyes are hard and I turn away, refusing to look at him, but that doesn't stop him from continuing on. "They're going to die and there's nothing you can do to stop it."

I freeze up, and cold washes over me. I turn around. "What did you say?" But when I look there's no one there. My parents are gone. The airport is gone. There's only darkness all around me. I run away, trying to find a way out of here. I'm screaming for my parents over and over, but nothing comes out. Tears are falling down my face as I continue to run until I trip over a notch in the floor.

My body flies up as a scream is released from my mouth. The pressure on my chest intensifies as my heart races faster and faster. I'm gasping for air as the ache continues to grow inside me. I reach for anything, but my hands only meet nothingness. I grab at my chest, willing my heart to stop. Just stop right now so the pain will be over with. I can't hear anything outside of the pounding inside my head.

It was only a dream.

I'm in Ashtyn's house. It was only a dream. I continually tell myself this, attempting to calm down my racing heart. It doesn't change the fact that they're gone. I'm drenched in sweat and there are tears still falling down my face. I take a deep breath and slowly let it out. My body crashes back down, and I cough uncontrollably as the weight is lifted from my chest. After I start returning to normal, I glance over at my phone on the bedside table. It's only five, but I know I won't be falling back asleep after that nightmare. Instead, I push myself out of bed and head to the bathroom for a shower.

The house is eerily quiet this early in the morning. I wander out on tip-toe toward the kitchen. As I grab the bag of coffee, the day Hudson taught me to make it comes crashing back to me. It's hard to think that was less than a month ago. It seems strange that our feelings for one another changed so rapidly in such a short amount of time. The rich aroma of the coffee quickly starts filling the kitchen, and it feels a little less cold in here. I pour myself a mug and sit at the breakfast bar, letting everything I've been holding in finally come out.

My parents, Hudson, me. It all flows out of me with each additional tear that drops. There are so many what-ifs to each and every scenario, but focusing on those will only break me further. I've always been a big believer that everything happens for a reason, and I have to believe my current situation is no different. I suck in a giant breath of air and let it out, letting the silent sobs break through my body.

Sometime later, footsteps come up from behind me. My body involuntarily stiffens as Ashtyn sits down and puts her hand on my shoulder. I turn slightly to look at her, and she grabs me, pulling me into a tight embrace. I can't even hold anything back now as violent sobs break through. I'm not sure how long the sobs wrack my body, but eventually they subside and I start to calm down. I take in a deep breath and slowly let it out. Realizing what just happened, I push myself back and look up at Ashtyn. "Sorry about that."

Her mouth tightens in a flat line, and I'm afraid of what she's going to say. "You have absolutely nothing to apologize for. I've been the bitch here, Chloe. I've been pushing you too hard. I should have never done that." She pauses briefly and then asks, "So, do you want to talk about it?"

I shake my head and reply, "What's there to talk about? They're dead and they aren't ever coming back. How do I ever feel okay again?"

"You don't. No part of that is ever going to be okay. You just heal and eventually, hopefully, it doesn't hurt as bad every day."

My voice squeaks out like a mouse when I ask, "How can you be so sure?" She shrugs and I continue. "That had to come from somewhere."

She lets out a small laugh and says, "I read a lot, remember? Some part of fiction is always based a little on reality. There's always some sort of drama or heartache. The characters heal, so I know you will too."

"You just said it yourself, Ashtyn. That's fiction. Books aren't real."

Like a modern day Scarlett O'Hara, she throws her hand up to her chest and says, "You did not just say that. I guarantee you, one of these days Rush Finlay is going to stroll through my front door and Flynn will have to fight him off."

"I'd pay to see that," I say in a full-blown laugh. Flynn can turn into a caveman sometimes when it comes to Ashtyn, and there's no way he'd let any guy, fictional or not, stroll in and take her. It's not bad in a possessive kind of way, just one hundred percent love. Of course, thinking of love makes my mind wander to Hudson. I miss him so much it physically hurts. I guess this is what it feels like to actually have your heartbreak. "I miss Hudson."

"I'm not going to pretend to know what's going on between you two. But I can tell you that you've gotten yourself into one giant clusterfuck," she replies thoughtfully.

"What am I going to do, Ashtyn?"

"What do you want to come from this?"

I don't even have to hesitate before answering. "I want him back. I know it sounds weird coming from me, but I'm pretty sure he's the one."

"If you feel that strongly, then you both need to have a conversation. When he gets back, you need to force him to sit down and talk to you. You're my best friend, Chloe, and all I want is for you to be happy."

"That's all I want for you too."

Shortly after, Abbie comes and breaks up our little heart-to-heart session to open presents. Maybe presents can make this day a little more cheerful. It won't be perfect without my parents or Hudson here, but maybe we can get it pretty close.

CHAPTER TWENTY-EIGHT

Hudson

We've been sitting at the airport for what feels like hours. Apparently Flynn's dad already promised his jet to one of his clients, so we're flying commercial on the way home. How quickly we were spoiled. Flynn and Jude disappeared a while ago for food, or maybe it was the bathroom? I don't remember. We've all gone on the hunt for something or other a few times since we've been here. Luckily, since flying in Flynn's dad's private jet we're VIP, so we get to sit in a special lounge, which is more comfortable than the regular terminal chairs, but I'm still bored out of my mind.

"We should have a party this weekend."

Jax always wants to have a party. I aimlessly nod my head. He's going to get what he wants anyway. Usually he needs a reason to have a party, so I ask, "What are we celebrating this time?" Obviously I haven't been paying close enough attention, because he throws one of the couch pillows at my head. "What the fuck?"

"I said, it's Christmas. Mom and Dad are gone because they thought we would be too. Flynn is going to be barricading Ashtyn and himself in his bedroom. What are we going to do? I think it being Christmas is reason enough for a party."

Nodding my head, I say, "Sure. Works for me. I'll text Clare and see what she's up to. Maybe she'll want to fly down and hang out with us too. She was pretty bummed the last time I saw her since she broke up with her boyfriend and all of that."

Jax throws another pillow at my head and asks, "Who the fuck is Clare?"

"The girl that I met when I went to Eugene," I say and throw the pillow right back at him. My aim sucks and it flies right over his head.

"Wait, is this the girl that answered your phone in the middle of the night and caused all of this drama between you and Chloe?"

I groan and say, "Yeah, but it isn't like that with Clare. She was drunk and puked on me. So I put her to bed and that's why I was in the shower."

He pauses for a minute before asking, "You think that's a good idea?"

"It'll be fine. Who knows if anyone is still in town, so that's one more person to fill the room. Besides, I don't even know what she's up to anyway. This whole conversation could be a moot point."

"True."

I pull my phone out and send her a text.

Me: Hey, I know it's super last minute, but what are you up to this weekend?

Clare: Flying. I was visiting with my family, but they're driving me crazy, so I'm heading back to the dorms early. Why what's up?

Me: Where are you flying back from?

Clare: San Francisco?

Me: My brother wants to have a party this weekend. Feel like taking a detour in Ashland?

Clare: Hell yeah I do.

Clare: Too much enthusiasm?

Me: Nope. Just enough. See if you can get your ticket changed to land in

Medford instead of Eugene.

I wait a few minutes for her response.

Clare: Done. My flight leaves here around five and then it's only a little over an hour flight. I was able to get it direct.

Setting my phone down, I look up to a very expectant Jax and I say, "Well, looks like she's coming. She was already flying today and now she's coming here instead of Eugene."

Nodding his head, he says, "I guess I'm riding home with Flynn."

"You could stick around and meet her."

He chuckles and dryly says, "I'd rather not be there when you let her down easy."

"Let her down easy?" I ask.

"Seriously, don't you think this chick wants to bang you?"

Now it's my turn to laugh. "No way. It's not like that with us. We're friends. Nothing more."

"Yeah, you feel that way, but does she? You did just invite her to come visit you."

If he would just meet Clare, he would know I'm not her type. She's a total straight-A student, nerdy type. Not that there's anything wrong with that, but she gave off the good girl vibe. I'm not a bad guy, but the whole band persona doesn't mesh well with the girl I met in Eugene. "I'm telling you, Jax, it isn't like that with us."

"Well, either way, I'd set her straight if I were you."

"Yeah. Whatever."

"It's your funeral."

Shortly after that, Flynn and Jude come back, just in time to board our plane. Hopefully in less than twelve hours, I'll have Chloe back and everything will be right in the world again. Just in case, I cross my fingers and toes. You can never be too superstitious.

As I'm waiting for Clare at the airport, the conversation I had earlier with Jax continues ringing through my mind. She's cool and we're friends. There's no way she'd be interested in more than that. Is there? I don't have time to contemplate that further because people start shuffling into the terminal and I spot her right away, although I don't notice it's her at first. My eyes are immediately drawn to her hair. The last time I saw her, it was mousey brown and she had that whole studious vibe going for her. Now her hair is dyed bright red and cut a little bit shorter. She's got on a pair of black skinny jeans, a Black Veil Brides tee, and Chucks. I guess breaking up with your boyfriend will make you change your appearance.

She quickly spots me and comes rushing over, enveloping me in a giant hug. "I'm so excited to be here. I was dying of boredom back in the dorms."

My body stiffens at first contact and I try to relax

myself, but I can't keep earlier thoughts out of my head. Letting go of her and leaning back slightly, I look her up and down. I hope this isn't her way of trying to get my attention. "Hey, it's good to see you too. Listen, I was thinking we could go grab a bite to eat and have a chat."

She nods her head and says, "Awesome. I'm starved and could go for some good food right now."

Motioning to the bag, I ask, "Is that all you have, or did you bring anything else with you?"

"Nope, this is everything."

I lead her out to my SUV, but the urge to say something before we go any farther comes over me. I turn around and she slams her body right into mine. I grab her arms and steady her, preventing her ass from hitting the pavement. "Whoa, what's up?"

My arms swing to my side and I back up a couple of feet. "I don't like you." Wow, real smooth, Hudson. She backs up and her head whips back as if I just slapped her in the face. Her eye's go wide, and she wipes away imaginary tears from her eyes. "Why the fuck am I here, then?"

Shaking my head, I step toward her and she retreats back. "Shit. That's not what I meant. My brother got in my head and that's the first thing that popped out. What I meant to say is, I love Chloe. We might be going through shit right now, but she's the one for me. I didn't think about the way you might see—"

She throws her hand up as she says, "You have no reason to continue. I don't like you like that."

I let out a sigh of relief and throw my head back, laughing. I knew it, but Jax had to put those dumb thoughts into my head. Now I just look dumb. But that still doesn't explain one thing. "No offense, but what's with the change in your look then?"

Looking down at herself and back up at me, she asks, "What do you mean?"

"When I met you, you were dressed kind of like a librarian."

"I think you recall me saying I broke up with my boyfriend?" I nod my head and she continues. "Well, he liked for me to dress that way. This is the way I always dressed until I was with him."

"But didn't you say he was in a band?"

"Oh, he is. He's in a jazz band. He's an economics major, and a couple of other guys and him have a band together. It's not serious, just something they do in their free time. He wants to be a senator someday, so he wanted me to play the part."

"You looked more senator's wife before, but I prefer this look better. It suits you."

Nodding her head, she thanks me and we get in the car to head out to lunch. Now that all of that is cleared up, I'm on edge, worrying about seeing Chloe tonight. Will she want to come with us? Or is she going to hate me forever?

After lunch, Clare and I come back to the house and start getting ready for the party. I'm not sure if anyone will even show up at this late of notice, but we still treat it like any other party Jax and I have had in the past. The kitchen counter is covered in liquor bottles and mixers. The surround sound is set up with a Christmas playlist, and now we're just hanging out.

After people slowly start trickling in, Clare and I park ourselves on the couch, and that's where we've stayed ever since. Occasionally I get up to refresh our drinks, but I don't want to move somewhere else and potentially miss Chloe's arrival. So here we are.

"When are you supposed to be back for school?"

"Classes start back again the second week in January. Why?"

She has no idea where I'm going with this, and I smile as I say, "We're flying out to Vegas for a New Year's Eve show and going on Flynn's Dad's jet, and I was wondering if you want to go with us? We're all heading out there tomorrow for rehearsals, interviews, and all of that stuff, but I thought I'd offer it up to you if you want to join us."

Tapping her finger to her chin and cocking her head to the side she says, "Let me get this straight. I could head back to school tomorrow and hang out in my dorm for the rest of winter break, or I could fly out to Vegas and hang out with a bunch of rock stars and spend New Year's Eve there. You know, I'm going to have to think about that for a bit."

"Don't be such a smartass," I reply with a chuckle.

She jumps slightly in her seat. "Hell yeah I want to go with you guys. That's awesome! But wait."

"Yeah?"

"Won't Chloe have a problem with that?"

After tonight, there's no way Chloe will have a problem with that. After we get everything straightened out it will all be fine. It can go back to normal, and Chloe and I will be back together again. "Don't worry about it. I plan on fixing our problems and she'll be right there with me."

"That's great for you. But is she going to be okay with you inviting another girl along?"

I shake my head. "You're my friend, Clare, and she'll understand."

She doesn't look like she believes me when she adds, "If you say so."

"I do."

"Um, is that Chloe over there?" She's pointing at a crowd of people gathered near the front door. I don't see Chloe anywhere.

"Where?"

"The girl that just stormed out? The gorgeous blonde?"

Shit. It couldn't be. How did I get so wrapped up in our conversation to miss her? "Hey, I'll be right back."

"Go get your girl. I'll be fine by myself."

I take off running toward the front door. It's more like a speed walk as I push myself through the small crowd that has conveniently gathered near the front door.

CHAPTER TWENTY-NINE

Chloe

This morning Ashtyn received a text from Flynn for the three of us to get all fancied up and head over to his house where a surprise was waiting. Ashtyn got the surprise of her life when she found Flynn waiting there for her. I'm truly happy for her, but I'm not sure how to feel about myself right now. Apparently Hudson, Jax, and Jude are throwing a party right now, and that's where Abbie and I are headed. Her face is full of pity as we both climb into Ashtyn's Jeep. I turn to her as we're buckling our seatbelts and say, "I'm not going to drop you off there. I wouldn't feel comfortable doing that. But I will stop in with you."

She pats my arm and replies, "I know this is hard for you. We'll just stop in real quick. I'll just make Jude leave with us."

I grimace, but I can't tell her no. It's Christmas, after all. Nodding my head, I turn the car on and back out of Flynn's driveway. This is the last place I thought I would be heading ever again, but off to the Hartleys' we go.

Fortunately or unfortunately, I'm not sure which applies right now, Flynn's house is just down the road from Hudson and Jax's house. Of course, Flynn's house is a lot more modest in comparison, but there's only one of him. I park on the street in front of their house, fully preparing myself for a quick exit. Abbie leans over and squeezes my hand, and I unbuckle my seatbelt. Letting out a small breath, I reach for the door handle. Well, I guess this is it. When I turn my head, Abbie is looking right at me and she hasn't moved to get out of the car.

"What's going on?"

"I just wanted to make sure you're okay before we head in. You've been on your phone like crazy lately, so I know you've seen it."

I fake confusion and say, "I'm not sure I know what you're talking about. What have I seen?"

"The video. The show they played in L.A. was televised."

"Okay, what about it? Yeah, I've watched it." I've watched that video so many times I have it playing on repeat in my head. They played flawlessly, and Hudson looked happy. Shit, they all looked happy and I can't blame them. They're making their dreams come true and it's got to feel good. I just wish he wasn't doing it all without me by his side.

"How many times?"

I lay my head on the steering wheel and let out a frustrated sigh. "Too many times to count. What's the big deal?"

"There is no big deal. I just wanted you to know that I'm here to talk if you need me."

"That's very sweet of you, Abbie, but I don't need anyone to talk to." She opens her mouth to say something, but I shake my head and get out of the car before she can say it. I'm not in the mood to talk my feelings to death about stupid drama right now. I'd rather just get this over and done with so I can go back home and curl up with a bottle of whatever I can find.

As soon as we open the front door, we're blasted with music. There aren't a ton of people here, and I'm sure the holiday is to thank for that. It is still Christmas after all. Surprisingly, there are still roughly fifty people here, so it's not empty and I can easily conceal myself. Once Abbie spots Jude, she flits away from me and I'm left alone to wander.

In the hopes to avoid everyone, I head straight for the kitchen. Jax, of course, is surrounded by a crowd of girls all vying for his attention. Once he spots me though, he leaves their sides and comes up to me. He wraps his arms around me and lifts me off the floor, spinning me around. I start laughing but stop when he whispers in my ear, "I'm so glad you came."

He puts me down on the floor and I reply with a wink, "Not now, but maybe later."

He throws his head back with a laugh that ripples all the way down his body. "There's my girl. Where have you been all my life?"

With my finger, I motion him closer to me and whisper,

"Why don't you make me a drink and I'll let you know."

"For you babe, anything."

He reaches into the fridge and grabs a container of something. Grabbing a random mug, he fills it up and hands it to me. Peeking down into my mug, I see a frothy white drink and I take a sniff before looking back up at him. "What the heck is this?"

Bringing his finger to his lips, he quietly says, "It's eggnog. The real deal. My mom makes it every year, liquor and all. Don't let anyone know though. They all get the cheap shit."

I raise my mug, and the milky drink slides down my throat. I'm usually an eggnog hater, but this is delicious. I can't hide the grin that is immediately plastered on my face, and I take another giant gulp. "Don't drink it too fast. It'll catch up to you." I nod my head at him and say, "Thanks for the drink. My lips are sealed. I think I'm going to wander and find Abbie. I'll find you later." He smiles and I turn around with my drink in hand.

It doesn't take me long to find Hudson, and I'm not prepared for the rush of air that leaves my body. He's not alone. He's leaning back on the couch, drinking a beer while a rocked-out redhead sits on the arm next to him. She keeps giggling like a fucking hyena at everything he says. I'm far enough away that I can't hear what they're saying, but I distinctively see the name "Clare" leave his lips. The mug leaves my hands and shatters on the hardwood floor in front of me.

You have got to be fucking kidding me.

I feel kind of shitty leaving Abbie, but I know Jude will

take care of her. He's a sweet kid and he would never fuck around on her. I hit the driveway when I hear footsteps pounding behind me.

"Wait. Chloe, wait."

Tears are still pouring down my face as I stop in my tracks. I don't turn around, but rather I wait for him to come to me. Ashtyn owes me for this. I knew it wouldn't be a good idea, but I wanted to be a better friend than I have been. What good would it do? Hudson wasn't sitting here pining away for me. No, instead he just moved on to the bitch who broke us apart. Moved on without even a backward glance. Seeing them sitting on the couch together killed what little part of me was left inside.

From any outsider looking in, the whole exchange looked innocent enough. They were just sitting there chatting. She had this twinkle in her eye, and she kept throwing her head back in laughter. All I was wishing was that I was her. I want Hudson to make me laugh again. I want everything the way it used to be. He didn't notice, but she kept finding a way to touch him. A brush of her hand against his arm. Pushing his flopping hair out of his eyes. If I had the power, I would have burned her hands with my eyes so she couldn't touch him ever again.

He sounds out of breath when he finally reaches me and he turns me around. "Why did you run off? Wait, why are you crying?"

Is he kidding me right now? He's flaunting his new relationship in front of anyone who cares, and he's asking me why I'm crying? I guess I thought he would be as broken up as me. Maybe I did fall in love with the wrong Hartley boy after all. "If you don't know why I'm crying, then you didn't know me at all, Hudson."

I turn to walk away, but he turns me back toward him. "Wait. Don't leave. I'm glad you're here."

"Why, so you can show off your new girlfriend? Make me jealous? Well, congratulations, you got just what you wanted. So please let me leave."

"No, I won't let you go."

I start to tell him to let me go because he's holding my arm kind of tight, but I look up and see the determination in his eyes. Maybe they aren't together? Maybe it was an innocent interaction and I read too much into it. Can that be it?

"Jax told me everything."

My breathing gets quicker. Where is this going? "What did he tell you?"

He bows his head and lets out a low sigh. "He told me about the phone call. That you two started to hook up and stopped. That you were heartbroken and a complete mess. Everything."

I nod my head. "Yeah, I guess he did tell you everything. So is that it?"

"That's not even close. Because while Jax knows the rest of the story, you don't. You're the one person that needs to know the rest of what happened that night. I didn't want to have this conversation over the phone and waited until we came face to face."

I don't think I can handle any more details. I don't want to know that they got drunk and it was an accident that will never happen again. Or whatever lame story he has prepared. He cheated and that's the end of it. If there's one thing I cannot forgive, that's a cheater. "You can save whatever story you have to tell me. I don't want to hear it."

I start walking away again, and this time he lets me. I get about fifty feet away when he says, "I didn't cheat." I stop dead in my tracks. There's no way I heard him right. Is there? I turn around and look at him when I ask, "What did you just say?" He's looking like a broken little boy when he replies, "I didn't cheat."

He didn't cheat? What does he mean that he didn't cheat? "Please explain." And he does. He tells me everything about what happened that night. All about Clare and her boyfriend. The party. Her throwing up all over him. He never knew I called. The long-ass bus ride back down. And ending with him only thinking about me the entire time to find me asleep, half naked, in his brother's bed.

When he finishes, I don't know what else to do. I fall to the ground and break down. If anyone is at fault here, it's me. I cheated. My perfect sweet Hudson only had me on his mind and never did anything wrong. I can't breathe as the realization of everything hits me. I've been in the wrong here. I'm not the victim, Hudson is. What the hell have I done?

He wraps his arms around me and I try to get away. He can't be comforting me right now. I should suffer in the pain and guilt I'm feeling right now. I'm the horrible person who did this, not him. Not sure what else I can say in this moment, I say the only thing that comes to my mind. "I'm so sorry. I don't know what I was thinking."

He walks us over to a bench that I didn't even know was there. He pulls me onto his lap and holds me close. He's rubbing my back while telling me everything will be okay and it's not my fault. How can he even say that? I push back slightly and look into his eyes. He really means it. How can he forgive me? "Hudson, it's not going to be okay. I cheated."

"Chloe, you're a bit of a wreck right now. I've been trying to tiptoe around you, but it's true. I'm sure another girl answering my phone in the middle of the night looked horrible. I know I would have been pissed. I get it. But—"

"But what?"

He brings his hand up to his neck and rubs it. I know there's something he wants to say, but either he isn't quite sure how to say it or he isn't sure if he wants to say it. I tense up, thinking the worst.

"I need to know that you choose me, Chloe. I can't take it if one day Jax decides he wants you and you go. I need to know this is never going to happen again."

"There was never a choice, Hudson. I was in lust with Jax. And he's way more screwed up than I am right now. But with you…I fell completely and head over heels in love with you."

He clenches his hands into fists and scowls. "Why? What makes me so much better than him?"

"Everything about you, Hudson. I can walk into a room and I'll know you're there because my heart starts racing and my body feels like it's on fire. You're sexy, incredibly smart, passionate, and you've helped heal me. I'm broken, Hudson, but you make me want to be better. Like I have a reason to live, and I don't ever want that feeling to go away."

He leans forward and gently kisses my forehead. "I don't want you to feel broken, Chloe. That's the last thing I would ever want for you. I only want you to be happy, whether or not that's with me."

Before he gets the chance to say anything else, I slam my lips down on his. If he doesn't believe the words coming out of my mouth, then he better believe my actions. And oh, have I missed these lips on my own. He's hesitant at first and returns my kisses with soft, gentle ones. We have been apart too long to go slow and gentle. I nip his bottom lip, which causes him to let out a shocked yelp. Taking the opportunity, I push my tongue into his mouth and explore what I've been missing. His tongue tastes of beer, and I relish the feeling of his against my own.

I let out a small moan as his hands tangle in my hair and slightly tug on the ends. I involuntarily rock on his lap and immediately know he's right there with me. He groans into my mouth and I start clawing at his shirt. I'm unaware of our surroundings until some loud catcalls come from behind us. I break the kiss and start to move off him when his hands lock around my back.

"Don't worry about them. Stay."

I see the determination in his eyes and stay right where I'm at. He doesn't need to tell me twice. A slight breeze flows through the air, and I realize it's freezing outside. With the snow on the ground, I should be shivering right now. Fortunately, the hot makeout session and shared body heat is keeping me perfectly warm right now. I'm focusing on the snow and the serenity around us—the cat callers already made it inside—when Hudson pulls my attention back to him.

Reaching into his pocket, he says, "I actually have a surprise for you. I'm sure Flynn has already given hers to Ashtyn, but I wanted to be the one to let you know."

I can't hide the shock on my face. "You got me a present?"

He kisses me on the nose and I melt a little in his lap. "Of course I got you a present. This one is sort of a group present from the band, but I have another gift waiting for you in my room. I told you, Jax told me everything, and I had every intention of winning you back tonight."

"I love you, Hudson."

"I love you too. Now open your present."

I let out a small giggle and take the small box from his hands.

CHAPTER THIRTY

Hudson

Chloe opens the small box painstakingly slowly. I'm on edge thinking I should have given her the other present first. What if she doesn't accept the invite? After she finally gets the envelope open, she lets out a small giggle, no doubt at my expense. She peeks inside the box, and with a look of confusion, she dumps the whole thing onto her lap. One by one, she picks up each item, seeming even more perplexed. As I watch her, I feel like this was a bad idea. I thought it would be cute in a cheesy way, but it doesn't work if she doesn't understand.

"I'm guessing these are all clues, so let me think about this real quick. Can you offer me any hints?"

I start to shake my head and say no but instead I reply with, "All of those things are related to a location."

She claps her hands. "Oh, a trip!" Looking back down at her lap, she slowly starts picking everything up. "Okay, so we have a queen of hearts playing card, a poker chip, and a Holly Madison bobblehead. Wait…no." She jumps up and then sits back down. "Are we going to Vegas?"

"We are."

She lets out a squeal of excitement, and I can't even be a little upset that she figured out the clues so quickly. She wraps her arms around my neck and says thank you to me about a million times before letting go.

"Wait. There's no way Ashtyn's mom would let us go to Vegas."

"We actually got the show because of Ashtyn's mom. The show we're playing is with a newer band, Half Unread, that's signed with Lost Souls Records. Her mom was already planning on bringing you girls with her, but the upside is we get to be there too."

"That's awesome!"

I push up from the bench and stand up in front of her. She cocks her head to the side. "Remember how I said I had another present for you?" She slowly nods her head, but she doesn't look any less confused. My palms are saturated in sweat and my heart speeds up. I start to second-guess myself, but this is what I want. Reaching my hand into my coat pocket, I grab the small box that has been weighing me down ever since I put it in there. She lets out a small gasp as I settle down on my knees so I'm not towering over her. Before anything is out of my mouth, Chloe jumps up to her feet with her hands covering her mouth.

Her excitement is radiating off of her as tears slowly start falling down her face, and she not-so-quietly says, "Yes! Oh my god! Yes!"

I can't help the laugh that builds in me as I grab her hand and pull her down to the bench. "Chloe, I haven't even asked anything yet." Her cheeks turn red and she turns her face away from me. I bring my hand up and cup her face, turning it back toward me. "Don't get embarrassed. Just wait." She nods her head and I take a deep breath. I've been practicing my speech all day, and now I can't seem to remember any of it.

I pick up her right hand and look her in the eyes. "Chloe, I've known from the first moment I met you that I wanted to spend the rest of my life with you. I also know we're both still seniors in high school and it's crazy to be thinking anything remotely close to that. But when you know, you know. With that being said, today I'm not proposing to you." Her head drops out of my hand and I gently lift it back up again. She has unshed tears in her eyes, and I gently kiss her on the lips.

"What I'm doing today is making you a promise. A promise that one day, when we're both ready, I'll move this ring from your right hand to your left, and that day will be the day I ask you to marry me. We've been through so much in the short amount of time we've been together, and I don't want anything to overshadow that day."

Those unshed tears start dropping and I panic. I start to get up, but she pushes me back down. Wiping at her eyes, she smiles and says, "That was the sweetest thing anyone has ever said to me." Motioning to her face, she says, "These are happy tears. At this point I think it's pretty obvious that when you do ask me to marry you, I'll say yes. But for now, I'll gladly wear your promise ring."

We just played a huge show in L.A., but even so I still have all of these jitters standing backstage. This is unreal, and I can't believe we're here right now. It doesn't feel like we've earned this or paid our dues. Shouldn't we be slumming it in dive bars for years before we ever see this kind of success? Don't get me wrong; we've worked our asses off as much as the other guys, but maybe we just want it more. Flynn is always spewing his mumbo jumbo off, focusing on what we want and not on what we don't want. All of that hippie shit, and I think it's going to his head. The funny thing is, since he planted that thought in my head, I've been focusing on what I want. Maybe there is something about the power of positivity. Who knows? I certainly don't.

This show isn't quite as big as the Christmas Eve one, but it's nothing compared to what Flynn was used to at the pub. Or the parties in Jax's and my backyard. None of us quite know what to do with this, but I'll tell you one thing: I hope it never ends. Being up on that stage with thousands of people cheering us on…there isn't anything quite like that feeling. Jax won't be the only one harassing Oliver for a tour as soon as we get back home.

We flew out here on separate flights from Oliver and Erin, so there wasn't any drama there. But Clare came with us, and Chloe alternated between cuddling up to me and shooting daggers toward her. Fortunately for me, it didn't seem to bother her, and I think she gets the reason for Chloe's animosity. I just hope one day those two can become friends. Clare is awesome, and I'm not attracted to her in the slightest. But she's fun to hang out with, and if Chloe were to put her anger aside, I think she would agree with me. For now, I guess I'll just have to wait and see, especially since Oliver has taken a liking to her. So it looks like, much to Chloe's disdain, Clare won't be going anywhere anytime soon.

"You guys are up next. How are you feeling?" I jump ten feet in the air when Oliver sidles up behind me. Dude can be like a fucking ninja sometimes. I think he does it on purpose most of the time because he's constantly scaring the shit out of me. I don't even have to say anything before his wheezing laugh starts up. I can't even be pissed. If it were anyone else, I would be laughing my ass off along with everyone else. I playfully punch Oliver in the gut and shake it off. The pre-show jitters are getting the best of me. But soon enough it doesn't even matter, because we're walking across that stage and I'm taking my seat at my drum set. All the jitters are gone and I feel ready to play.

Tonight starts off differently from a week ago in L.A. Maybe that show gave us a little more confidence? Flynn starts off with a bit of an intro, with Jax throwing a little bit of banter into the mix. He's always been one to share in the spotlight. The stage tonight is a lot smaller, so I can see the crowd in front of us. As we start playing our first song, same set list as the benefit show, I keep my eyes open this time. I want to see everything as it unfolds, and something amazing happens.

People are singing along!

It's so surreal. I have to blink a few times to make sure I'm not seeing things. But sure enough, these people aren't talking. They're mouthing the words to the lyrics as Flynn sings them. The result is a fucking huge burst of adrenaline through my body. I kick it into overdrive, and I can tell the other guys notice it too, because we all bring it up a notch. It doesn't take long before our set is over, and if it's possible, it flies by even faster than the last one. Soon enough, we're all huddled backstage and I look at all of the people around me. In a very short time, we've all become a giant family, and I couldn't imagine my life without these people by my side. It's weird how quickly you can build relationships with people, and these are ones that are built to last. As we do our celebratory shot after the show, I can't help but imagine what the rest of the year will bring for us. Nothing but good things for sure.

Everyone is counting down until the clock strikes midnight, and I pull Chloe tightly to me. A few days ago, I never would have thought she would be right here with me in this moment, but I'm not letting her go now. I look down at her hand holding on to mine, and my heart swells with love. Yeah, the ring isn't on her left hand right now, but it will be someday, and I can't wait for that day to come. Until then, it will sit firmly where it is. The shouting around us becomes very obvious as the countdown slows down. "Three…two…one…Happy New Year!" There's cheering and screaming as I lean down and put everything I've got into this one simple kiss. It says everything that I can't fully put into words. That Chloe's mine and I am hers. That we'll be together forever and never have to worry about us falling apart like we did before.

As we end our kiss, I gaze down at the beautiful girl smiling up at me. I wonder how I ever got so lucky to find an amazing girl like her, but I'm happy nonetheless. I half shout into her ear to get over the noise around us, "I have a surprise for you."

"What kind of surprise?"

"You'll just have to wait and see. Tomorrow night. I promise you it's going to be epic."

She nods her head and doesn't even question me. Now hopefully she'll enjoy it as much as the rest of us. I guess the only thing to do is wait and see, just as I said.

CHAPTER THIRTY-ONE

Chloe

"Babe, you ready yet?"

Reaching for my perfume, I give myself a little spritz before turning around and heading out of the bathroom. "Yeah, just a sec." Hudson's eyes trail my body and widen with approval. I do a little turn and pop my butt out with a giggle. "I don't understand why no one will tell me whose concert we're going to."

Shaking out of his daze, he stalks toward me and wraps his arms around me. "I guarantee you've never heard of these guys."

I push him back and put my hand on my hip. "That's what everyone keeps saying. But maybe I do. I could surprise you, ya know."

He steps back into my space and kisses me on the nose

before heading toward the door. "Well. now I can surprise you. Either way it will be fun. C'mon, everyone is waiting for us."

I check myself over in the mirror one more time, fully satisfied with my look. Well, almost. Ashtyn wouldn't let me wear heels and almost forced a pair of Converse onto my feet. Instead I went with the whole 90s vibe with a pair of black Guess combat boots and a floral turquoise and black babydoll dress. I would have been perfectly fine in heels, but whatever. I let out a sigh and then follow Hudson out of our hotel room.

This whole trip was supposed to be business, but I'm glad all of us girls got to come. The guys can't work twenty-four-seven. They do need some down time occasionally, and a concert is the perfect outing. Everyone seems super stoked over this show, so it should be a great time for everyone.

Just like Hudson said, when we make it down to the lobby everyone is already waiting for us. I look around and see all of my favorite people. Well, and Clare. I squeeze Hudson a little tighter in her presence. I know he says I have nothing to worry about, but I still don't know why she has to be here. Just because he invited her before we got back together doesn't mean he had to keep that invitation once we got back together. Fortunately, she seems to have all of her attention on Oliver. Maybe something will happen there and I won't have to worry about her anymore.

"Here you go. My dad ended up getting us these."

Hudson grabs whatever Flynn is holding and hands one to me.

"Thanks, Flynn. I can't believe your dad was able to get

us backstage passes."

Jax comes walking over and says, "Right? His dad seriously hooked us up. This is going to be epic."

I finally look down at the pass in my hand and flip out. I knew Flynn's dad was connected; I just didn't realize how connected. I start jumping up and down and screaming like a teenage girl. I am one, so I guess that's okay. Everyone's attention is focused on me, and I look like a crazy person in the lobby right now, but who cares?

Hudson grabs my arm and looks at me with wide eyes. "Hey, Chloe. You alright?"

Giggles start bubbling out of my mouth and I can't stop. Every time I try to stop and calm down, more come out. I just nod my head while I try to compose myself. I take in a giant breath and let it out slowly. I do that three more times and finally calm down enough to speak.

"I'm more than alright." Holding up my pass, I say, "Did you see who we're going to see?"

Everyone starts laughing and Hudson says, "Yeah, I'm well aware of who we are seeing."

"Hudson, it's the Sinners. O-M-G, I can't believe we're going to see the Sinners. And we have backstage passes. Is this really my life?"

Jax starts laughing and says, "I guess we were wrong, dude. How the hell do you know who the Sinners are, Chloe?"

These people are ridiculous. It's not like I've been living under a rock my entire life. Sure, I'm not usually in the know about most music. But the Sinners are not most music. Not even in the slightest. I lift up my hand and hold up two fingers and say, "I've got two words for you: Trey Mills. Enough said."

Jax lets out an obnoxious laugh and Hudson groans beside me.

"You have nothing to worry about, babe. I love you with all of my heart, but even I can recognize a true specimen of a man. You're ridiculously hot. Trey, on the other hand, is unnaturally hot. The kind of hot that shouldn't be allowed to exist in real life. He's like the Mona Lisa; you can look but most certainly cannot touch."

Shaking his head, Hudson replies, "Did you just compare the dude to a painting?"

I turn around and look at Ashtyn, begging for her help. "C'mon, you know what I'm talking about, right, Ashtyn?"

"Sorry, Chloe, you know I don't usually listen to that kind of music. I like a little more pop with my rock."

I shouldn't be, but I'm surprised when Clare steps forward to back me up. "I know exactly what you mean, Chloe. That man is a work of art. It's a little unreal how gorgeous he is." Turning toward Hudson, she says, "I guess it's just a girl thing."

Putting his arm around Clare, Jax says, "I don't care how hot this dude is. Are we going or what?"

We head outside to a waiting limo, also compliments of Flynn's dad. If I didn't know any better, I'd think he was trying to buy Flynn's love. I guess this is his way of trying to make up for lost time. I'm pretty happy I get to take part in this particular gift either way.

We make it to the venue and my entire body is buzzing. I mean, I've been to concerts with Ashtyn before, but nothing I was ever interested in. She always dragged me to whatever band she was interested in and I never paid attention. Unless of course one of the guys was hot. Then that would help pass the time, but how fun can it be to go to a concert when you don't know the words to any of the songs? Not very, in my opinion.

We find our way to our seats, and after a few minutes, Hudson puts his hand on my knee. "Hey, babe, calm it down a little." I look down at his hand and up to his face. "Calm what down? I'm just sitting here."

He chuckles and says, "You were bouncing your leg like crazy. I half expected you to bounce it right through the concrete."

Oops.

I calm myself long enough to sit through the two opening acts, but my nerves are still fried. When they finally take the stage, I'm not prepared for the emotions that fly through my body. I've always thought the people who start bawling when they meet a celebrity are silly and dumb. But now I get it. I don't start crying, but I'm overcome with so much emotion that I totally could. I'm in awe of the gorgeous men who take stage, but the minute they put their hands to their instruments, I'm in a complete trance. All of the guys play off of each other and create something so beautiful that I can't even describe it. I'm witnessing something epic, and I can't believe this is the first time I'm actually seeing them play live. I can tell you one thing: it won't be the last.

I'm so mesmerized with every guitar solo, every beat of the drum, and every lyric sung across that stage. We are in the presence of masters and they know it. With every wink and smirk. These guys are the epitome of the best, and they have rightfully earned that title. Unfortunately, their set ends sooner than I would like, but that only means we get to head backstage now. Bats start flying their way through my belly, and I'm suddenly aware that I will be coming face to face with the Sinners in a matter of minutes. I feel like crying or throwing up, but I hope neither one happens.

Clare taps me on my shoulder and motions me away from everyone else. We walk about ten feet away when she stops and turns around to face me. "Hey, can we talk for a sec?" Shocked at what all of this is even about, I just nod my head and she continues. "Look, I just wanted to clear stuff up real quick. I wanted to do this sooner, but you've been avoiding me. I'm setting the record straight that I don't have any feelings for Hudson. He's a great guy and fun to hang out with, but I'm not competition for you."

I want to pretend to be a badass, but I can't help the sigh of relief that slips out. Hudson and I love each other, so even if she were interested, it wouldn't matter. But there's always the what-ifs, especially if a girl sets her sights on pursuing a guy. Some are just adamant about getting the guy, especially if they're an upcoming celebrity. Ashtyn's the reader, but she's always telling me about stuff like this happening in her books. There was one specifically involving a baseball player and some slut at a bar. When the temptation is there, it can be hard to refuse.

My first instinct is to reply with some snarky comment, but instead I say, "Thank you for telling me that. It means a lot to me. Hudson likes you, and I would like to get to know you better and not feel like you're vying for his attention."

Again with the hugging. She jumps and wraps her arms around me tightly. "Oh my gosh! I would absolutely love that!"

I slip out of her grasp and smile at her before turning to the rest of the group and asking, "Well, are we heading backstage yet?"

Everyone nods in agreement, and it doesn't take long with our fancy vinyl passes to make our way into the dressing room where the guys are lounging around. All of my friends make their way in, but I'm stuck in the doorway. Is this really my life?

Sed, who I've decided Jax will be just like in a few years, asks, "Wait, if your dad is Carl Wilson, then why the hell aren't you guys signed with Lost Souls? Wouldn't that be the obvious choice?"

Flynn chuckles and says, "It's a long, drawn-out story, dude, but I wanted to make it on my own. Not be tied to my dad and make everyone think the only reason we're successful is because of him and not us. I'd always wonder, you know?"

Trey stands up from where he's sitting on the couch and shakes Flynn's hand. "I get that. Although we tour with my brother's band all the time, I wanted to make a name for myself. Have people know me as me rather than Dare Mills' little brother."

Nodding his head, Flynn replies, "Exactly. Same idea."

How are they just having a regular conversation together? Does everyone here understand who these guys are standing in front of us? If they did, they wouldn't be able to just carry on normal conversations. My heart is still racing and all I can do is stare. Hudson is over in the corner, chatting it up with Eric Sticks, while Jude seems to be deep in conversation with Jace Seymour. Everyone seems to have found someone to talk to, including the other girls. I feel like a loner standing over here by the door, but I'm glued to my spot, unable to move.

"Are you going to stand there all night or are you coming in?" I turn around to attach the voice to a face when I gasp. The Brian Sinclair is standing right behind me. I step to the side so he can move into the room and find the courage to say something. "You're Brian Sinclair." I totally face-palm it. Of course he knows who he is. I'm totally ruining this moment right now. Fortunately, he laughs it off and says, "That I am. So who are you wanting to meet?"

I cock my head to the side and ask, "What do you mean?"

"I can tell the difference between a groupie dripping with desperation and wanting a quick fuck with a rock star, and the true fans who have a favorite. I can already tell you're not a groupie. So which one of us is your favorite?"

I'm glad he didn't peg me as a groupie, but I suddenly feel nervous when I squeak out, "Trey."

His face breaks out in a big smile and he says, "Good choice." He walks away from me, and I'm not sure if I should follow him or not. I continue to stay glued to my spot near the door and watch as Brian taps Trey's shoulder and tells him something. He points over to where I'm standing and they both start walking over. My heart starts racing and those bats start up again. My mouth is incredibly dry, and I flick my tongue out and run it along my bottom lip. I'm suddenly shaking like crazy, and I try to give myself a pep talk to calm myself down, but it does nothing to calm my nerves. I take a deep breath, and suddenly they're both standing in front of me.

"Trey, this is—" Brian looks at me and then says, "I'm sorry. I didn't get your name."

I put my hand out there and reply, "My name is Chloe," although my voice cracks a little when I say it. Trey shows off a freakin' megawatt smile and grabs my hand and turns it to the side. He brings it up to his mouth and kisses the top. I'm pretty sure I melt in a freakin' puddle right there.

"It's a pleasure to meet you, Chloe."

And then I really do melt. Or faint.

The next thing I remember is waking up in the moving limo.

"What the heck happened?"

I look around, and everyone is fighting between relief and laughter. And then it all comes back to me. "Please tell me I did not just faint in front of Trey Mills." That sets everyone off. The laughter is coming from all directions, and I feel like curling into a ball of embarrassment. Hudson has the decency to look embarrassed for me and says, "Sorry, babe. I can't tell you that. One minute you're talking to him, and the next you're passed out on the floor."

He swooned the shit out of me, that's for sure. I'm not sure I could handle that on a daily basis though. I feel sorry for the girl he's with. Because I would faint every day around that charmer. I lean my head against Hudson's chest and ask, "What are you going to do with me?"

He chuckles and says, "I'm not sure I can take you

anywhere. I'll just have to lock you high up in a tower."

I giggle and add, "As long as you include daily visits, I'll understand."

He's quiet and I look up at him. "Always and forever."

"I love you, Hudson."

"I love you too, Chloe."

EPILOGUE

Hudson

10 Years Later

Leaning over, she wipes her hands down the front of her dress and asks, "Babe, are you sure I look okay? I don't want to show up tomorrow as worst dressed on Fashion Police."

She's asked me for the millionth time tonight, and I appease her again with my reassurances. Tonight is her night, and her anxiety is making my nerves go haywire, but I'll never let her see that. If there's one thing she needs, it's for me to be strong for the both of us. I squeeze Chloe's hand as she sits right beside me. I'm not sure who is more nervous tonight: her or me. She's worked so hard for this and I know she's got this.

I just know it.

We exit the limo after waiting forever in this damn line of cars and hit the dreaded red carpet. She fits perfectly in this crowd. Even after all this time, I still feel out of place. As a band, we've been to a million of these things, but not one as prestigious as this. I always dreamed of coming to this one in particular, for Chloe, but I never actually thought I would be here. Knowing that the woman sitting right beside me is the reason I'm here right now makes my heart soar. Chloe has come so far from the broken girl I first fell in love with.

"Chloe. Chloe. Can you answer a few questions for us?"

Smiling at the reporters, she saunters over and eagerly fulfills their wishes. "Of course."

Beaming up at her, the reporter's cheeks flush and she fumbles with a small notebook in her hands. "Thank you so much for coming over to talk with me." Chloe continues smiling, waiting for the first question. "Okay, so obviously everyone wants to know, who designed the stunning gown you're wearing?"

And the reporter is right. Chloe looks absolutely gorgeous. I couldn't tell you anything about the dress she's wearing, other than it fits her perfectly and makes her body look fantastic. She's just lucky I didn't rip it off her the moment I saw her in it.

"Thank you so much. My dear friend Clare from CM Designs made it. I'm happy with how it came out, and I'm shamelessly going to tell everyone to go buy her stuff."

I lean forward slightly in my chair as the clips start playing on the screen. And then we're waiting. The man at the microphone clears his throat and says, "And the winner for Best Actress in a motion picture is…Chloe Hartley."

I stand up and pull Chloe with me, wrapping my arms around the woman I am so incredibly proud of. I knew she had it in her, and this right here is proof of that. After kissing her face a million times, I let her go and watch her walk up to that stage and accept her award. Wiping away the tears in her eyes, she starts the speech she practiced a million times prior to this. She told me she knew she wasn't going to win the award, but in the million to one chance that she did, she wanted to be prepared. I knew she would win, and the odds were never a million to one.

"…Last but most certainly not least, I want to thank my husband. My rock. He's been there for me every day for the past ten years. Through my darkest days, when my parents suddenly died, to my happiest days, when I started living my life again. I couldn't have done any of this without him by my side. With his support, I was able to become the actress and woman I am now. I love you so much, Hudson."

The music starts playing to cut off her speech, but she's already finished and starts walking backstage to the many interviews I'm sure she will be enduring. If there's one thing I hate most about my career, it's the interviews. But Chloe doesn't seem to mind them. In fact, she thrives in this atmosphere. Chloe was always destined for the spotlight.

Somehow, we've become one of Hollywood's elite power couples. None of that means anything to me, but if it makes Chloe happy, I will continually be right by her side throughout all of it.

She called me her rock, but what she doesn't seem to realize is she's the same thing for me. I don't know where my life would be if we hadn't gotten back together when we did. I can tell you one thing: I wouldn't be as happy as I am now. Shortly after we got back together, Ashtyn's mom was able to convince Chloe to start up therapy. She didn't move back in with me, at least not then. It was a rocky road when she was working through everything, and for a while there I would be woken up to a sobbing Chloe on the other end of my phone.

I think those nights were harder on me than they were on her. I would have given anything to take her pain away, and I hated knowing there was nothing I could do to help her other than just being there in any way she needed me. If I had to give up sleep to help her, then that was what I was going to do. The first night I slept all the way through, I woke up in a panic, searching for my phone and feeling like I had failed her. When I noticed I hadn't missed any calls, I was so ecstatic I called her up right then and there. It was five in the morning on a Sunday, so she wasn't too happy about that, but I was just happy knowing she was okay.

After that day, things started getting better and better. It wasn't easy in the slightest, but she's the strongest woman I know. With the combination of her continued therapy and stopping drinking, she was able to come to terms with what happened to her parents. The day she finally worked up the courage to say goodbye and spread their ashes was the hardest day of her life, but I was right there by her side. I know how much she wishes her mom was here to celebrate with her today, but she's still watching, wherever she is.

My pocket starts vibrating with all of the many messages coming in from our friends and family. I ignore most of them but send a quick reply to Jax, Jude, and Flynn. It's killing Ashtyn that she can't be here tonight, but she's eight months pregnant with baby number three, and Flynn gets pretty crazy when she's pregnant. And I don't blame him one bit. Especially on a paparazzi-heavy night like tonight. Luckily, with Auntie Ashtyn and Uncle Flynn staying at home, our little ones, Monroe and Katrina, can spend time with their cousins, Conner and Gwen. It was shocking, to say the least, when Chloe found out she was having twins, but we wouldn't have changed a thing. Neither one of us could imagine our life without those two, and the last ten years have been the best of our lives.

Chloe and I had a rocky start, but I would never change anything about the past ten years of our lives. Everything we've been through together has truly solidified our relationship and made it possible for us to enjoy our lives. They say the people who support you at your worst are the people you want in your lives when you're at your best, and I believe that one hundred percent. We've been there for each other in the highs and lows of our lives, but the best part about it is we've always been there for each other. That's true love, and I can't wait to see where the next chapter in our lives takes us.

For now, we're going to spend the night celebrating her major accomplishment and savor every moment together. My past, present, and future will always be spent with Chloe by my side, and I couldn't be happier having that knowledge.

Continue reading for an excerpt of:

Freeing Jude

ASHLAND SERIES, BOOK 3

PROLOGUE

Abbie

Have you ever been called into the principal's office? Your heart is racing, your palms are sweaty, and the waiting is the worst, almost as bad as waiting for potentially bad news at the doctor's office. Not sure if the headaches you've been having are from something missing in your diet or cancer. You're waiting to receive your punishment and find out how much trouble you're in. That's me right now, only I'm not in the principal's office and I have no idea what I could be in trouble for. This is worse…so much worse.

The tension in the room is so thick you could cut it with a knife. But what makes matters worse is I don't know what I did wrong. I would think I'm overreacting, but the grim expressions on everyone's faces tell me otherwise. Bruce, the owner of the gym where I train, has a deep scowl, but that's not out of the ordinary. He's a serious man, and nothing is more important to him than gymnastics and training the best of the best.

He's sitting at his desk in his usual workout attire. He's got a tight gray t-shirt that shows off every line of his muscles—I guess since he's over forty he's got to compensate somehow—a pair of black workout shorts, and tennis shoes. He's long past his prime in the world of gymnastics, but since he was the best back in his day, he trains the best these days. When I got the chance to try out in front of him and potentially join the gym a few months ago, I thought I was nervous then. But that is nothing compared to the terror of thinking that I could lose it all.

It's not unusual to be called into his office to discuss how training is going. The part that worries me is the guy standing behind him wearing a flashy black suit that looks like it costs more than the building we're sitting in. I'm sure if something weird was going on, John would let me know. John is the amazing man in the chair to my right, and I can't imagine my life without him. He's one of the assistant coaches in the gym, and while it might be frowned upon, we've been secretly seeing each other. We skirted around each other in the beginning. A little flirting and innocent touching, but it didn't take long before that wasn't enough for either one of us.

I discreetly glance over at John and give him a small smile. His mouth is pulled into a tight frown and his left foot is bouncing up and down uncontrollably. If he's nervous, then this must be serious. If there's one thing I've learned about him in the past few months, it's that he never loses it. He's always calm and collected. The one in control no matter what the situation.

Bruce clears his throat, pulling me from my train of thought and gaining my undivided attention. "It's been brought to our attention that the two of you have been carrying on a romantic relationship together. As you both know, that's against the code of conduct you signed when joining this team." Okay, maybe a little more than frowned upon. Bruce makes a point of looking at the both of us individually. "Not to mention it being highly illegal with Abbie being underage. I don't think I have to tell you what could happen if the Olympic Committee found out about this."

No. No. No. That's not possible. We've been careful; there's no way anyone could have seen us. The one and only time John and I went on a date, he took us down to Newport, a good two hours away. Other than that, we've always stayed at his place in Ojai. *Who could have seen us?* The rapid pounding of my heart echoes in my head and I rub my saturated palms against the slick fabric of my warm-ups. I take a peek over my shoulder and I'm met with nothing. His head is still straight forward, trained on Bruce. Licking my lips, I open my mouth to say something, but he beats me to it.

"I didn't want to embarrass anyone, but since my job and reputation are on the line, I feel I need to explain what's been going on here." I hold my breath in anticipation of whatever is about to leave his mouth. I honestly have no idea what I would say. I'm grateful he's quick on his feet and able to say something for the both of us.

"I want to clarify there's nothing inappropriate going on. I've been aware for a while now that Abbie has a small crush on me and it's my fault I haven't done anything to deter her advances. Nothing physical has gone on between us, but I will admit there has been some flirting. It was completely innocent on my part, but I've seen the error in my judgment. I feel horrible that I've let it go on this far. I'm extremely sorry and I hope you can see past this bump in the road. This was a one-time thing and I can guarantee you it won't be repeated."

The air leaves my body in a whoosh and my stomach crumples as if I've been punched. This can't be happening right now. I can still feel his arms wrapped around my body as he whispered his love for me. The tingles traveled up my spine and I knew we were going to be forever. I gave him everything. He owns part of me that no other man has ever touched before. Sure, there was something fun about the forbidden aspect, but it was so much more than that. We're soul mates; he said it himself.

The waves gracefully roll up onto the shore and there's a slight breeze in the air. The salt tangles with his musky cologne and I'm in heaven as he holds me close. We're in our own little world out here. We can escape to this hidden area of the beach and no one can interrupt us. The only person who knows we're out here is an older homeless man who we gave our sack of leftover tacos to. But we don't know each other and he has no reason to rat us out.

We dance slowly together under the shimmering moonlight to music only we can hear. He grazes his mouth along my hairline and whispers into my ear. "I love you, Abbie. I know we shouldn't be doing this but I can't stay away from you any longer. We were meant to be together. It's like my soul wasn't complete until you came into my life and I finally felt like I was whole. I can't imagine my life without you and I know we'll be together forever."

His words make my knees go weak and I relax my body into his to hold myself up. He tightens his grip on my lower back and I know he'll never let me go. "I feel the same way about you, John. I love you too."

Every word leaving his mouth is exactly how I feel. It doesn't matter that I'm only fourteen and he's twenty-five. When you find your soul mate, you know. Age is just a number, right? I hold on to him tighter, hoping with everything inside me that he won't come to his senses and leave me. He's mine and I'm his. And I proceed to give him all of me that night, right there on the beach.

"Abbie?"

Shaking my head, I look up and around the room. Everyone's faces are directed toward me, and I must have missed something while trapped in my own thoughts. My head involuntarily starts turning toward John, but I refuse to. That will make me appear guilty. That's the last thing I want. "I'm sorry, I must have missed that. What did you say?"

Nobody looks like they want to say anything, and finally the guy standing behind Bruce speaks up. "Abbie, my name is Arthur. I'm Bruce's lawyer. These are some serious accusations being thrown around about you and John here. We're trying to get to the bottom of this. What do you have to say about it?"

Bringing my hand up, I run my fingers through my hair

and start to massage my temple. This whole conversation is giving me a headache and I want nothing more than to leave this office right now and never return. If everyone finds out about this, I will be humiliated. Publicly branded as the girl who sleeps with her coaches. "I'm not sure what you guys want me to say here. I—"

"Abbie!" My name echoes from outside and carries into the office. I whip my head in the direction of where it's coming from. Everyone's faces are still trained on mine, expecting me to give them an answer that I don't have.

"I'm sorry…I think that's my dad."

As if on cue, he comes barging into the office like he owns the place. His face is red like he ran here and his breathing comes out in a heavy wheeze. "Thank God." *Wheeze.* "There you are." *Wheeze.* "Abbie, we need to leave, now."

Arthur, the suit, clears his throat. "Excuse me, Mr. Moretti—"

He doesn't get to finish his sentence before Dad interrupts him. "I'm sorry, but you'll have to finish this meeting when we get back."

Wait, what? "Get back? Where are we going, Dad?"

"To Ashland. Abbie…it's your sister."

Ashtyn? What could be going on with Ashtyn? "What do you mean? What's going on with Ashtyn? It's six in the morning. I'm sure she's not awake yet."

His entire face crumbles at my last comment and only now do I notice his disheveled appearance. His eyes are wide and crazier than I've ever seen before. His hair is standing in multiple directions as if he's been running is fingers through it repeatedly. Judging from the wrinkled state of his clothing, he either went to bed in the clothes he was wearing yesterday or he fished them out of the laundry hamper. His face is pale and he's shaking. Something is wrong. Very wrong. "She's been in a car accident with Chloe. Honey, she hit her head badly and hasn't woken up yet. I don't know any more details than that. Your mom has been calling me all night, but I accidentally turned my phone off when I went to bed. When she couldn't get ahold of me, she sent Carl, her boss, to come check on me and deliver the news. He has his jet ready and waiting for us at the airport. We need to get going."

I don't hesitate. I jump up from the chair and follow Dad out of the office. What happened in that meeting doesn't matter anymore. I can figure that out later. The only thing that matters right now is getting to my sister and making sure she's okay. Screw that—she will be okay. I know she will. She has to. As those thoughts run through my mind, an unreal calmness settles over my body. She will be okay. What the hell just happened and, more importantly, why does it feel like it was supposed to?

Continue reading Jude & Abbie's story now from your favorite retailers.

PLAYLIST

"Closer to the Edge" 30 Seconds to Mars
"Pain" Three Days Grace
"Hail to the King" Avenged Sevenfold
"Knockin' on Heaven's Door" Guns N' Roses
"Last Resort" Papa Roach
"Riot Girl" Good Charlotte
"Pour Some Sugar on Me" Def Leppard
"Right Where We Belong" Boymeetsworld
"Goodbye Agony" Black Veil Brides
"Lithium" Nirvana
"Medicine" Sunset Sons
"Kids in the Dark" All Time Low
"Don't You Go" All Time Low
"Lips of an Angel" Hinder
"Mr. Brightside" The Killers
"Fighter" Christina Aguilera
"I Will Buy You a New Life" Everclear
"Ecstasy" Late Nite Reading
"Shots" by Lil Jon and LMFAO
"Follow You Down" Gin Blossoms
"Truly Madly Deeply" Savage Garden
"Iris" The Goo Goo Dolls

ACKNOWLEDGEMENTS

These are always so hard to write. I don't want to forget to thank someone really important and then feel like an asshole for leaving that person out. But there's not much that can be done about that so here we go!

To my husband Ben. You continually stick by my side through all of the ups and downs of this crazy journey. I'm so grateful for your never-ending support.

My family has been so supportive through this process. From telling random co-workers about my books to just downright telling me that they're proud. This is a very hard industry to work in and I'm extremely grateful for all of the support that I receive. I wouldn't be able to do it without all of you.

CM Foss, thank you for being my amazing beta reader and just all around go-to person. You're stuck with me now! #soulmates

Heather Hildenbrand, until I was introduced to you I was completely lost in this huge book world. All of your knowledge and coaching has helped me tremendously in setting goals and plans for myself as an author.

Murphy Rae, I'm not sure what I do without you. Your name is all over this book. You helped me take a messy manuscript and a couple of pictures and turned them into something I'm proud to have my name on.

Olivia Cunning, thank you so much for giving me permission to borrow your guys. Backstage Pass was the first rock star book I ever read and the entire Sinners series will always be my number one favorite. I'm very appreciative that you gave us a yummy guy like Trey Mills who would cause any girl to faint in his presence. ;)

I can't list you all but I have a special thank you to all of my friends in our little indie author group. I can't thank you enough for all of the knowledge you are willing to pass on. This community should be about supporting one another and not competing. I've been fortunate to meet so many amazing people that believe in that whole-heartedly.

To anyone reading this book, thank you so much for taking a chance on a newbie. This is my second book but I still feel very new to the industry and I love that you helped getting my name out there by reading my book. I truly appreciate it.

Last but again certainly not least, I want to thank the guys from All Time Low. Their music continually inspires me with my own writing. Since I released Finding Flynn, I actually got to meet the band but sadly playing Cards Against Humanity with them is still on my bucket list. I'll cross that off someday!

Preview of The Road that Leads to Us

By Micalea Smeltzer

Released October 27, 2015

Things are about to get rocky for Dean Wentworth and Willow Wade.

Willow Wade is used to living in the spotlight, with her father a famous drummer in the band Willow Creek—her namesake—it's been a lot to live up to and oftentimes she doesn't feel she's enough. But there has always been one person she could turn to.

Dean Wentworth knows a thing or two about how crippling a name can be. His family is worth billions after all. But Dean's always been content to do his own thing. Play his guitar. Work on cars. And geek out to his various "nerdoms".

But when Willow turns up unexpectedly, he realizes maybe there is more in life he wants.

Her.

One trip will change their lives forever.

1

Willow

Those bitches were gonna die.

That was a horrible thing to say about my so-called 'friends'—and I used the word friends loosely, because true friends wouldn't ditch you the day of your scheduled road trip because they'd rather be sunbathing in the Hamptons.

The fucking Hamptons.

Ew.

I mean, how clichéd could you get?

This was why I hated rich people.

It also sucked that I was one of those rich people.

Well, I wasn't, but my dad was.

So by extension so was I.

When you grew up with a rock star for a dad, cameras and eyes followed you everywhere. It was exhausting.

I couldn't just be Willow.

I was Willow Wade.

The daughter of the famous drummer Maddox Wade.

People expected greatness from me.

I just wanted to graduate college without slitting my wrists.

I fiddled with the radio, changing it to a country station—my dad would most definitely not approve—and let my blonde hair whip around my shoulders courtesy of the open windows.

The drive from NYU to my childhood home in Virginia was

only about five hours, but it felt ten times longer thanks to the crazy traffic trying to get out of the city.

I might've yelled at a lot of people.

And waved my middle finger out the window.

My parents would be so proud.

Not.

My failed road trip might've been the reason I was headed home and not out west, but I was excited to be back where I grew up.

My freshman year of college had been trying, to say the least.

For most people college was their chance to spread their wings.

Me?

I found it oppressive.

That was probably due to the fact that I had no idea what I wanted to do with my life.

Did I want to act? Sing? Dance? Join a traveling circus?

I thought by going to NYU it would force me to finally decide what I wanted to do for the rest of my life.

If anything it only made me question everything that much more.

When the sprawling Victorian home came into view I couldn't stop the smile that split my face if I wanted to.

For the first time since I left last August, I could finally breathe.

I was home.

I parked my car in the driveway and hopped out—pulling in a healthy lungful of clean mountain air.

So much better than the exhaust fume-filled air that littered New York City.

I grabbed my patchwork backpack from the passenger seat and slung it over my shoulder.

Slipping my sunglasses off my face and into my hair I headed for the front door.

I pulled the key from my pocket, rubbing my thumb against the worn hedgehog key cap.

I entered the home and nearly cried at the rush of familiarity.

I was still majorly bummed that my plans for a road trip hadn't worked out, and I'd probably mope about it for a week in a bout of teenage angst, but being home wasn't all that bad.

I'd missed my house.

My parents.

My siblings.

And even the hedgehogs.

My dad had a thing for hedgehogs, so by extension I guess I did too. They were pretty cute.

The house was eerily quiet as I stepped inside and I looked around for my brother Mascen and my sister Lylah.

Neither was anywhere to be seen.

I moved further into the house, skimming my fingers over the familiar pale yellow walls on my way to the kitchen.

No one appeared to be home and I needed food.

Humming softly under my breath I rounded the corner into the spacious kitchen and immediately regretted my destination.

"MY EYES!" I screamed, slapping a hand over my eyes. "My poor innocent eyes!" I gagged for added effect.

Catching my mom and dad making out in the kitchen like a couple of teenagers had not been on my to-do list for the day.

Neither had seeing my mom's bra or my dad's hand skimming up her skirt.

I turned around, walking away as fast as my feet would carry me. "I'm going to go throw up now!"

I heard them shuffling in the kitchen, no doubt righting their clothes.

Thank God there had been no exposed body parts.

I might've been traumatized for life.

"Willow!" I heard my mom call my name, but I was already headed for the stairs. "We didn't know you were coming home."

"Yeah, I kinda sorta forgot to call on my way out of hell," I muttered under my breath, hurrying up the steps.

"Willow." She called again and this time her voice was close.

I paused on the stairs and turned to find her standing at the bottom of the staircase with her hands on her hips.

"Are you okay, honey?" A wrinkle marred her brow.

With her wild and untamable blonde hair, kind blue eyes, and boho chic style, my mom was still a knockout at forty-one years old.

"Just dandy."

She narrowed her eyes on me. "Spill it, I know you're lying."

Groaning, I stomped up the rest of the stairs. "I don't want to talk about it."

I headed down the hall and up the attic stairs to my bedroom.

I knew my mom was following, but I acted like I didn't notice.

Kicking off my black and white Chucks I belly flopped onto my gray and yellow paisley bedspread. Wrapping my arms around the pillow I inhaled the familiar scent of the lavender fabric softener my mom always used.

The bed dipped near my feet.

"What happened, sweetie?" She asked.

I rolled over onto my back and frowned. "Everything."

"Talking about it will probably make you feel better."

"And so will this tea."

I smiled at the sound of my dad's voice as he appeared in the doorway of my room.

"Hi, dad."

"Hey, princess."

I might've been nineteen years old now, but I would always be my daddy's princess.

He handed me one of the cups of tea and gave the other to my mom.

Pulling out the fluffy white swivel desk chair he took a seat and clasped his hands together.

"We weren't expecting you home."

I snorted. "I kinda figured that out. I'm sorry. I should've called. Where are Mascen and Lylah?" I looked around like they might suddenly jump out from behind my bed.

He chuckled. "They're still in school. The high school hasn't let out for the summer yet."

"Oh, right," I mumbled, having forgotten that my college courses ended before their schedule did.

"What happened with your road trip?" My mom asked.

"My friends are a bunch of cunt waffles."

"Willow!" She admonished. "That's not nice."

"They're not nice," I reasoned. Waving my arms dramatically, I began to explain my tragic tale. "I showed up at Lauren's apartment, where I was supposed to pick her and Greta up—and someone please explain to me who the hell would name their child Greta. I mean, honestly."

"Willow," my mom warned.

She said my name a lot.

She even had different ways of saying it.

So I'd know when I was in trouble, or she was irritated.

She was definitely irritated at the moment.

Me interrupting her and my dad about to go at it like a couple of rabbits probably added to that—not just my tendency to ramble endlessly.

"Sorry," I said, even though I wasn't really sorry. "Anyway, I get there, and I'm knocking on the door, and I'm all like, 'Let's gooooo my kemo-sabes!' and then Lauren opens the door dressed in a robe. A robe. And informs me that they've changed their minds and roughing it isn't appealing. Instead, they're going to the Hamptons because Greta's parents have a place there beside Ryan Goosling or whatever his name is." I paused, pulling in a lungful of air. "I just don't understand who in their right mind would pass up a road trip in order to sunbathe and spy on a guy with a name that sounds like goose."

My parents stared at me and then their eyes slid to each other.

They both looked like they were fighting laughter at my pain.

Jerks.

I lifted the cup of tea to my lips and winced at the taste before setting the mug on the bedside table.

My dad, he tried, but he could not make tea to save himself.

"Princess, not everyone's like you."

"What's that supposed to mean?" I bristled.

He chuckled. "Simmer down, Tiger. All I'm saying is, you're adventurous. A sedentary life isn't for you. Most people aren't like that. They're afraid to put themselves out there into the unknown, but you're not."

"Are you saying I should join the traveling circus? Because that idea is looking more appealing every day."

"Nah," he laughed and leaned forward to tap his finger against my toe, "I'd miss you too much. Sending you off to college was bad enough."

I frowned at the mention of college.

"What is it?" My mom asked softly, picking up on the sudden shift in me. She was perceptive like that.

I shrugged, picking up one of the many throw pillows on my bed and hugged it to my chest.

"Nothing," I lied. "I'm just tired and cranky."

She looked at me doubtfully. "Are you sure that's it?"

I nodded.

I knew my mom and dad wouldn't care if I threw my hands up and said college wasn't for me. But that was the thing. I didn't know that. I was completely and utterly clueless. Maybe college was for me and I was just at the wrong one.

Or maybe it wasn't.

I didn't know.

And I was afraid I never would.

I was terrified of graduating from college with a degree in something I didn't even like and being stuck.

Stuck and Willow Wade did not go well together.

But it was hard to explain to anyone, especially my parents, what I wanted when I didn't even know.

Maybe, this summer, I'd get my shit together and figure my life out.

Not likely, but one could hope.

My parents looked at me with pity in their eyes.

They knew I was full of shit but they were too nice to call me on it—for now at least.

Jumping up from my bed I slipped my feet back into my shoes.

"I'm going to head out for a while. I'll be back for dinner."

"Don't you want to finish your tea?" My dad asked.

I tried not to gag. "Nope, I'm good. Y'all just…uh…get back

to whatever it was you were about to do before I got here."

I only made it to the door before I stopped, horrified. Swiftly turning around, I pointed a finger at them. "But don't do that on my bed, because that's just gross and weird on so many levels. Go to your own room."

My dad bellowed out a laugh but quickly sobered. "You don't need to leave because of us."

"I know," I replied, "I just need to get out."

Before either of them could stop me I bound down the stairs and out the door.

I was slightly out of breath by the time I reached my car.

I should probably work out more.

Nah, who was I kidding? That was never going to happen…unless balancing a Cheeto on the top of your lip counted as exercise because then I was totally ahead of the game.

I slid back into the car, my sore bum protesting at this fact, and headed into town.

I wasn't sure where I was going, and I ended up stopping at the local coffee shop/restaurant, Griffin's, for some food.

Armed with a coffee and muffin, I suddenly knew where I needed to go.

Well, more like who I needed to see.

Cramming half the muffin in my mouth and getting crumbs all over myself—so ladylike, I know—I hurried from Griffin's out into the warm sunshine.

Behind the wheel of my car once more I headed to my new destination.

When the building came into sight my lips lifted into one of the biggest grins I'd worn in a long time and I hadn't even seen him yet.

I parked my car at the side of the building and walked around to the open garage door.

Wentworth Wheels was emblazoned on the front of the building and inside several mechanics bustled around. They laughed and chatted loudly as they worked—trying to be heard above the sounds of their tools.

I stepped inside, inhaling the familiar scent of oil and rubber. Most people hated that smell, but I loved it. It brought back so many memories.

I craned my neck around, looking for familiar floppy brown hair, but he wasn't to be seen.

And then, there he was.

He came out from the back office, wiping down a piece of metal with a red rag.

When he looked up he saw me and a grin that matched my own lit his face.

Barreling forward I ran into his arms.

He caught me immediately and spun me around.

"Dean," I breathed against his neck, hugging him tight.

I'd missed him so much.

Dean Wentworth was my best friend.

We'd grown up together—his dad was the cousin of the guitar player in my dad's band—and he was one of the few people I could turn to with anything. His parents might not have been famous, but they had a lot of money, so he could relate to many of the same things I went through. I was also close with his younger sister, Grace, but my connection to Dean was stronger.

Sometimes there were people that just got each other, and that's how it was with us.

Setting me down he placed the piece of metal on a nearby

worktable and tucked the rag in the back pocket of his jeans before crossing his arms over his chest.

"Willow Wade in the flesh." He looked me up and down. "I feel like I haven't seen you in forever."

"It's been a while," I conceded.

I hadn't seen Dean since New Year's when I'd attended his family's annual party. It was kind of a big deal and not to be missed.

I hadn't talked to him much there because his girlfriend had been with him.

She was an insufferable bitch that I wanted to gag and toss over a bridge into a lake.

He could do so much better.

"How's Brooklyn?" I sneered her name.

I'd tried to be nice to her when they first started dating last summer, but she made her distaste of me obvious—I was too loud, too crazy, and far too opinionated for her.

"Wouldn't know. We broke up in February."

I clucked my tongue. "You got her the wrong chocolate for Valentine's day, didn't you?"

He laughed fully at that. "Probably. We just weren't a good match. She kept trying to hide my Pokémon cards and that wasn't cool."

By now the other mechanics were staring at us with interest. I recognized a few of them and waved.

"Come on," Dean nodded towards the open garage door, "let's head up to the apartment to talk."

"You're not going to get in trouble are you?"

"I know the owner." He winked, referring to his dad.

My Chucks squeaked against the concrete floor as I followed Dean through the garage, outside, and around the side of the building to the set of stairs that led to the apartment above the shop. Dean was nearly two years older than me, and as soon as he graduated high school he'd moved in here and gotten his certificate to be a mechanic. He'd known from the time he was three and could hold a wrench that he wanted to be a mechanic like his dad. If only I was that lucky.

Dean swung the door open and waved me inside.

It looked much the way I remembered—muted gray walls, black leather furniture, and old-timey western and sci-fi movie posters on the wall.

"Thirsty?" Dean asked, already moving into the small kitchen.

I slid onto one of the red leather barstools and nodded.

He opened the fridge and seemed to be searching for something. Finally, he pulled out a glass bottle of Orange Crush soda.

"Ah!" I squealed, reaching out with grabby hands. "I can't believe you still get these!"

"'Course," he shrugged, unscrewing the cap on another and leaning across the counter towards me, "they're your favorite."

"I haven't had one of these in forever." I gulped greedily at it.

"They don't have Orange Crush soda in New York City?" He questioned with a raised brow.

"I'm sure they do," I relented, rubbing the condensation off the glass with my thumb, "but not in a glass bottle. Plus, I wouldn't be able to have it with you. This is our thing."

He grinned at that. "I've missed you, Will."

"Bleh," I gagged, "I wish that nickname would die already. I have a vagina, therefore I'm not a Will."

He chuckled and leaned his head back, swallowing a large gulp of the soda. "I've missed you, Willow," he amended.

"Much better."

"I've got somethin' else for you." He began shuffling through a kitchen drawer. When he found whatever it was he was looking for he exclaimed, "Aha!"

He held the blue raspberry lollipop out for me with a crooked smile. "Been saving all of these for you."

"My momma always told me not to take candy from a stranger," I quipped, taking the lollipop anyway—there was no way I was passing up blue raspberry. It was my favorite.

"Guess it's a good thing I'm not a stranger." He winked.

I unwrapped the lollipop and stuck it in my mouth. "Mmm," I hummed, "that's good."

He laughed and grabbed one for himself. Sour apple.

We grew quiet for a moment, and then he broke the silence. "This feels good. It feels like you never left."

I sighed, looking down at the worn ends of my shoes. "I wish I'd never left," I muttered.

"Is it really that bad?" He asked. "College, I mean."

I pulled the lollipop from my mouth. "I don't know whether it's college or me."

"Ah, I see." He nodded.

"You know me," I continued, "I hate being confined. I thought once I graduated high school I'd be free to wander the world and do what I wanted, but then I felt like I needed to go to school, and maybe it is what I need but it's not what I want."

"So…maybe you take next year off," he suggested.

"But I don't know if that's what I want. That's the problem. I'm so confused."

"What's something you do want?" The white end of the lollipop stuck out between his lips.

"Well," I slid the barstool back and kicked my feet up on the counter, "I wanted to go on a road trip and my so-called friends bailed. Assholes." I muttered the last part under my breath.

He chuckled, crossing his arms over his chest. "Because you're such a delight to hang out with twenty-four-seven."

I stuck my now blue tongue out at him.

Sobering, he walked around and sat on the empty barstool beside me. "Why don't we go on a road trip?"

My eyes widened in surprise. "Me and you?"

"Sure, why not?" He shrugged, crunching down on his lollipop and chewing the candy. "I mean, we're friends, I just finished restoring my Mustang, and getting out of here for a little while wouldn't be the worst thing ever."

"Would your dad let you take off work for that long? My plan was to head south and then west all the way to California to visit Liam," I said, referring to my cousin who was only a few months older than me and like a brother, "and then come back up the northern route."

"My dad won't care." Dean shrugged, tossing the lollipop stick in the direction of the trashcan. It hit the edge and bounced off. Dean never had much aim. It was a good thing he stuck to fixing cars and playing music. I didn't think he went anywhere without his guitar.

Excitement flooded my body, nearly bubbling over.

"Are you sure?" I asked him one last time.

"Positive."

"We're really going to do this?"

He nodded.

"Thank you!" I squealed, nearly falling to the floor in my haste to hug him.

"Whoa," he grunted in surprise when my body collided into his. He wrapped his arms around me, hugging me back.

"Thank you, thank you, thank you!" I said a thousand more times before smacking a kiss against his stubbled cheek. "This is going to be epic."

Before he could respond, I was out the door and down the steps.

I had a road trip to pack for.

ABOUT THE AUTHOR

Born on a small southeastern island in Alaska and raised in southern Oregon, Alexandria Bishop is a PNW girl at heart. By day, she goes to battle with a tiny dictator aka her toddler and by night, she can be found typing ALL the words of her contemporary romance novels accompanied by a glass of wine or two ;)

When she's not in mommy or author mode, she can be found drinking copious amounts of cold brew coffee, bingeing her latest obsession on Netflix, or attending concerts of her favorite pop-punk bands.

She loves hearing from her readers and you can find her on social media here:

www.alexandriabishop.com
www.facebook.com/authoralexandriabishop
www.twitter.com/allieebishop
www.instagram.com/alexandria.bishop

Made in USA - North Chelmsford, MA
1161652_9781724348289
09.09.2020 1426